AN UNWITTING COMPROMISE

By Sue Barr

Published by: Tiger Lily Books
ISBN: 978-1-7770825-9-8
Cover Design by the Midnight Muse
Text copyright ©2021 Susan L. Barr

Can a woman have two great loves in her life?

All it takes is one night for Elizabeth Bennet's life to change forever. Finding herself pregnant with Mr. Darcy's baby, she is forced to make decisions that will have an impact on the rest of not only her life, but her family's.

Mr. Darcy, who cannot remember the night in question and therefore does not believe she is carrying his child, soldiers on in his pride and arrogance until it's too late. There is nothing he can do. She is now married and not only is she unattainable, but so is his son.

Chapter One

ELIZABETH TOSSED FROM one side to the other in what was the most comfortable bed she had ever lain on in her life. Yet, sleep eluded her. Not surprising as she was not in her own bed. She wasn't even in her own home. She was in a guest chamber at Netherfield Park while her eldest sister, Jane, recovered from a dreadful cold. A cold which could have been averted.

More than once, Elizabeth fought down feelings of anger at their mother's machinations. Jane had weak lungs following a childhood ailment and this trifling cold, as her mother had callously called it when she descended upon Netherfield to ascertain whether Jane should come home or remain, could have taken her sister's very life. What was Mamma thinking, sending her on horseback, knowing it would rain? All because of a dinner invitation from Miss Bingley and her sister, who didn't give two figs about Jane? Mamma knew full well Mr. Bingley would not be in attendance and had gambled a lot on the health of her eldest daughter in the hopes of her being entertained by the amiable young man the next morning.

And yet, Jane had not refused.

Elizabeth flipped onto her back and even though the room

lay draped in complete darkness, she stared at the ceiling. This evening was the first time Jane felt well enough to come downstairs for dinner, much to Mr. Bingley's delight and Miss Bingley's distaste. Although Mr. Bingley had taken such good care of her beloved sister, ensured her comfort and made sure she did not catch another chill, Jane, still fatigued from her illness, had reluctantly signaled her sister they should excuse themselves from company. Elizabeth, herself exhausted, gladly made their apologies to everyone assembled and then escorted her sister off to her room.

For a brief time, as she and Jane discussed the night's entertainment – and of course, Mr. Bingley – it was like they were back in their shared bed chamber at Longbourn. However, her elder sister could not disguise her yawns, so Elizabeth had kissed her cheek goodnight and retreated to her room rather than go back downstairs. The muted clack of balls let her know the gentleman had retired to the billiards room and the sound of the pianoforte told her the sisters remained in the main drawing room. She had absolutely no desire to spend time with any of them – save Mr. Bingley.

The two superior sisters continually disparaged her and her family's background, propped up in their beliefs by the condescending manner of their haughty friend, Mr. Darcy. Elizabeth knew exactly where *she* stood with the taciturn man from Derbyshire. The first time he'd laid eyes on her, at the local Assembly, he had declared her tolerable, but not handsome to tempt him. Nothing in his behavior since indicated a change in his verbal assessment. He probably thought of her as an unwashed peasant and very likely looked forward to the day she and Jane scurried home to Longbourn.

She turned onto her side and then sighed. Although bone tired, sleep continued to evade her. After three straight days ensuring Jane received the best of care, she'd run herself ragged.

Very likely sleep eluded her because she was overtired and her mind kept looping in circles, rehashing the disdain of Mr. Darcy and the lack of civility by his faithful companion, Miss Bingley. If she were at Longbourn, she would have thought nothing of taking one of Papa's boring tomes from his book room and put her mind to rest with something like the Canterbury Tales, or a pamphlet on four crop rotations.

She sat up in bed. That would do the trick. She'd sneak down to the library and see what was tucked away on the ill-used shelves. Decision made, she slipped on her robe and a pair of slippers, lit the taper, and crept out of her room. The last thing she needed was for Mr. Darcy to find her roaming the guest wing in nothing but her night gown and robe. His already low opinion would sink beyond all redemption if that happened.

A quick search, because the library truly was dismal with its offerings, she curled up on the couch with a book on animal husbandry. She had not even made it past the second page when her head fell back and she was asleep in front of the waning fire.

Her dreams were strangely pleasant, of a man whispering how beautiful she was. He covered her body with his own and feathered kisses on her neck and across her bosom. Warm hands caressed her leg from her knee, upward to her inner thigh. On a soft sigh, her legs fell open naturally and he stroked her in an unfamiliar, yet intimate manner. The dream was so pleasant, so vivid. She arched her back when pleasure coursed through her body. It was as though she were actually being kissed and fondled. It was only when his member entered and pierced her untried passage that her eyes snapped open to find Mr. Darcy impaling her, over and over until he expended with a tremor and whispered a name.

Elizabeth.

So shocked was she, that not a sound escaped her throat. He did not remove himself, but fell into a deep slumber, still embedded deep within. No matter how much she struggled and pushed, she could not move him. The smell of brandy was strong on his breath and she knew he had no idea he'd violated her in such a grievous manner. She became frantic when the door to the library opened and Mr. Bingley entered with a laugh.

"Darcy! I say, we have to get you to bed old man. You can't sleep down here…"

His mouth dropped open when he came upon them. Elizabeth pleaded with her eyes for him to turn around. Her legs and lower body were fully exposed. There was no hiding what had occurred. Mr. Bingley turned a dull red and with eyes partially closed, began a clumsy approach. It became obvious he meant to raise Mr. Darcy, but he was a large man and out cold. Lifting dead weight was no easy feat.

"Mr. Bingley," she gasped out as her lungs were compressed by Mr. Darcy's weight. "You need only raise him a little. I will try and slide out."

Mortified almost beyond reason, she gave silent thanks when he nodded his acceptance of her suggestion. He then sidestepped to the couch, grabbed Mr. Darcy about the upper chest and shoulders and gave a might heave. Elizabeth scrambled as best she could, almost whimpering at the burning sensation when she felt *that* portion of Mr. Darcy withdraw from her body. She swallowed her cries and fell to the floor. Mr. Bingley lowered the still sleeping Mr. Darcy and sought to lend her a hand, dropping it to his side with an apology when she reared back in fright.

She scrambled backward in an attempt to gain distance from not only the couch, but also Mr. Bingley's mortification and couldn't help but wince at the unaccustomed pain at the juncture between her thighs.

"Please, I beg you, Mr. Bingley. Do not tell anyone of this. I want nothing from Mr. Darcy."

"He violated you Miss Elizabeth and must be held accountable."

"No. He had no idea what he was doing." She shook her head, her curls bouncing around her shoulders, making her look even more vulnerable. "I will not trap him into a loveless marriage. I cannot do that to him, or me."

"What if there are... consequences?"

"I will not borrow trouble, unless required." She clumsily got to her feet, mortified to find her night gown bloodstained. Mr. Bingley handed her a throw which she wrapped around her shoulders.

"If my help *is* required, you must advise me so that I can be your witness and tell my friend what occurred."

"Thank you for your kindness. I... I must go."

"Miss Elizabeth," he began, but she had already fled the room.

He turned to look at his friend, face down on the couch.

"You've gone and done it now, Darce."

~~~

ELIZABETH WATCHED FROM the chair she had dragged to the window as the sun rose the next morning, casting its weak winter rays over a frost covered garden. She remained huddled in the blanket Mr. Bingley gave her before she fled the library. Her gaze never wavered from the vista spread before her, not even when the maid came to start a fire.

"You're up early, Miss Elizabeth."

She dragged her gaze from the window, looked over her shoulder at the young girl, and tried to smile. Tried to behave normal. No one could ever know what happened.

"I found I could not sleep, Hannah."

"Can I draw you a bath, Miss?"

"Yes, please"

She remained seated until the maid left and then stood. The blanket fell to the floor, followed by her soiled nightgown and robe which puddled around her feet. Calmly, she stepped out of the pile of clothing, walked to the fireplace, and ripped the two articles of clothing into the strips before feeding them to the fire. She then wrapped the blanket around her now naked body and waited in the chair for bath water to arrive.

Two hours later, her hair had dried enough to begin pinning it up. A light knock on her door made her start and gasp. Surely, it couldn't be *him*. Heart racing, she called out and almost sighed out loud in relief when Jane poked her head around the corner.

"It seems strange for us to have separate rooms."

"Yes, but tomorrow we shall be back to Longbourn and our normal life." As normal as it ever will be, she thought.

"You know Mamma will not be pleased we are returning to Longbourn after services. She expected us to stay a full week, at least."

"Mamma needs to learn decorum," Elizabeth snapped. "She thrust us into this viper's den without a thought to our reputations."

"Lizzy! Whatever could you mean?" Jane's eyes widened in surprise. "With Mr. Bingley's sisters in residence, our reputations are far from being tarnished."

"Regardless of how proper we both behave, how do you think this whole escapade looks, Jane? Sending you on horseback when it was obvious there would be rain? I know at the time Mamma thought you would spend only one evening, see Mr. Bingley the next morning and return to Longbourn unscathed. But even that is manipulative and does not show us in a favorable light."

By this time Jane had begun braiding and pinning up her hair. She looked at Elizabeth through the mirror.

"You are distraught and I can see the fatigue in your eyes. It looks as though you have not slept in days."

"I did not sleep at all last night."

"My poor sister. This has been almost as hard on you as it was me."

Elizabeth caught herself up, determined to put on a more cheerful face. Jane did not need to be dragged down because of her. This was her sister's last full day of being in Mr. Bingley's company and it had to count. Something good had to come out of this nightmare she currently lived. With that purpose in mind, she turned in her chair to face her sister.

"Thank you, Jane, for being the best sister a girl could ever have."

"You *are* maudlin this morning. Let us go break our fast and start a new day."

"Yes." She stood and smoothed down her skirt. "A new day."

Although she had every intention of behaving in a normal manner, she found herself clinging to Jane like a limpet, starting at every sound. Even Miss Bingley's sniping did not raise her ire and as soon as it was humanly possible, she fled to the garden. She found herself in the wood which bordered the grounds of Netherfield, located a comfortable stump to sit on and lost herself in thought. It was only when she couldn't stop shivering from the cold air, did she rise to her feet and made her way back to the house.

Like a wraith, she stayed to the shadows and moved to the main staircase. Mr. Bingley came upon her and asked if she'd be joining them for dinner, but when he saw the pallor of her skin and eyes wide with fear, he gave a polite bow and told her not to worry, he'd have someone bring her meal to her room. She almost wept in front of him for his kindness.

On the Sabbath, a mere two days following the incident,

several carriages were used to transport all of the Netherfield party to church. She made sure she was in the conveyance that did not have Mr. Darcy within.

The carriages pulled to a stop and when their door opened, Mr. Bingley was immediately at the foot of the small steps to hand Jane out. When her turn came, she absentmindedly accepted Mr. Bingley's hand, only to find it was Mr. Darcy who stood at the door. She took a step backward and almost fell into the carriage when the back of her leg struck the folding stairs.

His reflexes quick, Mr. Darcy grabbed her arm and held her steady.

"Are you well, Miss Elizabeth?"

She could not answer. Her eyes were locked with his and her throat worked to find words, but none came. Mr. Bingley, seeing her distress, stepped smoothly between her and Mr. Darcy.

"Forgive me, Miss Elizabeth. I was quite rude to leave you to your own devices." He turned and put a hand on his friend's shoulder. "Good thing you were here to lend a hand, Darcy. Shall we go to services now?"

Miss Bingley latched onto Mr. Darcy's arm, her head held high as he escorted her into the building, followed by her sister and husband. Mr. Bingley moved a few feet away and waited for Jane, whom Elizabeth took aside.

"Make my apologies to… I am going to walk home."

"I would argue with you, Lizzy if I could not see with my own eyes that you are truly unwell. I do so hope you did not catch my cold."

"No, nothing like that. I slept ill again last night and now have a terrible headache. What I need most is my own bed and some of Hill's willow tea."

"I shall inform Papa and check on you as soon as I can."

Later in the day, Mamma came into her room and

upbraided her for making Jane leave Netherfield too early. Her complaints were long and vociferous. She'd fully expected them to stay the week complete and cast dire warnings that if Mr. Bingley did not ask Jane to marry him, the fault lay squarely on Elizabeth's shoulders. The Lizzy of before might have made some saucy remarks. However, the Elizabeth which had returned from Netherfield let her mother's grievances fall about her shoulders without uttering a word.

The next morning brought no further relief, only astonishment as Papa revealed with much glee, his distant cousin would descend upon Longbourn at four o'clock that afternoon.

"Is this the cousin who will inherit Longbourn, Papa?" Jane asked.

"Oh! – that wretched man should not be allowed to cross our threshold before his time. He's probably coming to catalogue all the silver and valuables. I'll have Hill lock away the pieces that I brought with me to the marriage. He has no right to them." Mama cried out and fanned herself with a handkerchief.

"I think he is coming here for more than surveying his future inheritance, I believe his extension of an olive branch means he wishes to select a wife from our daughters." Papa mused out loud.

"Do you truly think that?" Mamma could not hide the hopefulness in her voice. "We are saved!"

"Now, now, Mrs. Bennet. Do not put the cart before the horse. He may come here and not wish to marry any of our girls. We all know the path to love is sometimes a rocky road."

"Don't be foolish, Mr. Bennet. Of course, he will wish to marry one of our girls, and what a fine thing that will be. Jane will marry Mr. Bingley and Lizzy will wed Mr. Collins."

"We shall find out soon enough. He wrote that he will arrive at precisely four o'clock."

And, he did.

Mr. Collins punctual to his time, was received with great politeness by the whole family. Mr. Bennet, indeed, said little; but the ladies were ready enough to talk, and Mr. Collins seemed neither in need of encouragement, nor inclined to be silent himself. He was a tall, heavy looking young man of five and twenty. His air was grave and stately, and his manners were very formal.

Upon entry to the family parlor, he turned to Mamma.

"Mrs. Bennet, may I compliment you on having so fine a family of daughters. I had heard much of their beauty, but in this instance, fame has fallen short of the truth."

"You are so kind, Mr. Collins," Mamma tittered like a school girl.

"I do not doubt you will see them all in due time well disposed of in marriage."

"Yes, indeed. In fact, our eldest Jane, is very nearly engaged to a young man at a neighboring estate."

Mr. Collins's shoulders slumped and Elizabeth, who'd sequestered herself in a corner near the fireplace knew he felt keen disappointment. She had not missed the way his eyes had roamed in a lascivious manner over her sister's form. For once she was glad of Mamma's propensity to spout an engagement which had not even been broached by the anticipated pair.

Mamma lowered her voice and she could not hear the rest of their conversation, but when Mr. Collins turned his hound dog gaze in her direction, she felt ill. As planned before he arrived, Mamma diverted his attention to her least deserving daughter.

It was going to be a long two weeks.

Chapter Two

THE DAY AFTER THEIR cousin's arrival, all the girls save Mary, voiced a desire to walk to Meryton. Papa, already tired of Mr. Collins intruding on his privacy in his library, encouraged his cousin to go with them. At the last minute, Lizzy complained she still felt out of sorts from her headache the other day and stayed back with Mary. She could not bear another minute of Mr. Collins trying to take her arm or staring at her bosoms.

That Mamma was not pleased was evident but she did not care. All emotion seemed to have been leeched from her body. Over the next few days, Mama's loud calls for her salts, Lydia's exuberance over the arrival of the militia and Mary's pounding of the piano did not rouse her normal vexation.

She and Jane had been walking about the garden when the carriage from Netherfield Park trundled up the drive. She fled to her room, citing a tear in her skirt, unwilling to face the knowing gaze of Mr. Bingley and the haughty one of Mr. Darcy. After they'd left, she ventured back downstairs to find out the purpose of their visit. Everyone, save Mary, was ecstatic over the personal invitation Mr. Bingley had extended to the family for a ball he planned on hosting next Tuesday, the twenty-sixth of November. Unable to call up any form of enthusiasm for the event, Lizzy remained silent. Papa finally called her into his library.

"Lizzy, you have not been the same since Mr. Collins arrived. You are not getting missish over his attentions, are you?"

"No, Papa." She pinched the length of skin between her thumb and fingers to stop her eyes from welling up with tears.

"Good. You know I would never make you do something you did not want."

You might if you had no choice, came the unbidden thought.

"I do know. Thank you, Papa."

Although she'd avoided her cousin's unwanted attentions for most of the day, he caught up with her prior to dinner and solicited the first two sets of Mr. Bingley's ball. She knew by declining his request she'd be forced to sit out the rest of the ball, which for once she did not mind, but too many questions would arise from that decision. No, it was best if she accepted and then made herself invisible for the rest of the evening.

The night of Netherfield Ball was upon them. Jane was quietly excited about her promised sets with Mr. Bingley. Mary had been practicing for hours at the pianoforte in the hope she'd be called upon to perform, and Lydia was beyond excitement, rattling on about dancing with the handsome Mr. Wickham. Lizzy vaguely recalled him from a card party at her Aunt Phillips, but he'd not paid her much attention.

Mamma had high hopes Mr. Bingley would propose to Jane before the night was out while Lizzy dreaded the upcoming hours, mentally preparing herself to behave with a modicum of normalcy. Until she knew for certain there were consequences from that night, she had to forge ahead and hide her burgeoning distress.

It was with this attitude that she met up with Charlotte Lucas, whom she had not seen for a week, and poured out her frustration on the oddities of her cousin. Their conversation was shortened by the man's appearance to claim the first set, so after a quick introduction, she reluctantly let Mr. Collins lead her out onto the floor.

The two first dances brought a resurgence of her previous distress. They were dances of absolute and complete mortification. Mr. Collins, awkward and solemn, apologised instead of attending to the movement of other dancers, often moving wrong without being aware of it. His poor performance mortified her. She knew, beyond a shadow of doubt, Miss Bingley watched and sneered. The moment the set was complete and she was released from his officious company she walked off the dance floor, determined to never be embarrassed in that fashion again.

She danced next with an officer, and when those dances were over, she returned to Charlotte Lucas. Deep in conversation, she was surprised to be suddenly addressed by Mr. Darcy.

"May I have the next dance, Miss Elizabeth?"

She couldn't breathe. Her stomach clenched and rolled. She felt as though it lay at the base of her throat. One word, and she'd cast up her accounts. His brow furrowed and Charlotte gave her a subtle nudge with her elbow. Taken so much by surprise in his application for her hand, she automatically accepted him. He walked away again immediately, and she was left to stew in silent despair. Charlotte tried her best to console her.

"I dare say you will find him very agreeable."

"Never."

"Are you well, Lizzy? You look very pale."

Her anxiety continued to spiral. How could she stand

across from Mr. Darcy after what happened between them? She silently castigated herself. He had no memory of that night in the library. She squared her shoulders. She could do this. For Jane, she would dance with Mr. Bingley's friend and act as though nothing was wrong in her small corner of the world. When the dancing recommenced, however, and Darcy approached to claim her hand, Charlotte could not help cautioning her, in a whisper, not to be a simpleton.

"Mr. Darcy has singled you out, Lizzy. Do not let your prejudice stand in the way of making a splendid match."

Elizabeth made no answer, and took her place in the set. They stood for some time without speaking a word; and she began to imagine that their silence was to last through the two dances. Would that it could, she prayed fervently. She had no idea of what to talk about with the man who'd unwittingly compromised her and stolen her virtue. Her prayers for continued peace were not answered.

"Have you been enjoying the ball so far?"

"Yes, thank you," she replied, and was again silent.

After a pause of some minutes, he addressed her a second time with: "It is your turn to say something now, Miss Elizabeth. I asked about the dance, and you ought to make some kind of remark on the size of the room, or the number of couples."

She fumbled for words. "The room is lovely. Miss Bingley has done a wonderful job of decorating."

"Very well. That reply will do for the present." They promenaded down the line before pausing for the next groups to do their steps. "I find private balls are much pleasanter than public ones."

She was quietly becoming exasperated. What happened to the taciturn, broody gentleman who stalked the perimeters of the room avoiding any and all conversation with those he thought beneath him? Why? Why was he suddenly so verbose?

"Do you talk by rule then, while you are dancing?"

"At times. It would look odd to be entirely silent for half an hour together."

Once again, they were silent till they had gone down the dance and he asked her if she were feeling better. In surprise, her gaze flew to his and met his dark grey eyes.

"Mr. Bingley and I came across your sisters the other day and they told us you were feeling indisposed and had stayed at home for the day."

She lowered her gaze and made no answer because Sir William Lucas appeared close to them, meaning to pass through the set to the other side of the room. On perceiving Mr. Darcy, he stopped with a bow of superior courtesy, to compliment him on his dancing and his partner.

"Such very superior dancing is not often seen. It is evident that you belong to the first circles. Allow me to say, however, that your fair partner does not disgrace you. I would think this pleasure will be oft repeated, especially when a certain desirable event takes place." He glanced toward Jane and Mr. Bingley dancing further down the line. "But, let me not interrupt you, Sir. I shall not detain you from your delightful partner any longer."

Elizabeth was left in no doubt as to where Mr. Darcy's thoughts had traveled as his mien took on an attitude of seriousness when his gaze followed Sir William's to Bingley and Jane. With fascination, she watched him forcibly bring his emotions under control and turn his attention back to her.

"Sir William's interruption has made me forget what we were talking of," he finally said.

"We were speaking of nothing. Sir William could not have interrupted any two people in the room who had less to say for themselves. What subject you might canvas next, I cannot imagine."

"What think you of books?" said he, smiling.

She came to a full stop and the lady promenading behind her almost tumbled into her back.

"I cannot do this!"

Elizabeth fled the dance floor toward the balcony, pushing through the doors into the cold night air. Of all the subjects to canvas. Books! She did not need a reminder of the very room where he'd accosted her.

"Miss Elizabeth!"

She cast a frantic glance over her shoulder and saw Mr. Darcy about to come outside after her. She picked up her skirts and raced down the stairs, careening around the paths in an attempt to re-enter Netherfield via the servant's entrance. If she had on a warm coat and sturdy boots instead of dancing slippers, she'd have run all the way to Longbourn.

For the rest of the evening, she hid in the ladies retiring room, venturing out only when Mamma and her sisters came to change into their outerwear at the close of the evening.

"Where have you been Lizzy?" Mamma demanded as she tied on her bonnet. "I have not seen hide nor hair of you since your dance with Mr. Darcy."

"Oh, he is in a foul mood," Lydia giggled.

"Why do you say that?" Jane asked.

"Lizzy abandoned him on the dance floor and he stomped about for the rest of the night looking even more dark and broody."

"Elizabeth Bennet, did you stand up Mr. Darcy?" Mamma practically screeched out. "How could you? What must Mr. Bingley think of your headstrong behavior? He might not offer for Jane after this."

"I am still not well, Mamma and had to leave before I fell sick on the dance floor. I am sure Mr. Darcy was not so very upset. We all know he does not like me."

"That is true, but every action reflects on Jane."

Elizabeth stared, open mouthed, at her mother's gall to spout nonsense about her daughter's behavior when she herself was the one that embarrassed them all on a daily basis. She snapped her mouth shut and threw her cloak around her shoulders. Mamma would never change and fighting in the retiring room where neighbors could hear was not acceptable.

The Longbourn party were the last of all the company to depart; and by a maneuver of Mrs. Bennet, had to wait for their carriages a quarter of an hour after every body else was gone. It was painfully obvious to Elizabeth their hosts heartily wished them away.

Mrs. Hurst and her sister scarcely opened their mouths except to complain of fatigue and were evidently impatient to have the house to themselves. They repulsed every attempt of Mrs. Bennet at conversation. Oblivious to everything around him, Mr. Collins complimented Mr. Bingley and his sisters on the elegance of their entertainment, and the hospitality and politeness which had marked their behavior to their guests.

Mr. Darcy said nothing at all but parked himself near the stairs and glowered in the direction of Elizabeth. Mr. Bennet, in equal silence, was clearly enjoying the scene. Mr. Bingley and Jane were standing together, a little detached from the rest, and talked only to each other. Elizabeth, for her own sanity, stayed as quiet and unobtrusive as possible.

When at length they arose to take leave, Mrs. Bennet addressed herself particularly to Mr. Bingley, to assure him how happy he would make them by eating a family dinner with them at any time, without the ceremony of a formal invitation. He accepted with alacrity, saying he would be returning some time next week.

As the Bennet carriages slowly moved away from Netherfield, Mrs. Bennet leaned into her husband and whispered loud enough for Lizzy to hear, "Mark my words, Mr. Bennet. Our eldest daughter will undoubtedly be settled at Netherfield in the course of three or four months. Plenty of time for the necessary preparation of settlements, new carriages, and wedding clothes."

"The bird has not even been flushed from the thicket, Mrs. Bennet. Prime your gun all you want, but you have to wait until he shows himself before you take aim. Even then, the bird can evade you. When he comes to see me, *then* you may move forward with all your plans."

The following morning, Mr. Collins finally broached the subject Elizabeth had been dreading since his arrival. On finding Mrs. Bennet, Elizabeth, and Kitty together soon after breakfast, he addressed Mamma in these words,

"May I hope, Madam, for your interest with your fair daughter Elizabeth, when I solicit for the honor of a private audience with her in the course of this morning?"

Before Elizabeth had time for any thing but a blush of surprise, Mrs. Bennet instantly answered, "Most certainly. I am sure Lizzy will be very happy and can have no objection." Gathering her work together, she turned to Kitty. "Come, Kitty, I want you up stairs."

Not wanting to be alone with her loathsome cousin, Elizabeth called out, "Do not go. Mr. Collins can have nothing to say to me that anybody need not hear. I am going away myself."

"None of your nonsense, Lizzy. I insist upon your staying and hearing Mr. Collins."

Elizabeth, not one to outright defy her mother, sorely wished to do so. After a moment's consideration she decided it would be wisest to get the whole embarrassing debacle over as soon and as quietly as possible. She sat down again, and tried to tamp down her growing frustration. Mrs. Bennet and Kitty walked off, and as soon as they were gone Mr. Collins began.

"Believe me, my dear Miss Elizabeth, that your modesty, far from doing you any disservice, rather adds to your other perfections. Almost as soon as I entered the house, I singled you out as the companion of my future life. But before I am run away with by my feelings on this subject, perhaps it will be advisable for me to state my reasons for marrying…"

The idea of Mr. Collins, with all his solemn composure, being run away with by his feelings, gave her a brief moment of levity, but as he droned on, and on, she emptied her mind and waited for him to end.

"… To fortune I am perfectly indifferent, and shall make no demand of that nature on your father, since I am well aware that it could not be complied with; and that one thousand pounds in the four per cents, which will not be yours till after your mother's decease, is all that you may ever be entitled to. On that head, therefore, I shall be uniformly silent; and you may assure yourself that no ungenerous reproach shall ever pass my lips when we are married."

It was absolutely necessary to interrupt him now.

"You are too hasty, Sir," she cried. "You have not asked the question for me to give an answer. Let me do now and not further waste your time. No, thank you."

She made to stand but he continued to speak over her.

"I have been told," replied Mr. Collins, with a formal wave of the hand, "that it is usual with young ladies to reject the addresses of the man whom they secretly mean to accept. I am therefore by no means discouraged, and shall hope to lead you to the altar ere long."

"I will not marry you, Mr. Collins." She rose to her feet and would have quit the room, had not her cousin addressed her again.

"When I do myself the honor of speaking to you next on

this subject, I shall hope to receive a more favorable answer than you have given me thus far."

For one brief second, she considered revising her answer. If she were with child, she needed to find a husband and father. However, with or without a child, she'd be stuck married to Mr. Collins, and he'd be perfectly within his rights to expect her to welcome him to her bed. The thought of his oily person hovering over hers in the privacy of their bedchamber made her want to expel her recently eaten breakfast. It was that thought alone which gave her the impetus to end this ridiculous dialogue.

"Mr. Collins," cried out Elizabeth, interrupting his one-sided conversation, "I have refused your offer of marriage – more than once, I might add – and will continue to do so."

"You must give me leave to flatter myself, my dear cousin, that your refusal of my addresses is merely the words of a young maiden who does not know her own mind. You should take into further consideration that in spite of your manifold attractions," – his gaze once again lingered on her bosom – "it is by no means certain that another offer of marriage may ever be made you. Your portion is unhappily so small that it will in all likelihood undo the effects of your loveliness and amiable qualifications. Therefore, I must conclude that you are not serious in your rejection of me, I shall choose to attribute it to your wish of increasing my love by suspense, according to the usual practice of elegant females."

If his lecherous leer hadn't turned her stomach, the very notion of him thinking she wished to increase his love by teasing, finalized her resolve to end this abhorrent proposal.

"I am not an elegant female intending to plague you, but a rational creature speaking the truth from her heart. I will not marry you."

"Fear not, Cousin Elizabeth, when sanctioned by the express authority of both your excellent parents, my proposals will not fail of being acceptable."

To continue arguing with a man so set on wilful self-deception, was an exercise in futility. If he persisted in ignoring her repeated refusals, the matter would have to go before her father. She was fairly confident he'd support her refusal. Even if Papa didn't lend support, no one could make her say 'yes' at the altar. And so, she simply rose to her feet and left Mr. Collins standing alone in the room. She briefly wondered when retribution would arrive in the form of her mother's anger and did not have long to wait. Within the hour Mamma demanded she go with her to Papa, who was reading in the library.

"Come here, child," Papa said when she entered the room. "I understand Mr. Collins has made you an offer of marriage. Is it true?"

"He has," Elizabeth replied.

"Hmmm… and this offer of marriage you have refused?"

"Yes, Papa."

"Very well. We now come to the point. Your mother insists upon your accepting it. Is not it so, Mrs. Bennet?"

"Yes, or I will never see her again."

"I see. An unhappy alternative is before you, Elizabeth. From this day you must be a stranger to one of your parents." He afforded her a sly wink. "Your mother will never see you again if you do *not* marry Mr. Collins, and I will never see you again if you *do*."

Elizabeth could not help but smile at his droll wit, but Mrs. Bennet, who had persuaded herself that her husband regarded the affair as she wished, was excessively disappointed.

"What do you mean, Mr. Bennet, by talking in this way? You promised me to insist upon her marrying him."

"My dear," replied her husband, "I promised no such thing. Now, I have two small favors to request. First, that you will allow me the free use of my understanding on the present occasion; and secondly, of my room. I shall be glad to have the library to myself as soon as may be."

Mr. Collins, indignant and now fully aware her refusal had been steadfast, could not be persuaded to look upon the next eldest daughter as a suitable wife. Fortunately, Charlotte Lucas stopped by for a visit and when she witnessed first hand the turmoil within the walls of Longbourn, offered to take Mr. Collins back to Lucas Lodge where he would stay to dinner.

The next few days were difficult for Elizabeth. Not only was she coming to terms with what happened in the library at Netherfield Park, but also the possibility she could be with child. She fell into an attitude of despondency, barely registering her mother's never-ending anger and words of near hatred. In no uncertain terms, Elizabeth was made very aware she was Mrs. Bennet's least favorite daughter. She received no warmth or love from the woman who birthed her.

The Lizzy from before would have made sport of her cousin's horrible proposal and tried to tease Mrs. Bennet into good humor, but Elizabeth of now did not have the desire, nor energy, and spent most of her waking hours avoiding Mrs. Bennet. Thankfully, she did not have to avoid her cousin, for he continued to take advantage of his welcome at Lucas Lodge and rarely darkened the doors of Longbourn.

At one time, Papa called her into his library and teased her over being missish in avoiding his bumbling cousin and allowing Mrs. Bennet's tantrums to affect her sense of humor. She almost lifted her sleeve to show him the bruises from her pinches. However, there was no way to curb Mrs. Bennet's nerves or her father's delight in all things absurd, so she weakly smiled and promised once Mr. Collins no longer stayed with the walls of Longbourn, her happy manners would return.

Unfortunately, her unhappiness soon had a partner in Jane when Mr. Bingley left for London as planned. What they didn't expect was his entourage to follow the next day. Although her eldest sister was heartbroken and Mrs. Bennet apoplectic, Elizabeth finally felt as though a great restriction about her chest had lifted. She could breathe again. That is until, after the Christmas dinner, she was forced to approach her father and tell him an abridged version of what happened that night at Netherfield. Within less than eight months, she very likely would have Mr. Darcy's baby and, for the sake of her sisters and their reputations, she needed to leave Longbourn and Hertfordshire before it became obvious.

AN UNWITTING COMPROMISE

Chapter Three

THE ROCKING OF THE carriage made Elizabeth wish to cast up her accounts again, but for the sake of Papa, who was escorting her to their uncle's house in Cheapside while they figured out a solution to her problem, she fought the rising bile with all her being.

At first, she was to have gone to town when Jane did right after Christmas with the Gardiner's, but with Charlotte's unexpected engagement to Mr. Collins and subsequent hasty wedding, her plans were paused. Everything in her longed to run to London, but too many eyebrows would have been raised if she had not stayed to witness her best friend's wedding ceremony. Now, more than ever, she had to maintain a façade of normalcy.

It had been so hard to lie to Charlotte. She'd begged Lizzy to come and visit in March and she was forced to fob off her queries with evasion and untruths.

"I would love nothing better than to come and see you happily settled, dear Charlotte." This much was true. "However, I have been invited to stay with the Marquess of Haversham, a distant cousin from my maternal grandmother's side."

"I have not heard you talk about them before." Charlotte had said, showing no small annoyance at her friend would not agree to her request. Elizabeth felt bad, knowing her good friend would think she prevaricated in order to avoid Mr. Collins himself – which wouldn't be too far from the truth.

"We have visited them regularly. You often wondered why Jane and I would tour the Lake District every second summer. In fact, we were at Cousin Percy's estate in Buckinghamshire. Papa never wanted us to be judged by our relatives, and so he kept this branch of the family quiet."

"Then I demand you attend me sometime this summer."

"Oh, Charlotte. This year I may actually *be* touring the North country with Aunt and Uncle Gardiner until the end of August, but I *will* come visit before I am thirty." She took hold of Charlotte's hands and squeezed. "I promise."

"I will hold you to that, Eliza Bennet. There is no one else I wish to share my joy with."

She threw her arms around Charlotte. "I will miss you, my dearest friend. I am so very happy for you and know you will make a wonderful Mrs. Collins."

Her next course of action, while she waited for Papa to get things prepared for their journey to London was to ask Mrs. Bennet and Aunt Philips how long they thought it would take for Charlotte Collins to fall with child. She then left them to do what they did best. Gossip. From their uncensored conversation, she gleaned women who experienced nausea only had to contend with it for the first few months. Rare was the lady who suffered the full pregnancy. She hadn't prayed for much lately, but she did pray the nausea she'd begun to suffer from would pass, and quickly.

Jane had left with Aunt and Uncle Gardiner at the end of December for London, and upon her arrival, had written to say she and their aunt would be in the same area as Mr. Bingley's townhouse next week. It was the perfect opportunity for Jane to renew her acquaintance with Miss Bingley and Elizabeth was anxious to find out if her venture had been successful – as in meeting Mr. Bingley. At the same time, she dreaded the reunion with her sister, having made the decision to share her secret.

Her eldest sister was the only one she could bear to confess all. Telling Papa had been a necessity; telling Jane was for her sanity. It didn't take much for her realize her father meant to confront Mr. Darcy for his role in her fall from grace and she stopped herself several times from giving him more information.

For one, she never revealed Mr. Bingley's witness of her shame. Some small part of her psyche reasoned that if no one knew, nothing would stand in the way of him returning to Jane. So far, Mr. Bingley had been away six weeks. The future for her sister looked almost as grim as hers. It was blessed relief when the familiar street their uncle resided came into view and she saw Jane waiting on the front step. She took Elizabeth's hands in hers as soon as Papa helped her down and squeezed.

"I am so glad you have come. And you as well, Papa," she said when he kissed her on the cheek. "Aunt Madeline has tea ready, and those lemon tarts you are so fond of Lizzy."

At the thought of food, Elizabeth pressed a hand to her mouth, shot a horrified look at her father and ran inside and up the stairs to the room she would share with Jane. Faintly, as she ran up the stair, she heard Papa tell Jane and her surprised aunt, that her stomach had been upset the whole trip. He put it down to bad eggs from their morning breakfast.

~~~

"THERE IS A MR. BENNET here to see you, sir."

Darcy's butler had interrupted his quiet in the study, something which he frowned upon as this was when he balanced his books and took care of all his letters of business. He preferred uninterrupted time so that he didn't lose track of his thoughts.

"Have him come back this afternoon. I am busy."

"He said it was personal and urgent."

He huffed out a sigh. "Very well, show him in."

Burke gave a polite half bow and left the room, returning in a few short minutes to announce the gentleman. Darcy stood politely as he walked in the room. He noted two things very quickly. Bennet was distraught, but also showing signs of deep anger. He wondered briefly if he was here because Mr. Bennet, or rather Mrs. Bennet, had discovered he'd persuaded Bingley to quit Netherfield permanently, but discarded that notion as fast as it had come because their argument would be with Bingley, not him.

"Good day, Mr. Bennet. What brings you here, to Darcy House?"

"It is a matter of some delicacy and I ask that you hear me out before you show me the door."

Darcy nodded his head as acceptance.

"Two weeks ago, my daughter Elizabeth came to me in great distress. She did not want to tell me of her situation, but I am afraid she had no choice. While at Netherfield, the two of you spent some time in the library… alone. I demand satisfaction and ask that you behave with honor and marry my daughter."

Darcy simmered with anger. How dare this useless father of five harridans come and demand he marry his daughter. A sting of remorse pinched his heart at lumping Miss Elizabeth and Miss Bennet with their sisters, but he ignored it. Bingley had escaped their snare and now the desperate parents looked to capture a bigger goose. One that laid golden eggs. He would have none of their treachery.

"Miss Elizabeth and I *did* spend a half hour in the library reading. The door remained open the entire time, with servants in the hallway. At no time did we engage in anything that resembled a compromise."

"Yes, Elizabeth told me how you ignored her completely yet did not turn a single page of your book the whole time." He was sure he'd pretended to read. Had he sat there holding his book along with his breath? "No, Mr. Darcy, the time Elizabeth spoke of happened a different night. The ladies had retired while the gentlemen played billiards."

"Your daughter's web of lies has caught her up. I *did* play billiards with Mr. Bingley and Mr. Hurst and was in their company the whole of the evening. At no time was I alone with Miss Elizabeth in the library, so you can tell Mrs. Bennet her second attempt at throwing a daughter in front of a rich man did not work. We have nothing further to discuss. I bid you good day."

"Not so fast. Because of your licentious behavior, Elizabeth is *enceinte*."

Darcy reeled in shock. The thought of Elizabeth, heavy with a child not his own, struck him in the solar plexus and he struggled to breathe. His vision dimmed around the edges before he gathered his emotions into a tight coil.

He finally managed to say, "I do not know why you tell me this when I had nothing to do with the creation of her bastard."

Bennet audibly sucked in a gasp of air.

"My daughter claims you as the father of her child, and she does not lie."

"In this case, she has. I am sure her and her mother's eye is on the prize of Pemberley and all my other assets, but I assure you, I am *not* the father. I have not even so much as touched your daughter's hand other than in a public ballroom, let alone aid in the conception of a child. The only way it could have occurred would be immaculate conception, and the Virgin Mary she is not."

"You churlish, rump-fed, Fustilarian!" Bennet cried out in disgust.

"If you were a younger man, I would call you out for such an insult."

"That was not an insult. It was a statement of fact."

Darcy pulled the lanyard to call his butler.

"At no time did I accost your daughter, nor did I get her with child. Good day, Mr. Bennet."

The door to the study opened and Bennet glared at him, hatred cold in his eyes.

"Do not take me for a fool, Mr. Darcy. I am a married man and know very well what a man experiences and discovers on *his* body when he has taken a maiden to his bed, or in your case the couch in the library. There would have been evidence, sir. Deny your share in this catastrophe in public all you like, but when you are in the safety of your chambers and sleep eludes you, well remember what you have done." He moved to the exit and turned within the door frame to face him. "I take no leave of you, Mr. Darcy. I do not wish you good health and I hope I never have to lay eyes on you again unless you are laid out for viewing because of an early demise."

Darcy kept his features steady, internally cursing the fact that Bennet had voiced his ridiculous claim in front of his butler. He was a man of honor and had not betrayed his own personal code. He briefly toyed with the idea of setting out to ruin the man for spewing such venomous libel, but discarded the thought before it could take root. He would have nothing to do with them ever again.

Burke returned a few minutes later and asked if needed anything further.

"No. Tell Cook I will not be home for dinner."

"Very well, sir."

In less than an hour, Darcy was ensconced in a chair at White's watching other gentlemen mill about the betting book. Left to his thoughts, he couldn't help but reflect on Mr. Bennet's words. Elizabeth was pregnant. He'd fled Hertfordshire because he knew he was becoming dangerously attracted to her. Thank goodness he hadn't acted on those impulses. He'd made a serious mistake giving into his desire and asking her to dance at the ball. Because he'd shown a brief vignette of interest, she now thought she could claim him as the father of her child.

If someone had asked him if Miss Elizabeth would allow herself to get caught up with man to the point of disregarding all rules of propriety, he would have scoffed and said no. In light of his conversation with Mr. Bennet, once again he was shown that those who had the look of goodness hid evil in their hearts. After growing up with the nightmare known as Wickham, and the near ruination of his sister this past summer by that handsome cad's plan to debauch and steal her dowry, he should have known better. All the more reason to be so careful in whom he chose for a mistress of Pemberley.

Caroline Bingley it would never be, no matter how hard or how often she gripped his arm in public. But there was still his cousin, Anne. Except her health was so fragile, she could never bear an heir and survive. Unlike Elizabeth. She'd most likely have a dozen children and think nothing of it. His thoughts stuttered to a stop. He had to stop thinking of her!

"Darcy! Why the scowl?"

"I was thinking of your sister," he quipped back.

"That would make any man scowl."

Charles Bingley dropped into the chair opposite and caught the attention of a man servant.

"Brandy," was all he said and settled his head back onto the chair with a huge sigh.

"Rough day?" Darcy asked.

"Yes. I am rethinking my decision to quit Hertfordshire."

"No!"

At Darcy's vehement outburst, Bingley straightened and stared, mouth open in surprise.

"Why ever not? Miss Bennet is an angel and I am sure she returned my feelings. I very much would like to call on her and see if it could grow into something more."

"Stay away from the Bennet sisters, or you shall have more than love growing between you."

"Whatever do you mean?"

"I have irrefutable proof the Bennet's sole purpose was to catch a wealthy husband for their daughters and they have no love for either of us."

"For us? What do you mean? Were you going to offer for one of the Bennet sisters?"

"Never!" Darcy paused. As angry as he was at Elizabeth, he could not share her degradation with Charles. He'd never be able to keep it from Caroline and she would spread the story all over England if possible. No, he had to keep her dirty secret, although disguise was his abhorrence. "I cannot tell you my source, but it is indisputable."

"An infallible source?"

"Yes."

"That makes me quite sad, actually." Charles returned to his slouched position. "I thought for sure I had found the woman I could spend the rest of my life with." He speared Darcy with a discerning glance. "Might I know the source of this revelation?"

"I would rather not say, but it was someone very close to the family who knows all their intimate secrets." That was all he could give him without revealing too much.

"Did they write you a letter?"

Damn, Bingley. He would not let this go.

"No, they came in person."

"That dire?"

"Yes, and I will say no more. We are lucky to have escaped when we did and I strongly urge you to quit the lease, retrieve as much money as you can and look elsewhere to purchase."

Charles accepted his brandy from the servant and took a drink. He gazed into the flames of the nearby fireplace; his expression thoughtful. Something Darcy was not used to seeing on his friend's face.

"So many things happened at Netherfield. There is something I should share with you, Darcy. It might have an impact—"

Bingley got no further because Darcy's cousin, the Viscount Ashton arrived and sat down to share a drink, or two, or three. It was a very drunk Darcy who wobbled his way, with the aid of his valet and butler, to his bed chamber in the early hours of the morning. It was only when he opened bleary eyes and surveyed his rumpled bed, did he have a brief moment of clarity from a morning at Netherfield, when he'd awakened in a similar confused state. At the time, he'd had vivid dreams of kissing Miss Elizabeth. Of caressing her silky skin and touching her in places he'd only ever dreamed about.

He still could make no sense of those dreams or the condition of his nether region, and so he'd buried them deep within his memory banks, refusing to inspect them in the cold light of day.

AN UNWITTING COMPROMISE

Chapter Four

THE DRAWING ROOM at Gracechurch Street was pleasantly quiet as the three women either read or worked on some sewing from their basket of mending. Knowing her father had very likely gone to confront Mr. Darcy, Elizabeth's nerves were stretched even tighter than they had been the past month. Because she'd been waiting, she was the first to hear the arrival of her father's equipage and carefully stowed away her mending in anticipation of what word he brought back.

She didn't have long to wait. Papa came and stood in the doorway to the room and held out his arms. She stood and ran into them and he hugged her tight. Without him saying a word, she knew Mr. Darcy had denied all culpability and she was on her own.

"Thomas! Whatever is the matter?" Aunt Madeline had risen to her feet alongside Jane.

"All will be known soon enough." Papa held her shoulders and made her look him in the eye. The familiar Bennet green irises were unwavering. Resolute. She was the only daughter who inherited this particular family trait. "I must discuss this with your uncle and we will find a solution."

She could only nod in reply. To speak would mean she'd have to loosen the tight cords around her throat and if she did that, great sobs of grief would escape. Papa dropped his hands and went to find his brother-in-law. Uncle Gardiner's network of friends was vast and varied. She knew they'd be canvassing his contacts for someone in need of a wife who wouldn't care that she carried the child of another man.

"Elizabeth," her aunt's voice brought her out of her reverie. "What is going on?"

She turned and faced the two most important females in her life. To survive this nightmare, she needed their love and support. There was no way she'd receive any of that from the home front. A jolt of revulsion went through her. Her mother would wail and cry and all of Meryton would know her shame. Mrs. Bennet's propensity for gossip would not curb her tongue and she would drag all her daughters down only so she could bemoan the fact of how ill her second daughter had used her. Aunt Gardiner and Jane were the only ones she trusted with the truth.

Her heart pinched at the thought she could never share this with Charlotte, the other person she, up until this past month, had unwaveringly trusted as well. Now, as Mrs. Collins, her allegiance lay with her husband. If Mr. Collins became aware of her fallen woman status, he'd post a letter to Lucas Lodge so fast, Meryton would have heard the news yesterday.

"I hardly know where to start."

As Elizabeth moved back to her chair, Aunt Gardiner dismissed the maid and shut the door. She settled back into her chair and faced her favorite niece.

"Every burden shared becomes a lighter load, Lizzy. Please tell us how we might help."

"Oh, Aunt, I am ruined!"

She burst into tears and covered her eyes, bowing into

herself as she rocked. Jane quickly kneeled and wrapped her arms around her waist and held on. Aunt Gardiner waited until she was spent and then handed her several dry handkerchiefs.

"Now," she said in a gentle voice, "what has happened?"

She wiped her face and blew her nose before speaking.

"As you know, Jane and I were forced to spend almost a week at Netherfield while she recuperated from a violent cold."

"I remember from both your letters. Did something happen while you were there?"

The events of that night finally tumbled past her lips. Jane gasped when she told of how she'd awakened to find Mr. Darcy atop her body – she did not share the full particulars as she was cognizant that her sister, as a maiden, should remain unaware of the more intimate details – but Aunt Gardiner pursed her lips and frowned.

"I am surprised by his behavior. I know the Darcy family well. This is quite unlike anything I have heard."

"In his defense, Mr. Darcy was very drunk and I would not be surprised if he has no recollection of this."

"You do not need to defend him, Lizzy. He is a grown man and is responsible for his actions no matter what state he is in."

"I do not wish to defend him; I am only stating fact."

"You obviously were not discovered, or the compromise would have been made public before they left Hertfordshire."

Elizabeth hesitated. There was still a chance Mr. Bingley may return to Netherfield and she would never – ever – ruin Jane's chance at happiness.

"He fell asleep and I was able to get away." She twisted one of the handkerchiefs into a tight ball. "I had hoped and prayed there would be no consequence, but I have not had my courses since that night and had to approach Papa before my condition became known."

"You may still lose the babe. Until you feel the quickening, anything can happen. You shall stay with us here until we know for sure."

"Aunt, I can never go home now. No man will want to marry me. I am not a maiden any longer. The minute he finds out, my shame will become public."

"Nonsense. When the time comes, you will find a good man and if he loves you, he will accept you for who you are and understand you had no choice in this matter."

"Oh, Lizzy. I wish you had told me." Jane moved back to her chair, tears welling in her eyes. "Now I understand why you did not want to go to the ball at Netherfield. And to think I looked upon Mr. Darcy as a gentleman."

"He is a gentleman. As angry as I am, I know he also made a mistake. I am disappointed he did not acquiesce to Papa's demand but not surprised. He always did look upon the citizens of Meryton with nothing but contempt. And we all know he only looked to me to find fault. I was barely tolerable when he first laid eyes on me, I am sure he now actively hates the very thought of me."

"Let us not borrow trouble before its time. Until it is a certainty, our life goes on as before, and that means we shall visit the modiste for those gowns I promised you."

"I cannot go to any functions, Aunt!"

"You can and you will." Aunt Gardiner's voice was firm, showing that she would brook no opposition from her niece. She turned at the sound of a light knock and called for the door to be opened, revealing the housekeeper.

"Mr. Bennet would like to see Miss Elizabeth in the study, ma'am."

Elizabeth followed the woman to Uncle Gardiner's study. After a soft knock on the door, she was invited to enter. Both men were seated near the fireplace, but Uncle Gardiner rose to his feet and indicated Elizabeth should take the vacated chair.

Papa wasted no time.

"Your uncle will canvass his contacts and see if there are gentlemen in want of a wife. Men who might be widowers in need of a mother for their children, or a gentleman requiring a companion or hostess who will not mind if you come with a ready-made family. I am going to write cousin Percy. If we are going to fish for a husband, we may as well cast a wide net and the Marquis has friends in places I could never aspire to reach."

"I do not want more family to know of my shame, Papa!"

"Lizzy, your cousin is the soul of discretion. We may not have had a lot of contact over the years because I hate coming to Town, but this I do know. I trust him as much as I trust this man," – he nodded in the direction of Uncle Gardiner – "and Percy will not betray you."

Papa and Uncle then talked of preparing her side of the marriage settlement so if a suitable gentleman was found, the articles of marriage could be facilitated quickly.

"We do not have much, Lizzy, as you well know, but we will be prepared for all contingencies."

After about an hour, she pled the beginnings of a headache and excused herself to go up to the bedchamber she shared with Jane. Although her thoughts were jumbled and pinging from one scenario to another, she finally fell asleep, not even waking when Jane slid in beside her.

The next day, Papa returned to Longbourn saying that he'd given permission to Uncle Gardiner to negotiate any marriage offers in his stead. The following week, her uncle asked her to come to the study. She entered to discover a stranger seated by the fireplace. He stood immediately upon her arrival and she noted his height and athletic build. Although older than Papa, he was handsome and had a ready smile.

"Elizabeth, I would like to introduce you to Mr. Henry Talbot."

"Miss Elizabeth."

The man's voice had a pleasant rumble to it and soothed her frayed nerves. She gave him a curtsy and he nodded back in acknowledgment.

"Mr. Talbot is a friend of your cousin, the Marquess."

"Oh!" Her eyes widened. Was he a titled gentleman? She mentally shook her head. No, Uncle Gardiner had introduced him as Mr. Talbot. "I am pleased to make your acquaintance, sir."

"Mr. Gardiner. May I be so bold as to ask your niece if she would accompany me to the little park at the end of your street?"

"I… ah… yes. Of course. Her sister Jane can accompany you."

"No, I would rather a footman, please. Our conversation will be a private one, which she can share with her sister when we return."

"Very well."

Uncle called for a footman and soon Elizabeth was walking the paths of the park. Mr. Talbot said not a word until they reached a bench and he asked if she'd take a seat. The footman stayed a few yards away at a respectful distance. Not too close to hear the conversation, but close enough for propriety. She almost laughed out loud at the thought.

Propriety flew out the window last November, Lizzy.

"Miss Elizabeth, I am aware you may be *enceinte*. Is that correct?"

She blushed and lowered her eyes. "Yes."

She gave a start when his finger touched the bottom of her chin and raised her face.

"No shame, Miss Elizabeth. I am aware of the circumstances surrounding your condition and will not allow you to bow your head because of it." He smiled at her look of confusion. "If we rub along nicely, I expect you to hold your head high and look people in the eyes. I will claim your child as my own, and male or female, they will inherit all that I have."

"Why?" she finally whispered.

"I am unable to have children. My wife, who passed away about ten years ago, thought the fault lay with her, but I have had a few paramours in my time and they have never fallen with child." He chuckled at her blush. "I am no innocent boy, Miss Elizabeth. I have seen over fifty summers and will not paint myself as a saint."

"I cannot judge your actions, sir. I do not even know you."

"No, you do not, but I would like to change all that." He took one of her gloved hands in his. "My doctors have informed me I have only a few short years before I leave this mortal shell. I have no heirs and no other family. All my properties will go to waste and my family's heritage will become nothing but words written on aging parchment."

"I am sorry to hear that." Even though she'd only just met the man, she liked his manners and his honesty. "But my child will not be your heir."

"I have a special license…" he chuckled again at her gasp. "Yes, I know… presumptuous of me. If you are agreeable, we shall marry three days hence. You are not far enough along to show and I abhor Town, so no one will be surprised if I tuck you away in the countryside. Upon my death, all that I have will go to you and *our* child." He stressed the word 'our.' "The entail on my estate and title – yes, I do have a title – are *in fee simple* and once our child is born, I will change my will to add their name and no one will ever contest it."

"Why three days?"

"A lady must have a courtship. Are three days not enough?"

For the first time in months, Elizabeth laughed.

"Sir, a half hour was enough."

"Have you no desire to know what title I have?"

"No," she shook her head. "I have never been one to hold the peerage in awe. They serve a purpose and unless you have a title where my son – if the child is male – must take a seat in the House of Lords, I can stay in the country and rusticate to my heart's content."

"Our son will have a seat in the House of Lords when the time comes. Do you still wish to move forward?"

She paused. If he had a seat in the House of Lords, his title was most likely earl or higher. Could she do this? Her thoughts flew to Jane and then the rest of her sisters. Their chances of marrying well increased with this connection. For the sake of her child and her unwed sisters, she would accept Mr. Talbot's proposal.

"Yes, sir. I do wish to move forward."

"Well, then." He moved off the bench, went down on one knee, and pulled an emerald ring from his coat pocket. Taking her hand in his, he removed her glove and slid the ring to the first knuckle of her finger while saying, "Miss Elizabeth Bennet of Longbourn, would you marry me?"

"Yes, Mr. Talbot, of…," she paused.

"Buckinghamshire," he supplied the answer to her unspoken question.

"Yes, Mr. Talbot of Buckinghamshire, I will marry you."

Upon her acceptance, he slid the ring all the way down her finger and then pulled her to her feet. Before she could even think or breathe, he kissed her lightly on the lips. Her eyes widened and she sucked in her breath.

"Fear not, Miss Elizabeth. I am not a libertine and will not exercise my husbandly rights. Not right away. I will wait until you are ready and only then, will I come to your bed."

Her cheeks heated and she knew she'd blushed deeply while putting her glove back on.

"I thank you."

"Let us get to know one another, shall we?" He turned and tucked her arm in his and continued their walk through the park. "Ask me anything you like."

"You are from Buckinghamshire?"

"Yes, although I have a lesser estate in Derbyshire."

She almost came to a grinding halt, but he tugged her arm gently and they continued to promenade through the park.

"I am aware of who the claimed father is, and have only laid eyes on the gentleman maybe three times in my life. I do not visit that estate very often. You will have no concerns from that quarter, I assure you."

She breathed out a sigh of relief. "Is it a grand estate, the one in Buckinghamshire?"

"It is a tidy little estate. The housekeeper, Mrs. Haskins, has run my house for many years and will be a fountain of knowledge for you to drink from. My head steward is a competent man and Mr. Bridges, my butler, has been with me from the time I was but a lad. He should have retired years ago, but when he heard my time was short, he swore not to leave service until I was no longer alive."

Lizzy marveled at his acceptance of death and his servant's loyalty.

"Your servants love you."

"Love is a word used too liberally. My servants and tenants respect and trust me, and I work hard to keep that trust."

"I shall endeavor to follow your lead."

"If what I have heard from *all* your relatives is true, you will exceed my expectations." By this time, they'd exited the park and were on their way back to her uncle's house. "Do you have anything else you would like to ask?"

"Why me?"

"We met at the dinner your cousin Percival hosted a few

years ago. You would not remember me, there were so many people in attendance and we did not have a conversation but I well remember your flashing emerald eyes, sparkling wit and vivacity. When Percy wrote of your dilemma, I came immediately to Town. He has always spoken of you and your sister Jane in such warm terms. I had no reservation with regard to your temperament and personality." He watched her closely while she digested this morsel of information. "I believe this could be the answer to our problems and have some companionship along the way. If nothing else, we will end up with a great friendship. Of that, I have no doubt."

There was so much to ask, but she didn't know how to form the questions. He made it sound so easy.

"We have arrived." Mr. Talbot took her arm and escorted her through the front door where he gave her a polite half bow. "I shall speak with your uncle and come by tomorrow morning to break my fast and then we can enjoy another walk and chat."

She watched him walk down the hall toward uncle's study, his whole demeanor of one who knew where he stood in society. There was not one hint of false bravado, just a steady assurance that he was a man who knew himself well.

"Lizzy, what happened?"

She turned to see her aunt framed with the door to the front parlor.

"I barely know myself."

"Come, have some tea and tell us what you do know."

She shared with them much of the conversation, with Jane breaking in only once to say Mr. Talbot did seem familiar to her. They both had attended the same dinner.

"I must admit, I do not remember half of the guests. Cousin Percy's idea of a small gathering consisted of at least fifty guests. Papa, Jane, and I were the small fish swimming in a big pond that night."

"Do not speak untruths, Lizzy. You had a fair number of men swirling about your skirts that night."

"Dear Jane, you are in grave danger of perjuring yourself. You know full well that if there were any handsome men swirling about skirts, they were yours. Do not run from the fact that you are the flame most moths are drawn to."

"Will you be seeing Mr. Talbot tomorrow, Lizzy?"

Aunt's question brought their attention back to the matter at hand.

"Yes. He is coming here for breakfast and then we are to go for another walk, if the weather holds."

"I do hope he finds you amiable, and you him. It would ease your burden if he were to propose."

"He already has. We are to be married in three days."

"What? Three days!" Aunt Gardiner stood and gathered Elizabeth into a hug. "You are saved. My dear girl, what a whirlwind."

Caught up in the joy her aunt and Jane expressed, she allowed herself to have hope. The next morning, as she awaited Mr. Talbot's arrival, she read the newspaper. It wasn't until she read an announcement in the Society pages, she finally admitted to herself that a small portion of her heart had hoped Mr. Darcy would attempt to find out if what Papa told him was truth. Now she knew, beyond a shadow of a doubt, her child would not be acknowledged by their father. Her path with Mr. Talbot was set and she would never waver from her course again.

Wondering what had made her sister drop the newspaper onto the floor, Jane picked it up and gasped when she came across the following:

Lady Catherine De Bourgh of Kent, sister to the Earl of Matlock, is pleased to announce the betrothal of her only daughter and heir of Rosings Park, Kent, Miss Anne De Bourgh to Mr.

AN UNWITTING COMPROMISE

Fitzwilliam Darcy of Derbyshire. Wedding will take place on the twelfth day of August, in the year of our Lord, 1812 at St. George's Cathedral of Hanover Square, London. The Archbishop of Canterbury shall preside over the ceremony.

On a dull Thursday afternoon, in the front parlor of Uncle Edward and Aunt Madeline's house on Gracechurch Street, Mr. Henry Talbot of Buckinghamshire wed Miss Elizabeth Bennet of Hertfordshire. His witness was cousin Percy, the Marquis of Haversham. Her witness was dear Jane.

Her uncle took care of the marriage settlement and all he would say was that she would be well taken care of and Henry would explain everything when they were alone. Henry placed the announcement in the Society pages, but Elizabeth never saw it because after reading of Mr. Darcy's engagement, she did not want to read the paper again. She wanted no knowledge of his wedding, nor of his having other children.

Not very many people noticed the tiny announcement as it simply stated:

Mr. H. Talbot of Buckinghamshire wed Miss E. Bennet of Hertfordshire in a private ceremony on Gracechurch Street, Thursday, January 23, 1812.

Chapter Five

THE CARRIAGE GLIDED to a stop in front of large stately home.

"This house is yours?" Elizabeth asked her new husband, a trickle of trepidation running up and down her spine.

"*Our* house, Mrs. Talbot."

"You said you had a tidy estate in Buckinghamshire. Not once did you mention a town house on Park Lane."

Henry laughed and caught her hand in his, kissing the tips of her fingers through her gloves. Her face flushed and she felt her tummy do a little flip. Her husband had promised to withhold his attentions intimately, but he obviously felt no boundaries in flirting and letting her know, in no uncertain terms, he found her highly desirable.

"I have been remiss in telling you everything but given that we had a whirlwind courtship of three days, I had not the time."

"Mr. Talbot," she lowered her forehead and looked at him with mock severity through her lashes. "We have had two whole days of walks in the park with nothing *but* conversation between us. You had plenty of time to fill me in. I think you have been putting off the inevitable because you thought I would run off and leave you at the altar."

"My nefarious plot has been discovered." The carriage had now come to a full stop. "Before we leave our little cocoon of safety, please know I have every confidence in your ability as my wife. Once you have been introduced as mistress of Talbot House and have had a chance to freshen up, the housekeeper will bring you to my study. You *will* have more questions and now that we are here, I can answer all of them with no reserve."

She was baffled by his air of mystery and after being handed out of the carriage she stood, mouth agape, and stared at the house which was to be one of her homes. It was nearly as big as the Duke of Devonshire's. Her Aunt and Uncle had taken both she and Jane by it on one of their visits and she'd never forgotten the grandeur of the stately home.

She snapped her mouth shut and took her husband's hand as they walked toward the flight of stone steps. The door opened as soon as their feet touched the top stair and just as she went to move forward, Henry scooped her up in his arms and carried her over the threshold.

"Mr. Talbot!" she knew her cheeks had flamed a bright red and wondered what the waiting butler and housekeeper thought.

"Regardless of your circumstance, you are still a bride and should be treated as one." He whispered in her ear. "As such, I decided to carry you over the threshold."

He set her down and steadied her with a gentle hand. He then tucked a finger under her chin and raised her face, holding her gaze in his steady one. Almost immediately, her nerves calmed.

"No shame, Elizabeth." He said before brushing her lips lightly with his. "Today is a day of joy." He turned and beckoned the two head servants to their side. "May I introduce my faithful retainers, Mr. Gibson and Mrs. Prentiss."

The housekeeper dropped into a deep curtsy and the butler bowed at his waist.

"Welcome to Talbot House, your grace." Mr. Gibson said, his tone full of respect.

Your grace?

She fainted.

Elizabeth awakened in an unfamiliar room, a cool cloth resting atop her forehead. The room lay in semi darkness, the curtains drawn.

"Sleeping beauty awakens," a soft voice murmured beside her.

She tried to sit up, but her head went fuzzy again and she pressed her fingers to her temple.

"Slowly, Elizabeth. I should have realized the shock would be great, but it was such a joy to know you accepted me for myself, I put off telling you about my title."

He placed a hand beneath her elbow and helped her sit upright. Soon a cup of tea was pressed into her hands. "Drink," he commanded and she complied.

"You are a duke, Mr. Talbot. A duke!" she chastised and then sipped her tea again.

"I am the eleventh Duke of Tavistock and thought I would be the last until I met you. If we have a son, he will be the twelfth, and my heritage will continue."

"And if not a son?"

"Then I will have a daughter and wife who will be outrageously wealthy and she will have the world at her feet. Why, she may even marry a Prince and become a Queen." He handed her a lemon tart. "The world will be her oyster and she the shining pearl."

"You wax eloquent, your grace," she said before taking a bite of the tart.

"Do not 'your grace' me, Elizabeth Rose. I am only Henry when we are alone."

"And Mr. Talbot when you are in trouble."

"Aye, and Mr. Talbot when I am in trouble. You are the only one who may, or dare take me to task."

"I am sorry I embarrassed you in front of all the servants."

"I was not embarrassed. More concerned than anything. In fact, the servants are thrilled you were unaware of my title. Their estimation of their new mistress rose with that knowledge. They believe you and I are a love match and our little bundle of joy will add to their felicity."

"Servants are not stupid, Henry. You have not had children previously, surely, they will suspect."

"You forget that my wife firmly believed she was the cause of our remaining barren, and many servants were here during those times she went through bouts of depression when nature made her acknowledge no child was in her womb."

"For your sake, I pray our secret remains between us."

"For the child's sake, I pray that as well." He took her hand in his. "Regardless, as I said before, once the child is born, I will change my will to record their name, making it ironclad they are my direct heir. There is no one who would contest the document, but you and I will both sleep better at night knowing it is all tied up with a nice legal red bow."

"Henry!"

"What? Are you feeling faint again?"

"No, I have only just realized Mrs. Bennet has no idea of your status and when she finds out… oh, I will never be rid of her."

"Let me take care of your mother. I am told I have a way with the ladies." He had the audacity to wink at her and she almost giggled. "She will be as docile as a kitten when I am through."

"You do know the scratch of a kitten's claw is more painful than a full-grown cat? You may rue the day you decided to tangle with Mrs. Bennet."

"Never. You forget I have a secret weapon."

"Which is?" she queried, her brow furrowing.

"I have been in contact with your father and know you have four unwed sisters. In order for me to facilitate their come-out and find them rich husbands," – he laughed at her mock look of outrage – "Yes, your father apprised me of your mother's tightly held dreams. As I was saying, in order to facilitate all of that, she must indulge me and take lessons in decorum alongside your three youngest sisters. I have hired a most excellent governess for them and expect them to be polished to perfection by the time we host our first ball after baby Talbot is born."

"You have such high hopes. Would that they come to fruition."

"I also have another surprise for you."

"Beside the fact you are a duke, have hired a governess to improve my family's quality and provided me lemon tarts?"

"Yes, I saved the best for last. Your sister Jane is coming to stay with us for Easter until after your presentation."

Elizabeth was overwhelmed and even though she barely knew the man seated by the edge of her bed, she almost leaped into his arms and hugged him tight.

"Thank you, thank you, thank you," she kept whispering into his neck, her cheeks streaked with tears of happiness. She dreaded facing all of this alone and to know Jane would be by her side, made everything bearable. "You truly are the best of men, Mr. Talbot."

"Thank you, my dear. I have to keep reminding myself you are not even one and twenty and should not be without family during this time." He kissed her forehead before settling her back against the pillows. "Do you feel up to some dinner? I do not expect you to dress up as I keep meals casual when there are no guests. Your lady's maid, Hattie, will attend you and then escort you to the small dining parlor."

Their meal was simple, yet tasty. Elizabeth passed on her compliments to the chef and by the smile on Henry's face, she knew she was well on her way to winning over the staff. Tomorrow, she planned on having a long talk with her husband over what her duties were and if Mrs. Prentiss was prepared for such a young mistress to overlook the household.

"I know you have been raised as a gentleman's daughter and from everything I heard your mother is an excellent mistress of Longbourn." At her raised eyebrow, he chuckled. "The exception being her overspending. But every descriptor has claimed her as an excellent hostess who sets a fine table. I also know that you spent a great deal of time with your father and are very aware of the financial side of running a house."

"Mr. Talbot—"

"I thought we agreed you would only call me Mr. Talbot if I were in trouble."

She couldn't help herself, she smiled. "Henry," she stressed. "Your households are many times larger than Longbourn. I am sure I have much to learn."

"Numbers are numbers, Elizabeth. Let us presume Longbourn has thirty tenant families and I have three hundred. If you needed one hundred pounds per annum per family for Longbourn, it stands to reason you will need one thousand pounds for mine. Do not let the size of my estates overwhelm you."

"You make it sound so easy," she sighed.

"That is because it is, my darling girl." He laid his hand over hers and squeezed. "You will be a magnificent duchess, which brings me to my next topic."

"Which is…?"

"As my wife, you need a more extensive wardrobe as well as something suitable for when I take you for tea with my cousin in a few weeks."

"I thought you said you had no relatives to inherit your title and lands."

"I do not. This is a distant female cousin and she is most desirous of meeting you."

~~~

DARCY CROSSED AND uncrossed his legs. Georgiana was in one of the three rooms assigned for taking a lady's measurements. His aunt, Lady Lucinda, the Countess of Matlock, had been unable to attend as some minor crisis had arisen with her son's wife. Georgiana's come out ball was still a few months off, but with every young lady vying for time with a modiste, the fitting could not be postponed. He wouldn't have minded so much, but as soon as he'd entered the shop, his senses had been assailed by a faint scent of honeysuckle and lavender. One he associated strongly with Miss Elizabeth Bennet.

His attention was diverted by the bell jangling over the door. He acknowledged the Duke of Tavistock and stood respectfully. His curiosity was piqued as he knew the duke was unmarried, unless he was here with a current mistress.

"Your grace," he said with a polite tilt of his head, hoping his gentle sister would not be placed in proximity of the older man's paramour.

"Darcy." The duke looked around the shop. "Are you here with your sister? She has her come out this Season?"

Surprised that Tavistock was aware of such small details about his family, he was slow to answer. When the duke raised an eyebrow he said, "Yes. Her curtsy is this year."

"My wife will also be presented to the Queen."

"You are recently married, your grace?"

"Yes, almost two weeks ago."

"Congratulations. I wish you much felicity in your marriage."

"I expect nothing less. She is absolutely delightful."

"Do I know her? Have I seen her at any balls or dinners?"

"I know for a fact you have. The Marquis of Haversham is her cousin, but her father hates Town and eschewed giving his daughters a proper season. Now that we are married, her cousin the Marchioness has agreed to sponsor her."

"I do not recall any cousins of the Marquis of Haversham." Darcy shook his head, wondering why the duke would think he'd have a slight connection. Most likely the girl's family had trotted her out beneath his nose at a function and he'd brushed them off. He was forever hounded by desperate mothers and fathers.

"Hmmm…," was all Tavistock said. "I am certain when you meet the duchess, you will remember her." His grace turned when the owner of the shop peeked out from behind a curtain and beckoned him, politely, to come and see what she'd prepared for his wife.

Darcy retook his seat and thought about the duke's cryptic remark, before shaking his head. He'd never met any relatives of the Marquis, and very likely never would. He started to pick up a fashion magazine, desperate to have something to do while waiting, when Tavistock stepped out from behind the curtain, a pelisse in his hand.

Something about the simple muslin garment triggered a memory of Miss Elizabeth walking across the fields of Netherfield the morning she came to attend her sister. She'd been wearing almost the exact same pelisse.

"Would you see if you have any material in the same color

as this?" Tavistock asked the assistant. "My wife is fond of it and I would like to have a gown with matching spencer made."

"Right away, sir, leave it with me."

He handed over the pelisse and then sat down beside Darcy. Not a word was spoken between them, but Darcy had the distinct impression the duke was studying him very carefully. For what reason, he did not know, but when Georgiana finally emerged from her fitting room, he almost sprang to his feet to greet her. His surprise knew no bounds when Tavistock also rose to his feet and asked to be introduced to his sister.

"Georgiana, may I present His Grace, the Duke of Tavistock." Georgiana paled and began to shake. He had to see this through, regardless of how terrified she was. "Your grace, my sister, Miss Georgiana Darcy."

"I am enchanted to meet you, Miss Darcy. I knew both your father and Lady Anne very well as I have a small estate not even ten miles from your beautiful Pemberley."

Georgiana rose from her curtsy and almost whispered, "Thank you, your grace."

"I will not keep you from you other engagements. Good luck in your upcoming season, Miss Darcy. I know you will do well as you have much of your mother in you. Lady Anne was a genteel, refined woman."

His sister's gaze flew to the duke's and she smiled. It was tremulous, but she smiled. The man had done much to bolster her confidence and Darcy was thankful.

"Thank you, your grace," Darcy said and with a firm hand beneath his sister's elbow, guided her out of the shop.

Over ices at Gunter's, Georgiana's excitement knew no bounds.

"A duke, brother! I met a duke!"

"Yes, you did, and you will meet more when you finally have your curtsy and subsequent ball."

"I have been so frightened, but the duke said I have much of mother in me, and she would not have been frightened."

"Good Lord, no! Do not forget, she was sister to Aunt Catherine. I will let your imagination wander down whatever path it wishes as you think about our mother's personality. She was one of the few people Aunt Catherine dare not browbeat."

"Truly?"

"Truly."

"I wish I could remember her."

"Me too, Squirt," he teased, using her childhood nickname. "Now, finish your iced treat so we can go home and prepare for our dinner invitation."

For the first time that day, Georgiana's brow furrowed.

"Will Miss Bingley be there?"

"Of course, she lives in his townhouse."

"Do I have to attend? May I be excused and stay home? I am not out yet, as you always tell me."

"It seems you fall back on that excuse when you do not want to do something you think distasteful."

"I cannot like her, brother. She fawns over you and then fawns over me to make herself look good to you and she is as false as Mrs. Hawkins's teeth."

"Georgiana Darcy! Wherever did you learn to speak like that?"

"I do visit the tenants at Pemberley, brother. I have been exposed to more than you know."

"Very well. However, I warn you, only say these things to me and me alone. I do not want anyone to think you are a gossip monger and spiteful to boot."

"I promise to always speak with a gentle manner and tone, unlike Miss Bingley."

"She *can* grate on one's nerves. Very well, you may stay home and leave me to face the lion's den alone."

"Thank you." She picked up her spoon and dipped into her raspberry ice.

~~~

LATER THAT EVENING, Darcy stood by the fireplace while Mrs. Hurst played the piano. Miss Bingley sidled next to him and stood far too close for his liking.

"By the by, Mr. Darcy, I have a most unpleasant task before me."

"And what might that be?"

"Miss Bennet paid us a call and now I must return the favor."

"She is still in town?"

"You knew she was in town?"

He silently chastised himself over mentioning he knew the Bennet's had been in town.

"I recall she and her sister speaking about how they sometimes come to London after Christmas with their aunt and uncle."

"Yes, the uncle from *Cheapside*," she said, her lip curling in disgust.

"And she has only now paid you a courtesy call? I thought you were great friends."

"Friends we are not."

"Yet, she took the time to visit."

"Oh, her visit was not recent. The poor waif arrived on our doorstep the first week of January. Louisa and I hurried her out as soon as humanly possible. I did not want Charles to stumble upon the fair country maid in her simple muslin dress."

"That was over three weeks ago!"

"I suppose it was." Exactly when Mr. Bennet paid *him* a call and it had not been courteous. Not even close.

This new information, of Miss Bennet attempting to get

her claws into Bingley the same time her father sought to snag the Darcy fortune, increased his angry belief they were all duplicitous. That anger had been the impetus which caused him to send an express to Aunt Catherine and tell her to post his and Anne's engagement announcement.

Regardless of the Bennet's bad behavior, Bingley's sister still should have behaved with better decorum.

"Miss Bingley, even in polite society one does not leave a return call for that length of time. It does not put Miss Bennet in a bad light, but you alone."

"Truly? Who would ever know? It is not as though the Bennet family have the type of connections that matter to people like us."

He felt a trickle of dread.

"And who, might I ask, are people like us?"

"Why, the upper crust, Mr. Darcy." She flicked her fan and preened. "Those of superior breeding and bloodlines."

"Miss Bingley," he said in a low voice, "as much as I did not think Miss Bennet a suitable wife for your brother, I have never denigrated their position in society. Yes, Mrs. Bennet's family is from trade, but Mr. Bennet is a gentleman. He raised his wife to a higher status in marriage exactly the same as Mr. Hurst did your sister. From what I heard while in Meryton, there has been a Bennet at Longbourn for over six generations. Quite possibly longer than that."

"Not for long. All of them will be tossed to the hedgerows upon Mr. Bennet's demise."

She hid her smile behind the fan but Darcy distinctly heard a soft laugh. His level of disgust rose even higher.

"I do not gloat over the hardships the Bennet ladies will face because you never know when something equally disastrous could befall your very own family."

His mind hearkened back to Georgiana's near miss last

summer. There but for the grace of God they might have had to hide away in shame and his sister would have borne the brunt of the *ton's* penchant for malicious gossip.

He assessed Bingley's sister. If Georgiana's near elopement had been uncovered, he was fairly certain Miss Bingley would have led the charge of the gossip brigade. With her inside knowledge of the Darcy family, she would have held court in the drawing rooms of every loose tongue in town. Not for the first time, he realized he had to narrow his friendship back to Charles alone. Miss Bingley had become too clingy. Too… possessive. He feared the next time they arrived at Pemberley for the wedding in August, she would attempt a compromise and thwart his plans to marry Anne.

He felt a familiar sense of revulsion at the thought of her laying supine on his bed. As much as he did not look forward to bedding Anne, his abhorrence of any kind of physical relationship with Miss Bingley was stronger. Why, he'd even bed Miss Elizabeth before he came within a barge pole length of Bingley's sister.

An image of Elizabeth reclined on a couch of some sort, hair loose about her shoulders wearing only her nightclothes, flashed through his mind. He could almost taste her skin, a faint memory of honeysuckle and lemon clinging to her hair. He shook out of his thoughts when Bingley approached, challenging him to a game of billiards.

They'd often played billiards while at Netherfield. With the incessant rain that had lingered for nearly a week before the ball, their usual pursuits to alleviate boredom had been severely curtailed. As such, the activity had given them something to do away from the ladies. One night, while the Bennet sisters were in residence, he made the mistake of imbibing in far too much brandy. At the time he was desperate to dull his senses to the presence of *her*. She'd begun to haunt all his dreams, and after that night, they bordered on the erotic. For the sake of his sanity, he made the decision to remove to London, needing to lessen the proximity between them. He had no desire to heed the petite siren's call and end up on the rocks of an ill-advised marriage.

He and Bingley set up the table and began to play.

"We had many a night of billiards at Netherfield. I hope you are prepared to lose, yet again."

"I did beat you once, Darcy."

"You did? I do not recall such a momentous occasion."

"There are many things you do not recall from that night. You were very drunk."

"Humor me, Bingley. Did I fall flat on my face and have to be escorted to bed?"

Charles paused and fidgeted with his cue stick. For some reason, his friend was uncomfortable talking about that night.

"I did find you flat on your face, and your valet and I had to drag your sorry arse to bed."

"I must have fallen somewhere soft. I had no bruises, that I recall."

"You... that is...," Bingley's cheeks were now flushed a deep red. "Your fall was definitely soft. You..., I came into the library, and... It does not matter anyway. I would have heard by now if it was otherwise."

"Heard what?"

"What ho! Are you playing without me?" Hurst burst into the room and grabbed a cue stick. "I shall play the winner."

Darcy noted Bingley's shoulders sag in relief at his brother-in-law's arrival, but his general good humor was replaced by a sense of melancholy. Maybe mentioning Netherfield had not been a smart thing to do. It brought back too many memories of the ethereal Miss Bennet.

Chapter Six

THE PAST TWO WEEKS had been a flurry of fittings and shopping. Elizabeth knew it was necessary, given her station in life and her upcoming curtsy, but in her mind, it was the closest thing to Dante's third circle of hell she'd ever experienced. Her cheerful disposition sank to an even further low when Henry insisted, she be kitted out with a riding habit.

For the first time in their marriage, she balked.

"I do not ride."

"At all?"

"No."

"Well, we shall have to change that."

"I do not think so, your grace."

Henry paused in taking a sip of his tea.

"You are defying me?"

"Yes."

"Hmmm…," was all he said. He then stood and placed a hand on the back of her chair. "When you are finished here, my dear, meet me at the stables and we will pick out a suitable mount and start with gentle walks. The doctor has said that is a safe activity for now and will acclimate you to your mare."

She felt all the blood leave her head and would have fallen

face down on her uneaten eggs if Henry had not caught her by the shoulders.

"Elizabeth, are you well?"

She sat back in her chair, feeling decidedly drained and raised her gaze to his. Her eyes welled up with tears and she struggled to hold them back.

"Please do not make me ride."

He squatted by her side, not caring how it looked in front of the ever-present footmen.

"My darling girl. If I had known your fear was so great, I would never have commanded you to try and ride." He waved the footmen from the room. "Please do not think me an ogre. It is not uncommon for people to have a healthy fear of horses. They are magnificent beasts. I thought if you could choose your own mount, you would be fine."

"There is a reason I like to walk everywhere. As a child I had a horrendous accident with one of Papa's horses. Both my arm and leg were broken. The poor animal had to be destroyed."

"Good heavens. How did that happen?"

"I do not know. Something spooked the horse. All I remember is the beast slightly rearing and then taking off at a gallop. No matter how hard I pulled on the reins, he would not stop. We were approaching the small stone boundary wall between Netherfield Park and Longbourn, and the horse attempted to jump. I could not hold on." She trembled at the memory. "I will never forget the creature's high-pitched cries as it struggled over and over to rise to its feet. I was trapped beneath the animal and finally passed out from the pain."

"How old were you?"

"Almost fourteen. Mrs. Bennet nearly gave me to the tenants to raise while I recuperated. I was not a good patient. Being confined to a bed for almost six weeks is not something I wish to repeat."

Henry stood and placed a soft kiss on the crown of her head. "You do not have to worry about riding a horse, my love, instead, I will teach you to drive a phaeton. You must have a way to get around my estate when we remove to Buckinghamshire."

She covered the hand that laid on her shoulder. "Thank you, Henry."

"Elizabeth," Henry paused as though he were searching for words. "Why do you refer to your mother as Mrs. Bennet?"

She went completely still and for one brief moment thought her breakfast would make a messy reappearance. To buy some time to gather her thoughts, she dabbed her mouth with a linen napkin and then carefully folded it beside her plate.

"Prior to my cousin's disastrous proposal, Mrs. Bennet and I had a somewhat contentious relationship. She never understood my love of reading, nor my penchant for long rambles in the woods as a way of clearing my mind. She could not fathom why I did not like to sit and embroider, or tear apart bonnets, or peruse page after page of fashion magazines. Things that held her interest did not hold mine. All things came to a head when I declined Mr. Collins's abhorrent proposal. She lost control and I did all I could to stay out of her way. As it was, my arms and legs were covered in bruises from her pinches and kicks. Her anger seemed to have no boundaries when it came to me. My only refuge was Papa's library. She did not behave as a loving mother; therefore, I do not think of her in that manner any longer. I have determined that I would never return to Longbourn as long as she was there."

"I see. Thank you for clarifying that for me."

"I am sorry if this makes me a lesser person in your eyes."

"Never. You do not have to worry about her ever again. I will take care of things." He turned to leave the room, then stopped. "Have your day dresses been delivered?"

"Yes, most came yesterday, which you well know as the bill

arrived with them. I shudder to think of the cost."

"It is nothing. We are invited to tea with the cousin I told you about. Wear the pretty jade green silk. The color brings out your eyes, and they are one of your best features."

"Thank you. What time shall I be ready?"

"We will leave shortly after one o'clock."

The clock had struck the half hour past twelve when Elizabeth's maid finished pinning up the last curl. She surveyed herself in the mirror, pleased to see that she at least looked sophisticated even if she did not feel it.

A light tap at the door had her turning in her chair, surprised to see her husband enter the room. He'd never come into her bed chamber once since their wedding. He dismissed her maid and stood gazing upon her.

"You are radiant. I still cannot believe I was lucky enough to marry you."

She blushed and lowered her head.

"Would you come here, Elizabeth?"

She stood and walked over to him. He gestured for her to turn around and face away from him. Before she could wonder at his purpose, she felt the cool weight of a necklace around her neck. Henry closed the clasp and then escorted her to the full-length mirror in her dressing room.

She stood, shock causing her mouth to open in surprise. She barely recognized herself. Her gown, a deep green with ivory highlights, fit her curves to perfection. At the time of the fitting, she'd thought the neckline too low, but seeing how the emerald necklace complimented the cut, she had to agree her modiste knew how to make a gown look spectacular.

"Henry, this is too much," she protested, her fingers lovingly caressing the stones. "We are only going to tea."

"Ah, but you are a duchess going to tea, not a beautiful country miss visiting neighbors."

"True. These gems are beautiful. Are they part of your family jewels?"

"No, I had this made specifically for you. It is my belated wedding gift and matches your ring."

"I do not need gifts, and besides, I have not been able to gift you with anything."

"Do you not yet realize that you alone are more precious than any physical belongings?"

Her husband had a way of making her feel as though she were the only woman in the world. Slowly, but surely, he was worming his way into her heart.

"I have made you blush, yet again." He crooked his arm. "Come, my duchess. We have an appointment with my cousin and she does not like it when guests are late."

It was only when the carriage made its final turn and they rolled up the well-groomed circular drive did Elizabeth finally find her voice.

"Henry, we are at the palace."

"Yes, I know."

"Why are we at the palace?"

"Because this is where my cousin lives."

"Please tell me your cousin is a distant relative to our reigning monarch."

"I am a distant cousin to our reigning monarch's spouse."

She turned to face her husband, whose eyes twinkled with merriment.

"Henry Talbot, you are in so much trouble. You may not wish to come home with me."

"Elizabeth Rose Talbot, if you have not realized it, I would follow you to the ends of the earth. You will do marvelous. My cousin is already in our corner and when I came to get permission to marry—"

"You had to get permission to marry?"

"Yes, darling. All royal cousins must have the monarch's approval."

"I am going to faint."

"No, you are going to take a deep breath and hold your head high." The carriage came to a stop and smart looking footmen hastened to ready the steps. "Chin up, Elizabeth. You have the name and bearing of a Queen. Remember, your courage always rises…"

"Now is not the time to quote my sayings back to me." She accepted his hand once he was out of the carriage and descended with as much grace as she could muster. She took a steadying breath and then looped her arm through his. "Lay on, MacDuff."

"Is that not from one of the Bard's tragedies?"

"Yes. Let us hope we do not end up like Hamlet."

He ensuing laugh was light and low. "Cousin Charlotte is going to absolutely love you."

That day marked a change in their marriage and after dinner, he poured them each a glass of wine before joining her on the small couch in the drawing room. They sat in a comfortable silence, watching the fire slowly burn down to embers.

Before long, Henry shifted closer to her on the couch, taking her empty wineglass and setting it on a small table. Without saying a word, he cradled her face and kissed her, his movements tender, yet deliberate. Although his actions held no urgency, she was left in no doubt of his desire. For one brief moment, the kiss deepened and then he broke contact and enveloped her in a warm embrace.

"I never thought my heart would become engaged after my wife died, however, you my darling girl, fill me with such joy. Call me a fool, but I am besotted."

"The feeling is becoming mutual. I know I am cherished

and my heart is in your safekeeping."

"I always told you I would only come to your bed when you were willing."

She rose to her feet and held out her hand.

"Although I am bearing the fruit of an intimate encounter, I can tell you that I am quite unsure how to go about this. Will you teach me, Henry?"

He accepted her hand and rose with her, bringing her fingers to his mouth and caressing them with his lips.

"Elizabeth, it would be my honor to finally make you my wife in every way."

He tucked her arm through his and side by side they ascended the stairs. When they reached the door to her bedchamber, they faced one another. He caressed her cheek and leaned down to captured her lips with his, deepening the kiss until she could not catch her breath. He drew her into a warm embrace, one hand rose to cup her breast, the other slid around her waist and dropped to the natural curve of her bottom. Heat flowed through her body and her head fell back as he took his time eliciting small mewls of desire from her throat.

"I will come to you in a half hour," he murmured against her mouth and all she could do was nod.

~~~

DARCY SHOOK OFF his fatigue and concentrated on bringing his stallion to a trot after allowing the beast a good gallop on Rotten Row. His sleep continued to be plagued by dreams which more often than not ended in scenes of intimacy and eroticism bordering on the ridiculous. All of them featured a country miss with 'fine eyes.'

He thought Mr. Bennet's trip to his study would certainly aid in him banishing her from his thoughts, and yet, the obsession worsened. His dreams were beginning to invade his waking hours. The first instance was thinking he'd smelled her particular scent when at the modiste with Georgiana. The second was when he caught a glimpse of a familiar bonnet weaving among the rows of books at Hatchard's. He'd almost followed that bonnet until he spied the Duke of Tavistock perusing books in the same area. The man unsettled him, so with a huff, he'd spun on his heel and exited the store. The first time in his life without a new book tucked in the crook of his arm.

And then there was today. On his way to Rotten Row to give Arion his head, he could have sworn he saw Miss Elizabeth walking on one of the lesser trails, a hulking footman nearby. When he'd pivoted the horse to look back and confirm it was her, the lady was no longer on the pathway. It was as though she and her footman had been figments of his imagination.

He scrubbed a hand across his face and pulled Arion to a stop when a familiar voice called his name.

"Darcy," Bingley called out as he brought his horse alongside Darcy's. "Jolly good fun to find you here this morning."

"You are usually not out this early," he teased his friend who was known to embrace Town hours with a passion.

"I have had a deuced time sleeping lately," Bingley confessed, and Darcy noted the light shadows beneath his friend's eyes and felt a pinch of remorse. His friend's normal ebullience had not returned in full since leaving Hertfordshire. "I had hope finding you here, exercising that great beast you call a horse."

"He is a beauty, is he not?" The sound of creaking leather accompanied Darcy's leaning forward to pat the side of Arion's muscular neck. "We had a good run today."

"Speaking of good horseflesh, I was thinking of making a trip to the next auction at Tattersall's and wondered if you would care to join me."

"Tempting, but I am off to Rosings for my annual visit with Aunt Catherine for Easter."

"And to visit your betrothed."

"Yes, my betrothed," was all Darcy could muster.

He gazed off into the distance. Was this what he looked forward to? Scowling whenever he thought of spending time with his future wife and her mother? He tried to envision Anne walking among the gardens of Pemberley and failed miserably. Her emaciated form was supplanted by a woman with bright eyes, chocolate curls and a light and pleasing figure.

He had to get Elizabeth Bennet out of his mind! This preoccupation with a fallen woman was beginning to border on the edges of insanity. He may as well ride straight to Bedlam and commit himself.

"I say, Darcy, did you hear a word I said? You have the most unpleasant look upon your face."

He shook out of his thoughts.

"Pardon me, I was ruminating on something unpleasant."

"Was it about my sister?" Charles teased. "She has a way of making you scowl like a character in a bad play."

"The only play your sister is suited for is *The Taming of the Shrew.*"

"Quite right!" Charles began to laugh. "Speaking of my sister, one of the reasons I came here – other than to exercise Baron and ask about Tattersall's – was to invite you to dine with us tonight."

He balked for only a minute. Miss Bingley and her cloying attentions, ranked right alongside with Aunt Catherine as women he did not want to spend time with. He caught the hopeful look on his friend's face and, for the sake of their friendship, decided to attend.

"Yes, my evening is free. What time?"

"The usual." Charles wheeled his horse around to face the

opposite direction. "I shall leave you here, Baron is getting restless. Until tonight," he called over his shoulder as he kicked his horse into a fast trot.

Darcy waved his riding crop in salute, although Bingley didn't see as he was already too far down the lane. He clicked his tongue at the back of his throat to encourage Arion to walk on. Now he had two unpleasant thoughts to bounce around in his brain. His unwanted fiancé and his unwanted admirer. He wasn't quite sure which was the lesser of the two evils.

A flash of light green caught his attention at the far end of the park. The same light green Miss Elizabeth's twin had been wearing. He kicked Arion into a fast trot, determined to see if it was *her*. Unfortunately, or fortunately dependent on his frame of mind when thinking back, the lady had entered a non-descript black carriage and was already driving off before he was close enough to see anything. For a brief minute he toyed with the idea of chasing down the carriage, but then, what kind of fool would he look if he tore off after an unmarked carriage, demand the driver to stop and find within an unknown female?

He gently brought Arion back to a canter and then further slowed to a walk. Enough. He *would* conquer these unnatural wants and desires. He had to. She was an immoral woman, pregnant with another man's child.

Chapter Seven

"ELIZABETH, STARING AT the road will not make your sister appear any faster," Henry teased from his desk.

She was perched within the deep cushioned window seat which faced the street. Every jangle of equipage had her leaning forward to see if it was Papa's carriage, only to sit back in disappointment when it did not appear. She cut a quick glance at her husband, who was writing letters to his steward at Edgecam Hall.

She looked forward to leaving London for Buckinghamshire. Henry assured her there were plenty of large gardens and pretty parks around the estate for her to wander without ever treading the same path twice. She had been taking her exercise in Hyde Park early in the mornings before the pathways became too populated with the cream of Society and their daily promenade of importance. To see and be seen was their mantra, and she wanted none of that. However, she curtailed her early morning walks in Hyde Park nearly a week ago after espying Mr. Darcy exercising his horse.

After he'd trotted by, she'd veered off the path and made her way as quickly as possible to her waiting carriage. Thankfully,

Harris, her assigned footman, never complained about their quickened pace.

The jangle of harnesses and rumbling wheels had her pivoting back to the window. This time, she was met with success and the familiar Bennet carriage slowed to a stop in front of Talbot House. She slid off the window seat and faced Henry, her hands clasped in front. She practically bounced on her toes; her excitement was so great. Henry set aside his quill and placed the lid back onto the inkwell.

"They are here!"

"Well then, let us go and greet them," he said, rising to his feet.

Before long, she had Jane enveloped in a tight embrace, rocking side to side, uncaring if the servants witnessed her reunion with her family.

"I have missed you so," she said through tears and then stepped to her beloved Papa and enveloped him in as tight a hug as she'd given Jane.

With his arm around his favorite daughter, Papa caught Henry's eye. He reluctantly removed his arm and gave Henry a slight bow of deference.

"Your grace, please excuse our atrocious manners."

"Call me Henry, or Tavistock. I am your son."

"Very well, Tavistock. I am glad we are here and you look well."

Papa was aware Henry had been ill prior to marrying his daughter, but not that it was terminal. Her husband looked as though he were still in the peak of good health. Only Elizabeth knew he would slowly become more fragile as the cancer caused his body to waste away.

"Bennet, after you have freshened up from your journey, join me in the library. I know Jane and Elizabeth have some catching up to do and we would only get in their way."

"Please, let us all stay together," Elizabeth keeping her arm looped through her sister's. "I wish to spend as much time with Papa as I can before he returns to Longbourn, and Jane will be here for almost a month. Besides, if you take my father into the library, we will not see him for the rest of his visit." She wagged a playful finger at her father. "You are forbidden from the library until tomorrow afternoon."

"My duchess has spoken," Henry said with a smile. "Very well, we shall all convene in the family drawing room before dinner and enjoy a good old fashioned chin wag."

"I have not heard that turn of phrase in a long time," she teased her husband.

"You forget, my darling, I am quite a bit older than you and have heard many things in my life. Some suitable for mixed company," – he gave her father a wink – "and some not."

"On that note, Jane and I will find our rooms and freshen up." Papa said, smiling widely at the rapport his daughter shared with his esteemed son-in-law.

Henry signaled Gibson to have a footman show the Bennets to their suite of rooms in the family wing. He then turned to Elizabeth and held out his hand. Without hesitation, she took hold of his and he twined their fingers together. With a finger beneath her chin, a familiar action she'd come to love, he raised her face in order to kiss her on the lips.

"Are you happy, love?"

She leaned into his chest, her cheek resting where she could hear the steady beat of his heart.

"Yes. I am so very happy."

"I am glad." He drew her close against his body and gave her a squeeze. "Now, go to your sister. I know you are anxious to help her unpack and gossip about the latest happenings in Meryton."

"Jane and I do not gossip. We share ideas and perspectives

which sometimes differ from our neighbors," she said with a twinkle in her eye. Before Henry could argue his point further, she raised herself onto the tips of her toes and kissed him full on the mouth. "I love you, Henry Talbot. You are the best of men."

With a swirl of her skirts, she left him standing in the foyer while she flew up the stairs to Jane, quite unaware that a lone tear streaked down his face. Papa stayed for two full days before taking his leave and she and Jane settled into a comfortable routine.

"So much has happened since Henry and I married. I can scarce believe two months have gone by." She frowned at the knot her thread had created on the handkerchief she was embroidering for her husband's birthday. "Tell me Jane. What all has happened since your last letter. I know you do not put every single morsel of information down on paper. It is almost as though you were writing a spy in France and fear your missive might fall into the wrong hands."

"Well," Jane began after she pulled the needle through her mending. "Lydia is driving us all mad after her latest dust up with Papa."

"I still find it hard to believe Lydia will be sixteen this June."

"She still behaves without any thought for propriety. Their governess, Mrs. Gravestone, is beyond frustrated with her behavior. Last week, Papa prohibited Lydia from all social gatherings and she will not attend the next quarterly Assembly."

"No! What did she do?"

"She was caught sneaking out to meet up with Mr. Wickham. Do you remember him? He is stationed in Meryton with the ___shire Militia."

"Vaguely. I met him at one of Aunt's card parties."

"Well, Papa discovered Lydia in the middle of climbing out

her window and since then has nailed them shut. He completely overruled Mamma's lamentations and said Lydia would not come out until she was eighteen. I believe he plans on sending her to that seminary Henry recommended."

Elizabeth knew the seminary Henry suggested was known to take in girls who would not or could not conform to societal rules. They had a good reputation for turning these wayward girls around. It hurt her heart to think Lydia would not behave in a manner fitting a gentleman's daughter.

"When I think back, I now realize Mrs. Bennet did not do our family any favors letting us all come out at fifteen. Lydia and Kitty never had the opportunity to learn some decorum from Aunt Madeline, as you, I and Mary did. They are in the first flush of young womanhood, completely under the thumb of Mrs. Bennet and have no control over their emotions and behavior. I am sad it has come to this."

"I too, Lizzy." Jane reached and took hold of her hand. "I am of the firm belief Mr. Bingley fled Netherfield so precipitously because he could not bear the thought of having Mama, Lydia, and Kitty as part of his family. Their behavior was atrocious at his ball, I do not blame him for quitting the lease and staying in London."

"That may be so, but I still believe Miss Bingley had a heavy hand in that decision. She was far too vindictive in her letter." She studied her sister's face, looking for any sign that she held some regret for Bingley and found none. "Has any other eligible man of good fortune leased Netherfield Park?"

"No," Jane said with a frown. "Uncle Phillips wrote Mr. Bingley about quitting the estate as he has another family interested in taking over the lease. The house stands abandoned, all the furniture covered, and the servants dismissed. It is quite distressing to the community."

"How true. Many people rely on the income a tenant at

Netherfield brings with them."

"Aunt Phillips told Mamma that it was fortunate the butcher had not slaughtered all the animals he expected to provide them over the Christmas season. Can you imagine how much money he would have lost?"

"Jane, you know I always believed Mr. Bingley had stronger feelings than you allowed him to have." She held up her hand to forestall her sister's protestations. "However, the longer I am away from Longbourn, the more I realize how weak his character is."

"Lizzy, how can you say that?"

"He singled you out for his undivided attention the minute he laid eyes on you at the Assembly. He left all of us with no doubt of his affection, as you well know. He even told Mrs. Bennet he would come to dinner the week following his trip to London. That alone tells us he had every intention of returning to Netherfield, but once you were out of his sight, he wavered."

"His sister wrote that he remained there to pursue Miss Darcy."

"*Pfffft!* Miss Caroline Bingley has her eye on Mr. Darcy and Pemberley and she actively promoted a union between her brother and Miss Darcy as a stepping stone toward that goal."

"I have yet to tell you Miss Bingley finally returned my call."

"She did?"

"I confess myself to have been entirely deceived in her regard for me. I still assert that, considering her behavior toward me in Hertfordshire, *my* confidence in her friendship was as natural as *your* suspicion. I do not at all comprehend her reason for wishing to be intimate with me, but if the same circumstances were to happen again, I am sure I should be deceived again."

"That is because you are a genuinely kind person, Jane,"

Elizabeth said and covered Jane's hand with hers. "You are incapable of seeing evil in anyone."

"Maybe so. Caroline did not return my visit till nearly the end of January, and not a note, not a line, did I receive in the meantime. When she did come, it was very evident that she took no pleasure in the activity. She made a slightly condescending form of apology about not calling before, yet said not a word of wishing to see me again. Her exit from Aunt Gardiner's house was embarrassingly hasty, which informs me in no uncertain terms that she no longer looks upon me even as a pleasant acquaintance."

"You are the mistress of understatement, sister mine. She has never looked upon us Bennet girls as pleasant acquaintances."

"If that was the case, then she was very wrong in singling me out as she did. Every advance to intimacy began on her side. And before she quit Aunt's house, she said her brother knew of my being in town. If he had cared for me in the way you believed, he would have paid a call upon receipt of that knowledge."

"There is such a strong appearance of duplicity in all this, it makes my heart sick." Elizabeth stood and began to pace. "These people descended upon Meryton perceiving themselves so high and mighty and above all of us in looks and manners. For myself, I have never experienced such rude behavior and ill manners in all my life. The way they cut and badgered us – to our faces! Can you imagine what they said behind our backs? I would take a shop owner's son any day of the week over of the likes of them as a partner in life. At least then I would know I was loved for myself and not what I brought to the marriage."

"The exception being, your shop owner is a duke."

"Yes, my shop owner Henry. And I did bring something to this marriage worth far more than a paltry dowry." Elizabeth faced Jane, a soft smile gracing her face as she cradled her still flat stomach. "I brought Henry an heir."

"You did."

"Enough of the Bingleys and their terrible choices, tell me what the Lucas family is up to these days. Charlotte's letters are slow to arrive. Mr. Collins and his esteemed patroness must keep her very busy."

The two sisters continued to speak about shared family and friends until their aunt and uncle Gardiner arrived to dine, along with their cousin the Marquis of Haversham, his wife, and their son Christopher (fondly known as Kit), Earl of Thedford. Now that their cousin was here, the Marchioness would see to her final fittings for her court gown, teach her how to properly exit the room after curtsying to the Queen, and host a dinner for close family and friends at their town house.

~~~

ON A MONDAY MORNING, the week before Easter, two grand carriages conveying Darcy, his favorite cousin, and their servants, trundled out of London toward Kent. When they passed the ten-mile marker, Darcy questioned his decision to marry Anne. The fifteen-mile marker had him worrying about her ability to be a fit mistress of Pemberley. Twenty miles out, he had great doubt she could even bear him a child. As he and his cousin, Colonel Richard Fitzwilliam – who was also his best friend – rolled into the estate called Rosings Park, he was extremely conflicted about his upcoming nuptials in August. What had he been thinking by proposing to the sickliest woman in all of England with a termagant as a mother?

There was nothing to be done about it now. The announcement in the society pages had started the clock ticking to his eventual marriage. As a man of honor, he would see it through, albeit with a world of regret resting on his shoulders. It was imperative that he lay down ground rules with Aunt Catherine now. She would not be allowed to descend upon Pemberley. His insides coiled in revulsion at the idea of her banging her walking stick on the marbled floors of his beloved home, demanding the servants acknowledge her.

Do you know who I am?

Those imperious words would ring through the halls day and night if she lived with them. Georgiana would never leave her room. His faithful retainers might up and leave unless he increased their pay almost ten-fold. Why, half the population of Lambton, a picturesque village nearby, might relocate elsewhere as five miles was too close for comfort to her insidious need to dictate everyone's life.

When the carriage came to a stop in front of the grand entrance to Rosings Park, he squared his shoulders and took a deep breath before the footman opened the door.

"Girding your loins for battle, cousin?" Richard teased.

Darcy flashed him a quick look of annoyance. His cousin knew him well and had quietly tried to talk him out of this arrangement, knowing he had no feelings for Anne other than a familial love.

"You might well think that. It suits my dark thoughts."

The door to the carriage opened and soon both men were standing looking up at the broad façade of Aunt Catherine's home.

"Dear Lord in heaven, she added another fireplace." Richard said after sweeping his gaze from one end of the house to the other.

"Counting on the deep reserves of Pemberley to keep her afloat for another year."

"You could always deny her requests for money."

Darcy barked out a harsh laugh. "I would like to see you try and tell our esteemed Lady aunt that her coffers will run dry with how she manages her estate."

"Oh no, I do not have to do anything other than be your faithful companion on your annual pilgrimage to the throne of Aunt Catty." Richard said, using the nickname they'd coined when children.

The huge oak doors opened and Rogers, the butler, stood within the door frame. Meanwhile the carriages had gone around to the side of the house where the servant's entrance was located.

"Lady Catherine is waiting for you in the gold parlor," Rogers intoned.

"Does his voice ever fluctuate when speaking?" Richard asked beneath his breath while they mounted the stairs.

"Not that I am aware of," Darcy replied before entering the great house and handing his hat and gloves to a waiting footman. "Good day, Rogers," he said by way of greeting.

"Good day, Mr. Darcy. Colonel Fitzwilliam."

Rogers gave them each a polite half bow and then led them to what the two men called the throne room. They moved through an antechamber, to the room where she, her daughter Anne, and Mrs. Jenkinson were sitting.

Her ladyship, with great condescension, arose to receive them and he heard Richard stifle a snigger. The way she stood and raised a hand to beckon them forward let him know she still considered herself two steps beneath the Creator of heaven and earth, and one step below the monarchy. All within the kingdom of Rosings Park, where her word was law.

His aunt was a tall, large woman, with strongly marked features, which might once have been handsome and whatever she said was spoken in so authoritative a tone, her self-importance was evident in the extreme. Anne, in turn, was pale and sickly. As always, she spoke very little, except in a low voice to her ever-present companion, Mrs. Jenkinson.

"Come, Darcy," his aunt boomed out after their formal greetings were concluded. "Sit by Anne. She is quite desirous of her betrothed's attention."

Darcy took a seat on the couch facing Anne, much to Aunt Catherine's disapproval.

"I expected you here at least two weeks ago. One would think you hold no affection for your affianced, remaining in London while she stays here at Rosings."

"She stays at Rosings, Madam, by your command," Darcy replied, holding onto his growing frustration by a tenuous thread. "Anne is more than welcome to stay with your brother, the earl. Then I would have the leisure of escorting her to various events."

"Anne cannot attend events! Her disposition is such that she must stay close to her home and remain indoors."

"Then, my attentions shall remain lacking as I have an estate to run and cannot be at Rosings for longer than the fortnight I have allotted."

"This is not to be borne! I demand you stay a month complete."

"No," Darcy said rising to his feet. "My valet should have my things unpacked by now and after I am refreshed, I shall come down for dinner."

He strode from the room, followed closely by Richard. His aunt's displeasure was clearly voiced to all who would listen.

The following Monday saw the residents of the parsonage and their guests attend for dinner. Their arrival was long and tedious. Mr. Collins kept bowing and scraping over everything his aunt said. Darcy remained silent, his anger rolling afresh when he discovered that one of the guests was a Miss Bennet.

He had to admit, when he first heard the name, his stomach had dropped past his shoes. Upon seeing her, he'd felt a measure of relief that it was one of the younger sisters and not *her*. He kept a close eye on the young woman from Hertfordshire, waiting for her to burst out with loud remarks or behave in a manner that would betray her uncouth upbringing.

Surprisingly, she was discreet, polite, and stayed close to the traveling companion her father had hired to see her and Miss Maria Lucas safely to Kent, and safely home to Longbourn in a few weeks. Frankly, he was surprised the man would do that, but then again, his lazy attitude had contributed to his second eldest daughter getting herself caught with child. Maybe his lesson in how to raise a proper daughter was finally hard learned.

When the meal began, the next hour was agony. He'd forgotten what a buffoon the parson was. Mr. Collins ate and praised with delighted alacrity every dish. Nothing escaped his compliments, first by him, and then parroted by Sir William, who echoed whatever his son-in-law said. It was so over the top, Darcy wondered how his aunt could bear it.

But then, he chanced to glance at her and knew the compliments would continue. Aunt Catherine practically preened beneath their excessive admiration, and gave most gracious smiles, especially when any dish on the table proved a novelty to them. The rest of the party did not supply much conversation. There was no need. Mr. Collins, Sir William, and Aunt Catherine spoke enough for everybody.

He did not want to be here, with Anne across from him and the sister of Miss Elizabeth seated next to him. Why couldn't her friend Miss Lucas or the traveling companion, whatever her name was, be placed beside him. Why, for the love of God, did it have to be a Bennet?

Anne barely lifted her head. She sat to the left of her mother, wrapped up in several shawls, the cutlery seemingly too heavy for her to lift to her mouth. Mrs. Jenkinson was chiefly employed in watching how little she ate, pressing her to try some other dish, and fearing she were indisposed. He could not wait for this parody to finish.

"Miss Bennet. I am told you are the cousin to Mr. Collins."

Both he and Miss Bennet jumped at Aunt Catherine's abrupt interest.

"Yes, I am." Miss Bennet – Catherine was her name! – replied in a quiet, genteel voice.

Darcy was astonished. The girl he remembered was brash, uncouth, chasing and being chased by drunken officers at Bingley's ball.

"Are all your sisters still at home? I remember Mr. Collins saying there were five of you, all out at once, which is absolutely preposterous. Five daughters out at once before the eldest is wed."

"My youngest sister is not yet out your Ladyship and my second eldest–"

"What of your education?"

Darcy cursed his aunt's propensity to interrupt. Miss Catherine had been on the cusp of spilling information about Miss Elizabeth.

"My sister Mary and I have a governess, Mrs. Gravestone, who is our chief source of study. My youngest sister, Lydia is attending a seminary for young ladies."

"That is good, very good. Obviously Longbourn is turning a profit. How else could Mr. Bennet afford all of these expenditures?" Aunt Catherine looked over to Mr. Collins, who'd been busy chewing his meat and hadn't paid much attention to the conversation at the head of the table. "You must be well pleased with all this, Mr. Collins, and your little cousin does you proud."

"Thank you, your Ladyship. My cousin Catherine has a vastly different temperament than her older sister – Darcy caught the singular use of the word sister – and I knew I would experience no shame in you making *her* acquaintance."

"Hmmm…" was all his aunt said to those cryptic words.

Darcy hid a sarcastic smile behind his napkin. From what he'd observed, there were only two – no scratch that – only one Bennet sister who could be paraded about without shame, and that was the eldest, and even she had been a willing pawn in the attempt to entrap his friend Bingley.

He finished his meal and then stood with the gentleman when the ladies retired to the drawing room, leaving the men to enjoy their port brandy in peace. Once removed from the lady's presence, Mr. Collins dropped some of his cloying demeanor.

"I forgot you were related to the Bennet family, Mr. Collins," Darcy found himself saying.

"Yes, I am the heir to Longbourn. I shall be glad to rid them from the house when the fateful event of my cousin's demise takes place."

"That will be a sad day, indeed. They have lived there a long time, I believe."

"The Bennet family had a chance to secure their safety when I was there last, but that hoyden, Miss Elizabeth, turned me down rather rudely."

"You asked for Miss Elizabeth's hand in marriage?" Darcy almost choked on his drink.

"Yes, it was expected by her mother that she would make an advantageous connection with regard to their future happiness. Her continued acceptance of my marked attentions and favors ensured me that she would not, nay, *could not* refuse my generous offer of marriage. Imagine my surprise when she so rudely declined and her father practically encouraged her to defy me. Despite her manifold attractions, which I *freely* enjoyed —you must recall them, they are quite bounteous—" He had the audacity to give Darcy a lurid wink, "I informed her she very likely would never receive another proper offer for her hand."

If what the parson so broadly hinted were true, the thought of Elizabeth submitting her body to this toad of a man made him physically ill. There would have had ample opportunity to engage in licentious behavior as Mr. Collins had lodged with the family for nearly two weeks during his visit. At the time, her condition would not be apparent, and when the cousin wed her particular friend, she would have been hard pressed to find another man to conceal her ruin.

The temerity of the chit. To think she tried to pass off that sycophant's child as his by grasping at the one and only time they'd ever been alone in a room as the foundation of her botched compromise. The familiar rage he now came to associate with Elizabeth Bennet's duplicitous nature, rose in his chest.

"But Miss Eliza did marry," Sir William said in a cheerful voice. "She met the gentleman through her uncle in London."

"Is that the uncle who lives in Cheapside?" Darcy found himself asking before his brain had engaged and stopped him.

"Yes, her Uncle Gardiner. Such a pleasant man," Sir William enthused.

"How wonderful."

"Whatever do you mean, Mr. Collins?" Richard finally entered the conversation.

"My high and mighty cousin forced to marry a tradesman when she could have had the heir to Longbourn," Mr. Collins gloated, actually rubbing his hands with glee.

"Now see here, Mr. Collins." Sir William was beginning to lose his congenial manner. "You have married my daughter and should not care who Miss Eliza married. I am not pleased with what you inferred about a young lady I've long considered as the jewel of Hertfordshire."

"Forgive me, Sir William. Of course, I am beyond ecstatic to be married to your daughter Charlotte. It is like we were formed for one another; we get along so well." Mr. Collins gulped audibly. "I must admit, my pride was pricked by my cousin's inconceivable refusal."

The butler arrived and stated Lady Catherine wished them to return to the drawing room.

"I think this Miss Elizabeth had a lucky escape," Richard said beneath his breath to Darcy as they exited the dining room. "Is she as…" he paused before continuing, emphasizing a certain word, "*bounteous* as the fool implied? If she is half as lovely as her younger sister, Miss Catherine, I can see why he willingly sampled her delights."

"More so. And I, fool that I was, bought into her act of gentility and decorum."

He ignored the astonished look on Richard's face and entered the drawing room where Lady Catherine and his betrothed awaited, heartily congratulating himself on avoiding the compromise attempt of that impertinent chit and her scheming mother. The jewel of Hertfordshire, indeed. That did not speak well to the other young ladies in Meryton if Elizabeth Bennet was the pinnacle of their aspirations.

Chapter Eight

A FEW DAYS BEFORE her court presentation, Elizabeth and Jane were quietly talking about the past week and all the preparation which went into such an event. They'd also been reading letters from family while waiting for dinner guests to arrive at Talbot House when Henry joined them.

"Such a lovely vignette. Two of my favorite ladies, situated so prettily. I should hire an artist and have him capture your likeness."

"Would you, Henry? Then I could hang the portrait in my private sitting room and always have Jane close by me."

"Consider it done. As it is, I have hired Sir Thomas Lawrence to do your official portrait."

Elizabeth frowned.

"Are you not pleased?"

"He will paint me fat."

Henry burst out laughing.

"Even when you are close to delivering, my darling wife, you will always be beautiful to me."

Jane blushed and hid a smile at their open and loving manner.

"I see you received a letter from your mother. Is she still unaware of my status?" Henry settled next to Elizabeth and took her hand in his.

"Yes, and because of your benevolence to my family, she is now aware you are wealthy. To that end, she is quite desirous that I... how did she word it?" She held up Mrs. Bennet's letter, found the correct passage and read out loud. "*...it is your duty to bring all your sisters to town in order for them to meet rich, eligible gentlemen, not just Jane.*"

Jane giggled at her sister's accurate impersonation of their mother.

"Leave the answer to me, Elizabeth. Your mother will wish to curry favor with her new benefactor and I will use that to our advantage. She does not have to worry about the hedgerows and can let her daughters find men they love in their own time."

"Of that, I have no doubt." She refolded her letter and placed it in her work basket. "No, I will reply. Mrs. Bennet will learn that I will not be swayed."

"You *are* formidable, Elizabeth."

"Please understand, Lizzy," Jane said, "You have not been married long. Mamma has barely had time to adjust to the fact you are not under her control any longer."

"And I never will be. Mrs. Bennet thinks Henry is a successful tradesman and I do not mind if her view never changes. I will not have my husband's title used for Mrs. Bennet's gain."

"But Lizzy, it is not just Mama. Please think of our sisters. Your fight is not with them."

Dear, Jane. Always the voice of gentle reason.

"We shall cross all of these bridges as we come to them," Henry said smoothly. "For all we know, Elizabeth and her mother might declare a truce and peace and harmony will flow between them again."

"You are the eternal optimist, my husband. Granted, in about ten years I might look with favor toward Mrs. Bennet, but not right now."

Henry kissed her on the crown of her head.

"Good. Keep an open mind. Life is too short to waste it hating someone."

Her face paled at his gentle rebuke. How obtuse she was. Henry was facing his demise in a few short years and here she was, behaving like a recalcitrant child, not willing to make amends with her mother.

"Henry, I am sorry. I will try and find forgiveness, truly I will. I think everything is still too raw and so much is happening…. I cannot…." Tears welled up in her eyes.

"Elizabeth, I know you love your mother. Those whom we love the most cut us the deepest with cruel words and actions. Your wounds will heal." He handed her a handkerchief. "Now dry your eyes and ask your sister the question you have been sitting on for almost a week."

Jane's eyes widened in surprise and she looked to Lizzy, full of expectation.

"Henry and I have a favor to ask of you." She cut a quick glance at her husband who nodded for her to go ahead. "We would like you to live with us. If and when you marry, you can choose to marry from here, or Longbourn, but we would dearly like you to stay with us forever."

"But Papa—"

"Papa agreed before he left. I wanted to wait until you were more comfortable with us."

"I do not know what to say."

"My dear sister Jane, you do not need to answer right this minute. It is a decision that should not be made in haste. Elizabeth and I will accept whatever you decide." Henry stood as the sound of footsteps could be heard in the hall outside the parlor. "I believe our first set of guests have arrived."

Elizabeth and Jane also rose to their feet as Gibson opened the drawing room door and announced Mr. and Mrs. Edward Gardiner. Their uncle bowed and their aunt dipped into a deep curtsy when Henry greeted them.

"Your grace," they both said in unison.

"Now, Gardiner, Madeline, I told you at our last dinner you were not allowed to 'your grace' me. We are family and as such, I am Henry, Tavistock, or Mr. Talbot when among those whom we do not want to know my title."

"I wondered why my sister Fanny keeps referring to you as dear, dear Mr. Talbot."

"Although I have not met the lady, I believe it better suits Elizabeth and our family if, for the moment, she thinks of me as just plain Mr. Talbot."

"As it was, I fainted when I found out." Elizabeth told them with a light laugh. "Imagine Mrs. Bennet's reaction? Why, she might expire from the news."

"My sister has always had a nervous disposition. And therefore, I agree with you on that front." Uncle Edward said, a sad little smile making an appearance.

Elizabeth adored the fact her favorite uncle was treated as an equal by her esteemed husband. She looked about the room. Almost everyone she loved dearly was here. All that remained was for Papa to be among them. She did experience slight guilt over not including the rest of her immediate family in her bubble of contentment, because she did love them and would defend them with great ferocity if anyone attacked them physically or verbally. She just did not have the same affinity with Mary, Kitty, Lydia as she did with Jane and Papa.

Her mother was another matter entirely. She didn't know if she could forgive Mrs. Bennet, but for Henry's sake, she would make the attempt. Her reverie was interrupted by Gibson announcing her cousins, the Marquis and Marchioness of Haversham and their son, Kit. The room soon buzzed with conversation and Elizabeth was quick to note the closeness of Jane and Kit.

What surprised her was how animated Jane was around the handsome young man. Yes, she would blush every now and then, looking demurely down, but if Kit moved or said something, her eyes would raise and follow his every move. What made it amusing was the fact that he mirrored her movements.

"Are you seeing what I am seeing?" Henry murmured in her ear.

"Yes, I find it fascinating."

"How so?"

"When Jane was in the presence of Mr. Bingley, only I knew how affected she was by his attentions. My sister guards her heart well and I am amazed she is so open in her admiration."

"Do you not think that maybe she instinctively knew she was not accepted within that clique of friends?" Elizabeth's eyes widened as she thought about that kernel of truth. Henry continued, "Here, she is accepted and can openly show her admiration, knowing she will not be cut down with snide remarks about family and friends. She is another Bennet rose opening in the warmth of love and admiration."

Elizabeth turned and looked at him fully. Henry's gaze was focused solely on her, disregarding their company.

"You are my rose, Elizabeth Rose Bennet Talbot, and like any flower given the correct amount of care and love, become more beautiful every day."

The opening of the drawing room door interrupted their tender moment.

"Dinner is ready, your grace," Gibson announced.

Henry escorted the marchioness, cousin Percy escorted Elizabeth, Kit took Aunt Madeline in and Uncle Edward, with a grin, held out his arm to Jane. They made a merry party and the conversation was witty and welcome.

Over the dessert course, the marchioness, who begged them all to call her Eugenia, informed them all that she would be hosting a tea the day before Elizabeth's presentation to the Queen. At Elizabeth's look of dismay, she smiled and said, "I am inviting only my sister and her niece, whom she is sponsoring for her come out. I thought this would be a lovely way for you to begin your entrance into the social scene. Baby steps, if you will."

Elizabeth had to smile at the innocent phrase, 'baby steps.' Fortunately, the little bump she now sported remained invisible behind the layers of her skirts. She'd felt the quickening a few days back and since then, both she and Henry would lay quietly together in the morning, his capable hands on her stomach, waiting for their child to kick and squirm.

"Jane and I look forward to having tea with you and your sister. Have we met them before?"

"Yes, a few summers back when you were at Haversham Hall they came with us for a dinner party. I believe it was the same one your husband attended. You made quite the impression on all of us, if I remember correctly. Her son, the Viscount Ashton, thought for sure Jane was a goddess come down from Mount Olympus. If he hadn't been betrothed, I think a well-worn path between their estate in Derbyshire and your fathers in Hertfordshire would have formed."

Jane blushed at the words and looked down.

"My cousin Ash is no fool." Kit said and raised his glass. "To the ladies of Longbourn."

"To the ladies of Longbourn," everyone said together and toasted Elizabeth and Jane.

Henry could not take his eyes off Elizabeth. Another set of eyes kept careful watch on the eldest Bennet sister.

~~~

DARCY ARRIVED BACK from Rosings the day after Georgiana's curtsy in order to be there for her debut ball at Matlock House that evening. Over breakfast, his normally quiet sister enthused over the acquaintance she'd made the day before her curtsy. The Duchess of Tavistock.

"Is it not strange, the Marchioness of Haversham is Aunt Lucinda's sister, and yet we have never met her husband's cousins? I was so scared to meet the duchess. She is almost my age, brother, not yet one and twenty. Oh! – and her sister. She is *the* most beautiful woman I have ever seen and she made me feel so welcome. From what Lady Eugenia said, her son, the Earl of Thedford, is quite enamored with her. The duchess was presented yesterday, although I did not see her. I am told the Queen not only extended her hand, but kissed the duchess on the forehead. Such an honor. In all, the whole process took about four hours. Carriages lined the street and around the corner."

Darcy was amazed at how verbose his usually shy sister was about her new friends.

"If they allowed the young ladies to retreat in a normal fashion, the whole thing could be over in less than one hour," he couldn't help but tease about all the pomp and circumstance of a formal curtsy.

Georgiana looked at him as though he'd lost all sense.

"Fitzwilliam! It is against royal protocol to turn your back on their Majesties. Of course, we must back out of the room. There is only one main entrance."

"I stand corrected. Forgive my ignorance."

"You are not ignorant; you are a man who likes things

straightforward and simple."

He sat back in his chair and assessed his baby sister. Not a baby any longer, but a young woman venturing out into the world. Given what Georgiana had to say about the Duchess of Tavistock, his grace had made a good choice in wife. For his sister's sake, he hoped their graces would attend the same social functions. Georgiana desperately needed a welcome friendly face in a crowd of strangers. And it wouldn't hurt her chances of making a good marriage if her new acquaintance was a duchess whose husband was cousin to the Queen.

"I am glad you made new friends, Squirt. Now you have another layer between you and Miss Bingley. If you surround yourself with people like the duchess and her beautiful sister, they will not approach – no, I take that back. Miss Bingley would."

"She is, at times, abominably rude. I do not know why you allow her in your company. Her brother is a very amiable and handsome man, but his sister will make it nigh impossible for him to marry happily."

"Why do you say that?"

"There only two types of women Miss Bingley would accept for her brother. The first type must be titled and rich, which will never happen because Mr. Bingley is from trade. Unless the family was in dire straits financially, no one would marry so below their station. The other type of woman Miss Bingley would accept for her brother is one who is related to you. Seeing as I am the only person of the correct sex who fits that category, she is doomed. I like Mr. Bingley, but I could never marry him. He cannot seem to make up his mind from one day to the next. I want a man with purpose."

"Who are you and what have you done with my sister?"

"After my folly at Ramsgate I had a lot of time to think. Mr. Wickham tore the blinders from my eyes and made me see our world for exactly what it is. I had started to become jaded and frightened, but now – after meeting the duchess and her kind sister – I want what they have. Love and respect. I am told the duke and his wife regularly play chess. Is that not wonderful? And she is an avid reader and every morning they walk about the garden of their home. I asked her why she did not walk in Hyde Park and she told me she saw some nefarious man there and has not returned since."

"The duchess is beginning to sound like the perfect woman."

Georgiana laughed. "I said the same thing. She, the duchess, said she was just a country girl at heart and a perfect woman she was not. She said, '*I cannot forget the follies and vices of others as soon as I ought, nor their offences against myself...My good opinion once lost is lost forever.*' Is that not profound, brother? I could almost hear you say the same thing."

Darcy could not answer. How was it that the Duchess of Tavistock quoted almost verbatim something he'd said at Netherfield Park? Did she know Miss Bingley? It was something Bingley's sister would do, spout words that dropped from his mouth in order to show how close they were. There was no other way his words would loop around to his sister.

That evening, Darcy stood up with Georgiana for the first set of her debut ball at Matlock House. After that she partnered with her cousin Ash, and then Richard. The remainder of her card was filled with many hopeful suitors, who'd waited a long time for the wealthy girl to arrive on the scene. One of them was Mr. Bingley, managing to snap up the much coveted the supper set.

He stood with Darcy while waiting for his dance with Georgiana. Miss Bingley had attempted to stand near him, but Darcy had neatly sidestepped her maneuver and was now safely ensconced between Richard and a large column.

"Have you met the elusive Duchess of Tavistock and her sister?" Darcy asked Richard as Georgiana skipped by on the arm of Baron Sidway.

"I have not had the pleasure, but I do remember the summer my brother met the two sisters at Haversham's estate. I think that might have been the one and only time he regretted his betrothal to Lady Clarice. He laid eyes on the elder sister and declared her an absolute angel. Ash was ready to throw off propriety and ride to Hertfordshire before Mother took him aside and reminded him the banns had been read and the marriage settlements were signed. He was not backing out of their betrothal."

Why did *all* things keep pointing in the direction of Hertfordshire? Would he never be rid of that blasted short time in his life?

"I for one do not see what it is about Hertfordshire that drive men crazy."

"Was that where Bingley rented an estate?" Richard caught Bingley's attention, who'd been watching Georgiana with avid interest. "Charles, what is your opinion of Hertfordshire?"

"I thought everyone very hospitable and friendly. I had a marvelous time there. Why do you ask?"

"It seems you and my cousin must have been at two different Hertfordshire's. His memory is not as pleasant as yours."

"No small wonder. He held most of them in disdain and was continuously at odds with a few of the young ladies, most specifically Miss Elizabeth."

"Miss Elizabeth, eh?" Richard slid a sly look at Darcy, who grimaced and wished his cousin would stop tormenting him in this fashion. "Was she that ugly?"

"Ugly? Miss Elizabeth?" Bingley sputtered. "No, she was lively and very witty. She had a light and pleasing figure. She was much admired by everyone. I valued her friendship."

"You did not think of her a woman of loose morals? That she used her bountiful assets to curry the attention of gentlemen?"

Bingley's face grew red with anger. "Who has been saying these things! She may not be a relative of mine, but I will call out anyone who dares to say such derogatory things about Miss Elizabeth."

"Calm down, Bingley," Darcy interjected. "Her cousin hinted, quite broadly, that she had allowed him favors of an intimate kind."

"Then he is a liar!"

"You seem quite adamant about this." Darcy said, perturbed that his good friend would leap to *her* defense.

"Darcy, there are things you are unaware of. Things I cannot speak of at a ball."

"I agree. The subject is distasteful. I have no desire to hear anything further about that family. I am more interested in Georgiana's new acquaintance and had hoped to meet her tonight."

"Are you speaking of the Duchess of Tavistock, Mr. Darcy?" Caroline had finally crept close enough to join their conversation.

"Have you met her, Miss Bingley?"

Darcy asked because he needed to know if it had been she who'd quoted his words to the duchess.

"No, but I have not had the pleasure. Everyone is quite taken with her grace and beauty. I have been told her elder sister is even more beautiful, if possible."

"How could such gems stay out of our sight for so many years?" Richard groused. "Their parents must have hidden them in the country, knowing all the rakes and rogues would descend the minute they made an appearance."

By this time, Georgiana had been escorted back to Darcy's side by her last dance partner.

"You met her, Miss Darcy," Miss Bingley said.

"Met whom, Miss Bingley?"

"The Duchess of Tavistock."

A genuine smile graced Georgiana's face. "Yes, I did. She is a lovely woman and I hope we become good friends."

The music for the next set was beginning. Miss Bingley left with her partner and Bingley held out his arm for Georgiana to take.

"Where did you say she hailed from, Georgi?" Richard called out as his cousin and Bingley moved toward the dance floor.

"I believe she said a little town called Meryton."

Completely flummoxed, Darcy stared open mouthed at his sister lining up across from Bingley. Returning to his senses, he snapped his mouth close and stared at Richard. Was it a coincidence? Two sisters? Both beautiful, the eldest an 'angel' according to not only Bingley, but his cousin the Viscount. And the duchess repeating a phrase that only Miss Elizabeth and Miss Bingley had heard… it was too much.

He asked Richard to come with him to the card room.

"You look as though you have seen a ghost." Richard said as soon as they were seated, concern flitting across his face.

"I might have. More like a demon."

"Was not Meryton the place where Bingley's estate was?" Richard mused. "Mighty coincidental, think you not?"

"There is no such thing as coincidence. I am trying to figure out how Miss Elizabeth managed to trick the Duke of Tavistock."

"Whatever are you talking about? Could he not have met the lady and fallen in love?"

"No. If it *is* Miss Elizabeth, then she deceived him most

grievously. I fear he may be cuckold by that woman."

"Cuckold! What are you implying?"

"I have knowledge that she is pregnant and she is now trying to pass off the parson's bastard as the dukes."

"Are you positive about this?"

Darcy nodded in the affirmative.

"What are you going to do about it?" Richard ran a hand around the back of his neck, a sure sign he was troubled.

"I must speak with the duke. He might hate me, but he deserves to know the truth."

"Should I come with you. If he calls you out, you might need a second."

"Yes, I think I need your support, but not for the possibility of a duel. I am not looking forward to ruining that man's opinion of his bride."

"Do you really think you have to do this?"

"Richard, if it was me, I would want to know." Darcy stood and straightened his vest. "I shall send a note first thing in the morning."

~~~

THE NEXT AFTERNOON, Richard and Darcy heard from the duke, who insisted they meet in a private room at White's.

"Mr. Darcy, Colonel Fitzwilliam," the duke said when they entered.

Both men bowed and greeted him in return, and they seated themselves across from him. A footman brought them brandy and soon all had a drink in hand.

"What was so important that you needed to see me on such short notice?"

"Before I tell you, might I ask if your wife is the former Miss Elizabeth Bennet of Hertfordshire?"

He thought he saw a look of quick surprise on Tavistock's

face, but it smoothed out so fast, he couldn't be sure.

"Yes, my wife is Elizabeth Bennet."

"Sir, I am not one to bear gossip, but deceit of any kind is my abhorrence and I feel I must relay to you some intimate knowledge of your wife, which is not kind."

"Are you referring to the fact she was *enceinte* when I met her?"

Darcy opened and closed his mouth several times.

"You… you are aware of that?"

"I am," came the calm reply.

"Are you aware of who the father is?"

"Very aware." The duke rested his half full glass of brandy on his knee and looked Darcy in the eye. "Do *you* know who the father is?"

"I have reason to believe her cousin, Mr. Collins is responsible, and by the time your wife became cognizant of her situation, he had already married her best friend."

"You know this for a fact."

"No… I do not, but it was hinted at quite broadly by the man."

"I was there, your grace," Richard added. "The cousin left no one in doubt that a liaison of some sort had been enjoyed."

"Interesting. This cousin is your aunt's parson, am I correct?"

"Yes." Once again Darcy was surprised at how much Tavistock knew of his family. "He was appointed by my aunt, Lady Catherine de Bourgh last year."

"Does he have proof? You have stated you abhor deceit and I would assume, gossip, yet on the word of a man everybody knows is a sycophantic fool, you approach me." Darcy was left in no doubt the duke was deeply angry. "And it seems, this man, if you can call him that, has no qualms about casting aspersions against a lady when she is not in the room to defend herself."

"Sir, there were no others who could have been involved and gotten your wife with child."

"No?" Tavistock quirked an eyebrow in his direction. "There was no drunk young man in the library of a rented house who could have taken my wife's virtue while she slept on a couch? There was a witness, but that person has not come forward."

"I know you are referring to me, but let me assure you – I did not have sexual congress with Miss Elizabeth – pardon me – her grace. Mr. Bennet has already tried to lay the blame at my feet and I told him in no uncertain terms the child could not be mine."

Richard was staring at Darcy. Not once had he shared with Richard the claims made by Mr. Bennet, but he hadn't thought the duke would bring that up. He should have known better. Even now Miss Elizabeth wanted the duke to think her child had a better lineage than Mr. Collins.

"I suggest you have a long conversation with your friend. Or even better, it would be in your best interest if you dropped the subject and worried about your own future. I know your betrothed is a sickly woman and the chance of an heir, or any child for that matter is remote." Tavistock set his cut glass on a side table and stood. "If I ever hear you disparage my wife again, in any manner or any form, there is no place in England you can hide where I would not find you. I *will* bring the anger and might of my Royal cousins down upon your head. You will rue the day you slighted Elizabeth Rose Bennet Talbot, Duchess of Tavistock. Good day, *gentlemen*."

With that, he strode out of the room.

"What the hell was that all about!?" Richard practically yelled at him. "You were named in her compromise and did not think to share that tidbit of information with me?"

"I did not compromise her. For some reason, she has lied."

"Tavistock said there was a witness. Do you think a footman or maid know about this?"

"I would not take the word of a rented servant. She has money now. She could buy their statements and send them off fat, dumb and happy."

"She no longer needs you to marry her and has wealth beyond even what you have. Why would she do that? Why does she still insist that you are the father?"

"I wish I knew."

Richard leaned forward until his elbows touched his knees. He clasped his hands in front of his body and held Darcy's gaze.

"Given that she remains insistent about the parentage of her child, coupled with the fact Tavistock said there was a witness and told you to have a conversation with your friend, which I assume is Bingley, have you ever – even once in the deep, dark recesses of your mind – accepted she might be telling the truth?"

Richard's words hit him hard. If she had told the truth, then the child she carried, the next Duke of Tavistock if male, was *his* child. Should have been *his* heir. Something he'd never have with Anne.

"You need to speak to Bingley. The way he defended her virtue, saying he would call out those who disparaged her… Something is not right. When you belittled her, he said there were things you were not aware of."

Darcy nodded and the two cousins left White's with much on their minds. As soon as he was back at his townhouse, he'd send a note to Bingley, asking him to come to dinner that evening. Unfortunately, just as he'd gotten out his writing supplies, Burke came in bearing an envelope with black borders.

Anne was dead.

Chapter Nine

THE BEGINNING OF MAY saw Elizabeth and Henry prepare to remove to Buckinghamshire. Before she was showing too much, Elizabeth wished to visit Longbourn and make amends with her mother. From there, Jane would return to live with them at Edgecam Hall until she married or wished to return to Longbourn. If things continued the way Elizabeth anticipated, marriage for Jane was on the horizon, and her eldest sister could very well be the next Countess of Telford. Their cousin Kit was head over heels in love and his affection was returned ten-fold by Jane.

Mama – Lizzy had begun to address her mother in a more familiar manner to honor Henry – still did not know her son-in-law's importance. So, it was a humble Mr. Talbot and his wife who planned on staying at Longbourn for the week, enjoying hospitality of friends and neighbors who'd never had a chance to give her good wishes on her marriage.

Their carriage rolled to a stop in front of Longbourn. Papa, Mamma, Mary, and Kitty all waited near the front door. Lydia remained in the school for young ladies.

"You are come! You are come at last. I finally get to meet

you, Mr. Talbot. Oh, you are such a handsome man. Is he not handsome, Mr. Bennet? So handsome! So tall! I have such a fine son-in-law. Lady Lucas will be so jealous. Her son-in-law is not near as handsome as you, Mr. Talbot. Oh! – where are my manners? Come into the house. Hill! Hill! Bring the tea to the front parlor."

The whirlwind that was Mamma continued to flutter around Elizabeth and Henry. Jane was busy hugging her sisters and Papa. Henry smiled and nodded and never said a word. Elizabeth slipped her hand in his and squeezed and he gazed down at her, a silly smile quirking one side of his mouth, a sure sign he was amused.

"Is she always like this?" he whispered as Mamma bustled about, ensuring their trunks were unloaded to her satisfaction.

"No, today she is quite calm."

He laughed and then covered his mouth with hand and pretended to cough when Mamma glanced at them. "Elizabeth," he growled. "Are you trying to get me into trouble with your mother?"

"Yes. I like when her focus is on you."

"Later, in the privacy of our room, I will seek retribution and penance."

Her insides quivered at the intimate promise.

They made their way to the drawing room, where Mamma and Kitty began preparing the tea. Once everyone was seated, Mamma turned her attention to Henry.

"You have a house in town, Mr. Talbot? I've heard it is quite charming."

"I think it is."

"And you have invited my Jane to live with you?"

"We have. Elizabeth would like her sister close by. I hope you do not mind."

"Mind? Why would I mind? Jane deserves a season in town.

Do you have many connections Mr. Talbot? Any men a young lady with Jane's qualifications could meet?"

"Mamma! Mr. Talbot is not a marriage broker." Elizabeth found herself straightening in dismay. Henry placed his hand on her arm and she sat back in her chair.

"I have a small social circle, Mrs. Bennet, but I am not averse to making sure my new sister is introduced to suitable young men."

"Oh, that is good. It's just too bad you weren't a lord. I would so like to see her marry someone important. Jane cannot be so beautiful for nothing."

"I will see what I can do," Henry said and hid a smile behind his tea cup.

She noted Papa also was hiding his smile and Jane, well Jane blushed very prettily and said nothing. Henry then stood and asked Mamma if they could be shown to their room. Mamma looked at him with a blank face.

"You wish to share a room with Lizzy?"

"She is my wife, Madam."

"But... but, I thought she'd stay in her old room, with Jane."

"Were we not married, that would be acceptable. However, she is not, so we shall share a room."

"Oh, what will Lady Lucas say about this."

"How would she know unless you told her?"

"I... ahh.... Oh! – I would never gossip to Lady Lucas about such things."

"Good, then the matter is settled and only family will know that the husband of the former Elizabeth Bennet wished to share a room with his wife." He extended his hand to Elizabeth and helped her to her feet. "My valet should already have our trunks unpacked and I know Elizabeth's maid will have a bath prepared. We shall refresh ourselves and return for dinner."

"Lizzy has her own maid?" Mrs. Bennet's eyes widened and then she smiled. "That is a fine thing. My girls could use the services of a new maid."

"Mrs. Bennet. Elizabeth's maid is not here to cater to your daughters. Hattie serves no other than my wife."

"But—"

"No."

Henry placed Elizabeth's hand on his forearm and escorted her from the room while Mamma sputtered. Once clear of the room, Henry lifted her hand and kissed the back of it.

"Was I too harsh?"

They'd reached the stairs and he let Elizabeth precede him.

"No," she said over her shoulder. "But I wish I was a fly on the wall right now. It might prove quite entertaining."

"You know your sister Jane will tell you what happened."

They'd reached the top of the stairs and Elizabeth faced her husband.

"Jane will cover everything with light and happiness. Papa will only see the satire and humor. No, if I want a true rendition, I will have to petition Mary. She only speaks the unvarnished truth. Good or bad."

"I look forward to getting to know your sister Mary. Truth bearers are hard to find these days."

"Be careful what you wish for, dear Henry."

He closed the distance between them and lifted her face for a kiss.

"Then, I carefully wish for a nap with my wife before she takes her bath," he whispered against her mouth.

An hour later, a happily sated Elizabeth slid into the freshly warmed bath water while Henry slept fitfully on rumpled sheets. Dinner that evening was a lively affair, with Mamma apologizing for not knowing Henry's favorite foods.

"Mark my words, Mr. Talbot. Tomorrow evening, I will

have two full courses with all your favorites, if I can manage to winkle them out of Lizzy."

"Certainly, Mamma. I will speak with Cook first thing in the morning before I go on a long-awaited ramble."

"Surely you are not going to walk alone?"

"Mamma, I have always walked alone. My sisters are welcome to come, but they do not rise as early as me."

"Do not worry, Mrs. Bennet. I shall escort my wife. I have a great desire to see this Oakham Mount she is forever talking about." Henry said before turning to Papa. "I also would like to take a tour of the estate. Longbourn has some pretty aspects. Are you up for a ride later in the day, Bennet?"

Her father hated leaving the solitude of his library, although he did ride the grounds on a regular basis to keep Longbourn running smoothly. Yet, this was Henry's chance to let him know how their relationship and marriage was progressing in a setting where big ears were not listening at the door.

"Of course. My estate may not be as grand as yours—" Papa stopped at Henry's warning glance. Mamma did not know about the estate in Buckinghamshire. She only knew about the house in town. "—as your cousin's," Papa quickly inserted in place of what he almost said, "but it is sufficient for our needs and has been in my family for nearly four hundred years."

"Until that horrid Mr. Collins kicks us all out upon Mr. Bennet's death." Mamma wailed. "How can the law allow a complete stranger to remove a family out of the only home they've ever known?"

"We have talked about this before, Mrs. Bennet. There is nothing I can do about it and Mr. Talbot has agreed to find you and the girls a lovely house when the time comes. Hopefully, not for another ten or twenty years."

"While I am thankful for Mr. Talbot's generosity, I cannot stand the idea of Charlotte Lucas becoming mistress of my home. Already Lady Lucas is gloating over the fact Longbourn shall be her daughter's one day." She fluffed a lace handkerchief up to her eyes. "Kitty informs me the Collins's live very comfortably. Well, well, I only hope it will last. If she is half as sharp as her mother, she is saving enough. There is nothing extravagant in their housekeeping, I dare say."

"Charlotte has always been a practical woman." Elizabeth couldn't help but defend her friend. "Like the Bennet girls, she has learned well how to manage a household."

"Yes, yes. Mrs. Collins will take care not to outrun their income. They will never be distressed for money. Well, much good may it do them! And so, I would imagine, they often talk of having Longbourn when your father is dead. They look upon it quite as their own, I dare say, whenever that happens."

"They never spoke on the subject around me, Mamma." Kitty ventured in a timid voice.

"No. It would have been strange if they had. But I make no doubt, they often talk of it between themselves. Well, if they can be easy with an estate that is not lawfully their own, so much the better. I should be ashamed of having one that was only entailed on me."

"Mamma, let us talk of other things. You know how this subject distresses you," Jane asked, turning to Henry. "Shall we tell Mamma how Uncle Gardiner has provided Lizzy with some lovely fabrics to refurbish her private parlor?"

"Lizzy has a private parlor? Oh, how grand!" Mamma interrupted. "Your house must be very large, Mr. Talbot."

"Our house suits our needs, and that of my wife and any children we might welcome into our family."

"Lizzy's increasing?" Mamma turned to her with excitement lighting up her eyes. "Oh! – dear girl, make sure you have a son."

Elizabeth flashed Henry a look of dismay. They'd agreed

not to say anything to her mother in case she discovered how far along she truly was. He shook his head very slightly and the look upon his face told her he had things well in hand.

"Madam, calm yourself. We have no definitive news and will advise if there is any change." Henry turned his attention to one of her sisters. "Miss Mary, your governess Mrs. Gravestone tells me you are quite diligent in practicing the pianoforte Might I ask you to treat us to one of your performances when we return to the drawing room?" Mary blushed ever so slightly and said yes. "Perfect. I look forward to it."

It was a very tired Elizabeth who collapsed onto the guest bed a few hours later. She'd taken to having naps in the afternoon to help battle her ongoing fatigue, but that daily luxury had been replaced with a more vigorous activity she'd enjoyed with her husband. Prior to falling asleep, she thought about Henry riding with Papa on the morrow.

She wished she could tag along. A few days before they left London, Henry had gone to his gentleman's club, for business he'd said, and returned in a dark mood. He then spent a few hours holed away in his study, only coming out once to ask her the full name of her cousin in Kent and how he was related to her father. She expected some part of the conversation between Papa and her husband to revolve around the Reverend William Collins. For what reason, she had no clue.

She also had no clue her husband entered the room to find her fully clothed, asleep on the bed. He didn't call the maid, but efficiently stripped her down to her chemise. Before pulling the covers over her sleeping form, he knelt beside the bed and kissed her stomach through the material of her chemise.

"Good night, my child," he whispered. "Be kind to your mamma. Do not kick too much and let her sleep."

~~~

THE EARL OF MATLOCK, his wife, two sons and Darcy arrived at Rosings Park together the day after the news of Anne's death. Aunt Catherine was beside herself with grief. The earl was the executor of Anne's will and after the service and burial, they convened in the library, where Sir Lewis de Bourgh's attorney handed Uncle Robert the will he'd brought with him from London and everybody settled into a chair.

For the most part, Aunt Catherine stared listlessly at the wall. The only time she became animated was when the disbursement of Rosings Park was mentioned. At the age of twenty-five, Anne had become the legal owner of Rosings Park. Aunt Catherine remained in the main house only at her pleasure. This was news to everyone. They'd all believed Sir Lewis had left everything to his wife.

Anne's last will and testament, witnessed at the time of her twenty-fifth birthday, stated in clear and concise its terms, that if she was not married by the time of her death, Rosings Park would go to Colonel Richard Fitzwilliam on the condition he give up his commission and take over the running of the estate.

"This is not to be borne!" Lady Catherine shouted and banged her walking stick on the floor. "She was as good as wed to Darcy; the will is not valid."

"They were not married, Catherine."

"The announcement was in the *Gazette*; they were as good as married."

"Not as good as standing in front of a minister and saying 'I do' before signing legal documents. The will is valid, Catherine." Uncle Robert's voice rose in tandem with Aunt Catherine's.

"You only say that because your son benefits from the death of my daughter."

"Catherine! Enough. No one expected this, least of all Richard. Anne had her reasons, of which I had no prior knowledge." He picked up the will to continue reading. "Now, we have some sundry bequests to distribute to various family members and staff."

"I shall not stand for this travesty."

Aunt Catherine stood and stormed from the room. Her walking stick banging at regular, fading intervals as she traversed the hall and proceeded upstairs.

"Now that the drama has unfolded as expected, shall we continue?"

Uncle Robert read out the bequests, one being all of Anne's jewelry to be given to Georgiana, and all her personal books be given to Darcy. Her faithful companion, Mrs. Jenkinson, was to be pensioned and provided with a cottage on the grounds of Rosings Park, hers to stay in rent free until her death, or marriage.

"I have some other business to take care of and ask that Richard and Darcy stay back for this."

Everyone, including the solicitor, exited the room and when they were alone, Uncle Robert glared at the two cousins.

"I have in my possession an express post from the archbishop removing Mr. William Collins as rector of Hunsford. The archbishop received a damning letter from none other than his grace, the Duke of Tavistock, in which he stated that after having a conversation with one Colonel Richard Fitzwilliam and one Mr. Darcy earlier that day, he felt compelled to have the man defrocked." Uncle Robert settled his glasses back on his nose and looked down the letter bearing the archbishop's seal. "The duke's letter said, and I quote,

The Reverend William Horatio Collins, did with malice and intent, egregiously malign the character and virtue of her grace, the Duchess of Tavistock, previously known to him as Miss Elizabeth Bennet of Longbourn, Hertfordshire. Mr. Collins

alluded to Mr. Fitzwilliam Darcy of Derbyshire and Colonel Richard Fitzwilliam of London that he had engaged in licentious behavior with the gentle woman while staying at the home of his cousin – Mr. Thomas Bennet of Longbourn, Hertfordshire – whereupon he allegedly enjoyed her company in an intimate and sinful manner. If the above is true, Mr. Collins has behaved in a manner unbecoming of a minister by partaking in the sin of adultery, if the above is untrue, he is guilty of the sin of lying. Both are cause enough to remove the man from office and holy ordinance, etc., etc..."

Uncle Robert removed his glasses and refolded the letter. "What the hell have you two been doing?" Shocked, Darcy stared at his uncle. "You have one of the most powerful men in England, cousin to the Queen and therefore to the prince Regent, naming you as a witness to a smarmy parson's tale of illicit acts of sex."

"Alleged acts of sex."

"You believe the parson lied?"

"I have reason to believe he lied."

"Then how, on God's green earth, did the duke catch wind of this?" Darcy shifted uncomfortably in his chair. He hadn't felt this way since the time his deceased father had him on the carpet for something he'd done wrong as a willful lad. "How would Tavistock have any knowledge of a third-rate parson who caters to my sister's spiritual needs in the wilds of Kent?"

"I asked to meet him at White's earlier in the week."

"For what purpose?"

"I would rather not say, Uncle."

"No. You do not get to prevaricate. Not on this. I am friends with him. I have met his wife prior to their marriage. She and her eldest sister were guests of the Marquis of Haversham, whose wife, by the by, is my wife's sister and Richard's aunt! The

Duchess of Tavistock is Haversham's cousin and now also the Queen's by marriage. You *will* tell me what you have done."

"Very well." Darcy felt much disquiet. All the pieces of the puzzle were beginning to fall into place and he did not like the picture it was making. "When Mr. Collins alluded to a sexual liaison with then Miss Elizabeth, I felt the duke should be made aware in case she was attempting to cuckold him with another man's child."

"You WHAT?!" Uncle Robert jumped to his feet and began to pace. "You do not even know if she is pregnant. What were you thinking?"

"I did know she was pregnant."

Uncle Robert came full stop and faced him.

"You had better begin explaining, and leave no detail out."

"This cannot leave this room. Tavistock warned me that if one iota of gossip about his wife reached his ear, he will make my life miserable. He categorically stated there was no place in England where I could hide from his wrath."

"Why you? Why is he so focused on you, of all people?"

"Because, earlier in the year, Mr. Bennet attended my home and implied I was the father of the child his unwed daughter carried."

Uncle Robert fell into his chair.

"Are you?" he finally managed to ask.

"At the time I categorically refuted her claim."

"And now?"

"I have to speak to Mr. Bingley, who was my host at the time of the alleged event, to see if he has further details of which I am unaware."

"If you took a woman's virtue, you would be aware. There is indisputable physical evidence."

"Apparently, I was drunk."

"What a mess you have made of all this." Uncle Robert

speared his son with a hard look. "And what was your role in this fiasco?"

"I went with him in case Darcy was called out and needed a second."

"Of course, you did." Uncle Robert picked up another document and waved it about. "The fall out of this debacle widens. It turns out the duke has instructed his solicitors to examine the entailment to the estate Mr. Collins expected to inherit. Mr. Collins is apparently a third cousin down the maternal line and if that is the case, he is not qualified. There is no direct male heir and the entail is broken. Mr. Bennet can leave his estate to whomever he chooses."

"Why would you have this knowledge?"

"I would assume the archbishop wished me to break all the bad news to Mr. Collins at the same time. He will have to find another place of residence, and Longbourn is no longer available to him."

"I feel for his wife. She is a very genteel sort of woman and will be punished alongside her husband."

"She has family that can help sort things out. Mr. Collins may have to become a clerk. He has a scholarly bent, having gone into the church. Something will be found, I am sure."

"Not if this scandal follows him."

"Tavistock will not visit his anger upon Mrs. Collins. His aim is to remove the idiot from the church and let the cards fall where they may. No one will learn of his mistake, unless he persists in spreading further rumors, which will not end well for him. I have been instructed to relay all this information and the duke's dire warning when I see the parson tomorrow."

"What will you tell Aunt Catherine?"

"That Richard, as the new owner of Rosings, wishes to find a different rector. She need not be apprised of the reason because you can be assured, she would never keep silent, regardless of who threatened her."

"That is true.

"Uncle, there is nothing more I can do here. I would like to return to London tomorrow after Anne's interment. I have much to do on my own estate and need to move forward with my life."

"Agreed. If you stay here, Catherine will continue to insist you were as good as married."

"Good night, Uncle. I shall see you in the morning before I leave."

"Darcy," Uncle Robert called out and he paused before opening the door. "I have to ask. Why did *you* not notify the Archbishop of Mr. Collins's heinous behavior. This never should have gone further than our family."

"I am aware of that now, Uncle. I have no satisfactory answer."

He left the room and ascended the main staircase. About to turn left to go to his usual suite of rooms, a low keening noise made him pause. The sound came from Anne's room. He hesitated only briefly before turning and after knocking softly on the door, opened it to find Aunt Catherine sitting on the floor, her skirts puddled around her. She clutched in her arms one of Anne's old dolls and was rocking back and forth, tears streaming down her lined face.

He approached and waited. She did not acknowledge him. Not knowing quite what to do, he followed instinct and sat on the floor next to her. When she didn't shy away, he shuffled over and placed an arm around her shoulders.

Quite unexpectedly, she turned in his arms and began to cry. Great, heaving sobs rent her body. Caught unaware by her fresh outpouring of grief, he stayed where he was, letting her expend her tears. Finally, she was spent and with her head still resting on his shoulder, the two of them sat in complete silence.

"She was not supposed to die before me," Aunt Catherine finally said in a quiet voice.

"I am sorry this happened."

"No, you are not. I am not blind. I have always known you did not want to marry Anne."

"Not true," he began to protest.

"Do not mock my intelligence, Fitzwilliam Darcy. I was surprised when you finally told me to announce your engagement. I concluded you had fallen in love with someone and they rejected you. There was no other reason for you to turn to Anne. Not after all this time."

"I had not fallen in love, nor had I been rejected."

"But you *were* disappointed by someone whom you hold in high esteem. I know you, Darcy. Almost better than you know yourself."

"It is neither here nor there, Aunt. We cannot change what has happened." He shifted his weight on the floor and she straightened, as though realizing for the first time they were both sitting on the floor. He pushed himself to his feet and held out his hand, helping her to stand. "I am leaving tomorrow to pick up Georgiana and we are off to Pemberley. If you find that you need to get away from all this, please come and stay with us."

Aunt Catherine smiled at him and he was caught by surprise. He'd forgotten what a handsome woman his aunt actually was. "You are kind, Darcy, and I may take you up on your generous offer, but not at this time. Richard has not the first clue on how to oversee an estate and I must remain to ensure he does not run it into the ground. He is also in need of a wife. We know he is well versed in the art of flirtation, but to find the correct woman is beyond his capabilities. He will be taken in by the first doxy who practices her arts and allurements on him."

As his aunt continued to expound on the multitude of reasons why she would remain at Rosings, Darcy felt the corner of his mouth life. His aunt would continue on, as strong as ever. He stepped closer and kissed her temple.

"What was that for?"

"I love you Aunt Catherine. I will say my farewell now, as I know you do not like to rise with the morning lark."

"Bah! I can rise early if required. I will see you at breakfast. You will not slip away so easy from me, boy."

"No, I do not suppose I will."

He turned on his heel and exited the room, closing the door carefully behind him. Soon he was laying in his bed, thinking over the conversation he had with not only his aunt, but his uncle. He'd created a formidable enemy in the Duke of Tavistock, which was quite puzzling. The duke was known to be an amiable man, well liked by many. It was no small thing that he was taking up the cause of his wife in persisting the child was, by blood, a Darcy. Before he left for Pemberley, it was imperative he speak with Bingley. He had to know if what they alleged was true.

What he would do with that information was anybody's guess.

Chapter Ten

ELIZABETH AND HENRY extended their stay at Longbourn to two weeks before leaving for Edgecam Hall. They dared not stay longer as her body continued to shift and grow along with the baby and soon her gowns would not effectively hide the little bump. The baby was quite active and Henry spent every morning with either his hand or his ear on her belly.

"There! He kicked again. He is going to be a fine boy, Elizabeth," he said and waited for the baby to move again.

"Yes, she will be an excellent walker," she teased back, knowing how much he longed for a son.

She looked down at his large hands spanned across the small swell of her stomach. He was always so very tender with her. She would miss him dearly when that fateful day came and he left her forever. But he was hers for today and she'd take every day God allowed them to be together.

"What delights do you think your mother has for me this morning, seeing as it is our last breakfast here at Longbourn?"

"I have not been consulted. We shall both find out together."

As it was, Mrs. Bennet had made Elizabeth's favorites, which brought a tear to her eye.

"Muffins, hot rolls and hot chocolate?" Henry looked at her plate. "These are your favorite breakfast items?"

"I was usually up before everyone else and would grab a hot roll for my walk and finish with a muffin and hot chocolate when I came home." She smiled and bit into the hot roll. "This is my idea of heaven, Mr. Talbot."

Henry walked to the sideboard, where a more substantial array of foods was arranged. When he took his seat beside Elizabeth, he teased, "No wonder your figure is light and pleasing. You eat the same amount as a sparrow."

"Your cook must be feeding Lizzy better than a tiny bird, Mr. Talbot." Mamma said. "I have noticed her gowns are a little too snug for comfort. Although I bemoaned the fact, she set out every day, at times coming home with hems six inches deep in mud. She is of the same frame as her Grandmother Bennet. She also walked to keep fit and trim. You should encourage Lizzy to return to her daily constitutional."

Elizabeth nearly choked on her muffin when Mamma said her gowns were too snug. Truly, it was providential they were leaving in a few short hours. As it was, a little over five months pregnant, her center of balance had shifted, her feet were beginning to swell and she no longer wore stays. After birthing five children, and losing a few in between, her mother knew the signs of pregnancy. Elizabeth's saving grace was that Mamma's focus had been on impressing her new son-in-law. If they stayed longer, it might shift to her headstrong daughter. It was imperative they leave today.

"That is my plan, Mrs. Bennet. I enjoy walking with Elizabeth."

"You go walking with my daughter?"

"When I am not busy with business."

"What is it that you do, Mr. Talbot? I have never been told but I know you are successful; the cut of Lizzy's clothes can only come from an expensive modiste. And you drive a handsome carriage."

There was a small pause and Elizabeth held her breath.

"I took over the family business, Mrs. Bennet," Henry said smoothly. "It is very successful and runs like a well-oiled machine." He concentrated on his breakfast and Mamma didn't seem to notice he hadn't truly answered her question.

"Oh, that you could stay a month complete. We have not visited half the people who wanted to see Lizzy and her handsome husband."

"I saw everyone that I wished to, Mamma. The Lucas's held such a lovely dinner party, and almost everyone except the Gouldings attended."

"It is a good thing Lady Lucas held the dinner party when she did, the most dreadful thing has happened."

"What happened?"

"Mr. Collins has been ousted as Lady Catherine's parson. He and Charlotte are moving back in with Sir William and Lady Lucas and he has to find other employment. Apparently, he can never be a minister in the Church of England again."

"Oh no! Poor Charlotte. I wonder what happened?" Elizabeth felt a frisson of alarm for her former best friend.

"No one knows, not even Lady Lucas. It is all very hush hush." Mamma pushed her plate away and scowled. "I hope those Collins's don't think they can come and live here like vultures, waiting for Mr. Bennet to die."

"He cannot, Mrs. Bennet."

"Why do you say that, Mr. Talbot?"

"Your husband is the master of Longbourn. Mr. Collins cannot arbitrarily decide to live with the Bennet family because he has no other home. It is the law."

"Good. For all I know he would spend all day counting the silverware to ensure everything is here when he does take over."

"I wonder if I should write Charlotte," Elizabeth mused. "This will be such an unsettling time, and I believe she and Mr. Collins are expecting an addition. She hinted as much in her last letter."

"Poor Lady Lucas, I know she economises as best she can, but with two extra mouths and possibly a third, I do not know what Sir William is going to do."

Mamma looked out the window, an unfamiliar pensive look settling on her face. Although her mother and Lady Lucas were eternally engaged in an unspoken feud over who was the queen of Meryton society, they'd been friends and neighbors for over twenty years. News such as this would be distressing.

"Mr. Collins has a scholarly bent, Mamma," Elizabeth said softly. "I am sure he will find some work as a clerk. There is nothing wrong in working for a living."

Mamma turned and smiled. "That is true. My father was an attorney. Your Uncle Edward is quite successful with his business, and Mr. Talbot is also successful in…" she frowned and looked at Henry. "What were you successful at again, Mr. Talbot?"

"The family business, Mrs. Bennet."

"Oh yes, the family business."

Henry stood and placed his hand on the back of Elizabeth's chair.

"We really should make sure our trunks are packed and ready to go, Mrs. Talbot."

"I shall see if Jane has collected everything she wants from the still room and will meet with you at the carriage."

Mamma rose as well and bustled out of the room, calling for Hill to check on the footmen and Jane's trunks. The pianoforte in the other room went silent, and Mary came into the hall.

"Will you join me in fetching Jane?" Elizabeth held out her hand and was happy when Mary slid hers into a tight grasp. "I will miss you, Mary," she said as they walked to the still room.

"I doubt that."

"Whatever do you mean?"

"You have Jane, you need no other."

"That is where you are wrong. I need all my sisters. Like your music, each sister brings her own melody and chords to the song that makes up the ballad of the Longbourn ladies." She stopped and faced Mary. "How would Mozart's music sound if he never added the bass notes, or the beautiful contraltos?"

"Boring. Mundane."

"Precisely. Such is every Bennet girl. You are the rhythm. Most desperately needed and quite often overlooked, but without you, keeping us steady, our notes would go too fast, or go too slow."

Mary threw her arms around Elizabeth's shoulders and began to cry.

"I will miss you desperately, Lizzy. You *and* Jane, it is like one of my limbs is being torn off and I do not know what to do."

Elizabeth soothed her sister with long strokes down her back until she settled.

"I am not going to the ends of the world and Henry has already said my sisters can visit in a few months. Right now, our marriage is new and we are getting used to one another."

Mary took a step back and looked down at her sister's stomach.

"You are having a baby!"

Instinctively, Elizabeth's hands cradled her abdomen.

"Yes, but we thought it best to not tell Mama at this time. She would insist on coming and staying with us, and like I said,

Henry and I are still learning about each other. Mamma is too high strung for *my* nerves right now."

"Can I tell Kitty?"

Elizabeth shook her head. "I cannot trust she would not tell Lydia in a letter, which in turn would get back to Mamma."

"Then, your secret is safe with me."

Mary looped her arm with Elizabeth's and they continued to the still room where Jane was putting the last bottle into a blanket lined box. She was grateful Mary had not questioned her further about the baby. As it was, they'd have a hard time finding a reason for the baby's birth occurring seven months after the marriage. Being away from town and squirreled away at Edgecam would help with the ruse.

She couldn't wait to see Henry's country estate. He assured her there were enough paths and walking trails that she would never repine the loss of her favorite walk to Oakham Mount. The sisters made their way to the front of Longbourn, where Mamma, Papa, Kitty and Henry waited. All their trunks were loaded onto a wagon, a footman finished securing Jane's box of bottles as Henry's valet and Lizzy's maid entered their carriage.

"Good bye, Lizzy. I shall miss you," Papa said as he hugged her tight. "Take care of my daughters, Mr. Talbot. I expect letters from you all but cannot promise to return them promptly."

"That I well know, Papa. You are a witty, but terrible correspondent."

"Good bye, Mamma." Elizabeth brushed the cheek of her mother with her lips. She was not afraid of her mother embracing her, she never had in recent memory, if ever. The relationship between she and her mother was complicated and filled with remorse. Hopefully, now that she was mistress of her own home and out from beneath her mother's feet, she could begin to mend the deep hurt inflicted, sometimes unwittingly, by her flighty mother.

"Goodbye, Lizzy. Take care of your husband. Good ones like him don't hang about on trees, waiting to be picked."

"I know, Mamma. Mr. Talbot is the best of men."

"Goodbye, Mrs. Bennet, Mr. Bennet." Henry gave them a polite bow. "Sisters Mary and Catherine. Hopefully soon we can have you come for a visit. Your sister will keep in touch and let you know our future plans."

"Oh, Jane!" Mamma hugged her eldest tight to her chest. "I shall miss you so and expect you to write me soon with news of all the young men who come to court you." She stepped back and caressed Jane's cheek. "You cannot be so beautiful for nothing. Make sure Mr. Talbot finds you a titled gentleman. A duke would do nicely for you."

Jane blushed deeply and looked to the ground. Papa smirked and Elizabeth swiftly took Jane's arm, saying, "We must be on our way. Good bye, everyone. I shall write when we arrive."

Henry quirked an eyebrow at Papa and then turned to Mamma.

"Mrs. Bennet, I will do my very best to entice a titled gentleman to court your eldest daughter. I do have some notable connections in town but cannot make promises. The heart is a fickle thing. Sometimes we cannot choose whom we fall in love with."

"Oh, so true, Mr. Talbot. Why, I never thought my Lizzy would marry a tradesman, but here you are and she is almost radiant from your attention."

"I love your daughter very much and have never regretted your brother bringing her to my attention."

"Bless you, Mr. Talbot." Mamma dabbed her eyes with a lace handkerchief. "Now shoo," she cried out. "The day is wasting and you do not want to be on the highway at night with all those brigands who terrorize good folk as they travel."

Soon, their caravan of carriages trundled down the gravel drive of Longbourn, through the village of Meryton and were joined by a dozen armed outriders as soon as they were out of sight of the village.

~~~

EDGECAM HALL WAS everything Elizabeth expected, and more. The approach to Henry's ducal home was long and lined with ancient oaks. Their branches overstretched the graveled drive and provided welcome shade in the summer heat. Beyond them, she peeked a substantive parkland and the glint of water, which she discovered to her delight was a lake with a well-kept path encircling its shores, giving her much to admire on her daily rambles.

Edgecam Hall itself was a study of Elizabethan splendor. Largely U-shaped, two great spires anchored the house in place, prefaced by a magnificent fountain around which carriages circumnavigated before dropping off guests or family and then trundling off to the stables. Upon entry, after traversing the length of almost fifty servants, she was in awe of the grand staircase which swept up to the second floor, priceless masterpieces marching in tandem with the steps on the wood panelled wall.

"You said you had a tidy estate, Mr. Talbot. I believe that was not only a vast understatement, but most assuredly a lie."

"Nay, I have seen larger houses. I am but a humble duke, with a humble home." Henry grinned at her indelicate snort before handing off his hat and gloves to the waiting butler while a several maids divested Elizabeth and Jane of their outerwear.

Mrs. Hastings, the housekeeper, waited patiently before taking the ladies to the second floor and their chambers. Jane's room was a few doors down from hers in the family wing and soon Elizabeth was shown into her suite of rooms.

"Your footmen will have your trunks up here shortly your grace and I know your maid will have you unpacked and well situated before dinner. In the meantime, would you like a bath to wash off the dust from your travels?"

"That would be lovely, Mrs. Hastings," Elizabeth said with a smile. "This room is exquisite. Did the duke's previous wife decorate it?"

"She did, ma'am. The late duchess was a very refined lady. Her tastes were quite simple. The only thing we changed, as per the duke's instructions, were the coverlet and the curtains. He had your Aunt Gardiner pick out the material and forward it to our seamstress here at Edgecam Hall."

Elizabeth looked at the bed linen and then the windows. She couldn't have chosen better herself.

"It is all appreciated."

"May I show you the rest of your suite while we wait for your bath water?"

"Please, do."

Mrs. Hastings opened one of several doors which led to a large dressing room. Four armoires filled the area, with a small couch upon which to sit and a gilt-edged mirror dominated one wall. From there she showed her the bathing room, her private parlor and off the private parlor was another door which she said led to the duke's own bedchamber.

Although her bedchamber was lovely, Elizabeth knew she most likely would never sleep in the pretty bed. Ever since she and Henry had become intimate, he insisted she stay with him through the night, and she didn't see that changing any time soon.

~~~

"I WAS ABOUT TO send out a search party for you."

Elizabeth, after several wrong turns, had finally found the drawing room where Henry and Jane waited before going into dinner.

"I was sure Mrs. Hastings said turn right at the bottom of the stairs, but after I had walked into the several wrong rooms, I realized I was lost. One of the footmen took pity on me and escorted me here."

"You will find your way soon enough." Henry poured her a glass of wine and she accepted it with a smile. "Tomorrow, I will give you and Jane a tour."

"And then you promise to show me the walking paths?"

Henry laughed. "I should have known that is what you would most like to see. You will not be disappointed. We have a lovely deer park to the west of Edgecam, and behind the house, in the southwest corner, we have a maze."

They were just about to head to the family dining room when the butler, Mr. Bridges, announced the Earl of Thedford. Elizabeth looked at Henry, who gave her a smug smile, while Jane twisted her fingers together and blushed a rosy pink.

Kit strode into the room and gave them all a polite bow, and even though his words were directed at Henry, his eyes never left Jane.

"Forgive me for intruding, your grace. I have urgent business with Miss Bennet."

"Did you now?"

Kit finally looked at Henry and a dull flush of red rose up from his neck to his face.

"I was going to write, but it took less time to ride here than pen a letter and send a footman."

"You are fortunate there is only twenty miles between our estates. We are about to have dinner; would you care to join us after you freshen up?"

"Yes, but might I have a moment with Miss Bennet?"

Henry looked toward Jane and she nodded.

"Very well. Elizabeth and I will enjoy a conversation by the fireplace while Bridges lets Cook know another guest is here for dinner. You may talk with my sister Jane over there." Henry indicated with a nod of his head the two chairs in the far corner of the drawing room. From there they could watch, but not hear what Kit had to say, although Elizabeth had an inkling of what drove her cousin to abdicate all forms of polite courtesy and arrive on their doorstep the very day they arrived in Buckinghamshire.

She was not proven wrong and given the wide smile wreathing Jane's face, she knew another wedding was about to take place. The two of them turned, and arm in arm approached Elizabeth and Henry.

"I am sure you have gathered I have asked Jane to marry me, and she has said yes."

Elizabeth took hold of one of Jane's hands and squeezed, her own eyes filling with tears.

"Should you not have asked permission, or at least courted the poor girl?" Henry teased.

Kit looked at Jane, love shining in his eyes. "Jane and I talked about this before she went to Longbourn and I had planned on courting her. To put it simply, I missed her too much and want her by my side as soon as possible. She is of legal age and does not require permission, although we would like your blessing, seeing as you are acting in her father's stead."

Henry turned his attention to Jane and smiled. "In the presence of such felicity, how can I say no to a beloved sister?"

"We shall read the banns and marry in August."

"Could we marry at Christmas?" Jane asked, surprising Kit.

"You do not wish to marry sooner."

"I would marry you tomorrow, but I ask for more time because I want Lizzy to stand up with me."

"Are you away in August and cannot attend?" Kit asked Henry, who looked at Elizabeth before answering. She gave him a nod of approval.

"Elizabeth is with child and will be entering her confinement sometime in August. She cannot travel to Longbourn at that time."

"I have always dreamed of marrying with my sister standing up with me," Jane almost whispered.

"How can I deny such a simple request?" The earl kissed her forehead. "You will be the best Christmas present I have ever received."

"Thank you." Jane lifted herself up onto her toes and kissed his cheek, then blushed furiously and looked to the floor.

By this time, Bridges had returned and said the earl's room was prepared. Kit left them briefly to freshen up and then joined them in the dining room. The meal was delightful not only by merit of good food, but also of laughter and love that permeated the room. The next day, Kit made for Longbourn bearing a letter from Elizabeth to her father.

Dearest Papa,

With the arrival of Kit, Mamma will indeed be in raptures over the fact that Jane managed to capture an earl. Seeing as she most likely will be calling for her salts as well as the carriage to visit neighbors, please advise her of my good fortune with regard to Henry's rank. I think now would be as good a time as any to let her know about the baby. If you are going to be inundated with cries of joy, you may as well get all of them done in one fell swoop.

Your loving daughter,
Elizabeth Rose Talbot
Duchess of Tavistock

Chapter Eleven

DAYS MELDED INTO WEEKS, and then into months. July came and went and August arrived, bringing with it unbearable heat. Elizabeth suffered terribly the few short weeks before her expected time. As dawn broke on the morning of August twelfth, she felt the first sharp pangs of childbirth. She lay in bed as still as possible, hoping it was another minor contraction, similar to the ones her body had been producing over the past few weeks in preparation for *the* day.

Another clenched and released her abdomen. She wished she had Henry's pocket watch so she could see how much time passed between the pains. While waiting for the next one, she swung her legs over the side of the bed, slid swollen feet into a pair of Henry's slippers and shrugged on one of his robes as hers no longer closed sufficiently. The bottom of his robe trailed on the floor behind her as she made her way to the water closet to attend her most urgent need. A need that cropped up with annoying frequency the bigger she grew with child. Once complete, she washed her face and then rubbed and talked to her belly.

"You may not come out today, little one. Please go back to sleep and make your appearance tomorrow."

"You are well?" Henry called from their shared bedchamber.

She moved to stand in the doorframe and caught him grinning in an almost boyish manner.

"You are in a good mood, Mr. Talbot."

"Am I in trouble, sweet Beth?" Henry had taken to calling her Beth not long after they'd arrived home from Longbourn. "You promised to only call me Mr. Talbot if I am in trouble."

"You are not in trouble. I find I am already weary and have only just risen, which makes me testy. What has you in such good humor?"

"The sight of my beautiful wife, looking like a stranded waif in my robe and slippers."

She looked down her body, seeing only the swell of her abdomen.

"At least you can see your feet, mine disappeared about a month ago."

"Shall I have Hattie bring you breakfast in bed?"

"No, thank you. I wish to go for a walk. I feel an overwhelming desire to be outdoors."

"Then I shall send her up to assist you with dressing." He whipped a cut flower from behind his back and presented it to her. "A rose for *my* rose."

Unexpected tears filled her eyes.

"It is lovely, thank you."

She offered her cheek for a kiss, but he cradled her face in his hands and kissed her full on the mouth.

"I have missed you, Beth. I have missed the feel of you beneath me. My passion for you has grown, not diminished."

"I have missed you as well," she returned with a smile.

Because she took longer to complete the simplest of tasks, it was at least two hours before she was dressed, broke her fast, and was walking sedately in the garden at the rear of the house on her husband's arm. Henry had forbidden her from going too far from the house in case she went into labor. Although frustrated by his dictates, she knew he had only her and the baby's health in mind. The lake would still be there after the birth.

On their second round through the ornamental grasses, a sharp pain cut through her abdomen and she came to a full stop, breathing shallow to ease the discomfort. The birthing pangs had grown steady since she'd awakened, but this one was different. Stronger.

Henry placed a hand on her back and held her hand, which she gripped tightly.

"Are you finally going to tell me you are in labor?"

"You knew?"

"Of course, I knew. I have watched you grow with this child from the first day we met. I know your body as well as I know my own."

"I cannot have this baby today!"

"I think our child has determined you will," he teased gently.

"No, you don't understand. This is *his* day. I will not share it with him, in any form or matter."

"What do you mean?"

"Today is the twelfth of August. He is marrying today. I cannot bring this child into the world on the same day he is marrying another." She burst into tears, stopping only when another contraction ripped through her body.

"Elizabeth Rose Talbot. You are stronger than this." Henry chastised her as she fought to control her breathing. "It matters not what *they* are doing, it only matters what is happening right here, right now in this very garden. Today, you will bring into this world our son or daughter. I do not care what anyone else is doing and neither should you."

She brought his hand to her mouth, kissing it over and over.

"I love you Henry Cuthbert Talbot and I am sorry for being such a ninny-hammer… Oh…. Ah, ah, ah…." She squeezed his hand hard enough that he actually gasped. "Help me to my room and call the midwife. I cannot bear this any longer."

With speed and alacrity, he complied.

~~~

"HAVE YOU DECIDED on a name yet?"

"I was thinking William Henry Andrew Talbot."

"WHAT?"

"You do not want William as part of his name?"

"No, the names are adequate. I understand you wish, in some small way, to acknowledge the child's natural father. My concern lay in the fact his initials will spell out W.H.A.T., and we simply cannot do that to the poor boy. Would you mind if we rearrange the names to Andrew Henry William Talbot?"

"Wonderful," she replied sleepily, her fingers lightly touching the downy cap of dark hair on her son's head. "Andrew Talbot. Sounds wonderful and fitting, don't you think?"

"Yes, I do. As wonderful and fitting as his mother, Elizabeth Rose Talbot." Henry leaned down and kissed first the crown of Andrew's head and then her forehead. "I love you both, my darling Beth."

~~~

DARCY MARKED THE twelfth day of August, what would have been his wedding, by getting rip roaring drunk. He hadn't wanted to marry Anne, but he also did not want to remain single. He'd yet to meet a woman who appealed to him.

Liar, his subconscious screamed at him. *You met a woman you admired very much and cast her out of your life like dirty laundry.*

The mystery of Elizabeth Talbot, nee Bennet, remained unsolved. After Anne's death and his eventual return to London, he'd sent a note to Bingley's townhouse only to discover his friend gone to Scarborough to visit relatives and with no intention of returning until the New Year.

In subsequent letters, he'd been informed between splotches and squiggles, that Bingley was thoroughly enjoying his time with family and was looking to buy an estate near his aunt and uncle's home. His return to London was delayed indefinitely.

Darcy saw this news as both disturbing and humorous. Disturbing in that he wanted to ask Bingley about his time at Netherfield Park but would never commit his questions to paper in case the missive fell into the wrong hands. He found humor in the fact that Miss Bingley would be in agonies with the stifled society of Scarborough and therefore relentless in badgering her brother to return to town.

At the beginning of October, he returned to London. His life continued apace with balls and soirees, nights at the opera and dinner parties. The only difference being that he now squired around his highly eligible sister. Aunt Matlock was a godsend and made sure Georgiana met the proper class of people, but his sister had yet to find anyone that made a dent in not only her shyness, but her stubborn determination to marry for love.

He and Georgiana marked the following Easter by going to Rosings to visit Richard and Aunt Catherine. He'd kept up a steady correspondence with Richard, but the letters from his cousin had decreased over the course of the year as he became more comfortable with being a gentleman rather than a soldier.

During his visit, Darcy had to hide more smiles than he thought possible as Aunt Catherine, now that she was officially out of mourning, had begun to canvas the local families, seeking a suitable wife for the determined bachelor who owned her home. More times than Darcy could count, Richard had looked to him for help and he'd all but shrugged his shoulders as though to say, 'better you than me.'

He and Georgiana were introduced to the new parson, Reverend Peter Hawkins, after services Easter Sunday. Darcy dared not ask Richard what happened to the previous parson, nor did he inquire about the entail on Longbourn. He most certainly did not want further incentive to dream of her, or revisit his deep secret longing. The sooner he could banish her from his tortured memories, the better.

He should have known Richard would not let the matter rest.

"Any news from Bingley concerning your little problem?" Richard asked as they enjoyed port in the same room where everything had come to a head with Mr. Collins.

"He has elected to remain in Scarborough, maybe returning sometime this summer. My problem remains unsolved."

"You could always travel to where he is and visit."

"Never. If I even set foot in the same county as Miss Bingley, she would have a wedding trousseau ordered before I arrived at the front door. In between the lines of ink blotches in Bingley's last letter, I was able to make out she still thinks I will come and make an offer."

"For a man who has so many setting their cap at him, it is a wonder you have not settled down."

"There are few women of whom I can abide even ten minutes in their company."

"Does the Duchess of Tavistock fall into that category?"

"No," he was uncomfortable talking about Elizabeth, but he could no longer denigrate her character. She'd proven herself an honorable woman, he only needed Bingley to confirm what deep down he knew as truth. "The few times we had conversations, more like debates, I always felt she took the opposing side, even if she did not believe her side of the argument, just to prove a point. Her mind was so very agile."

"High praise, coming from you. I have never heard you speak of any lady in this manner."

"That is because I have not met any like her."

"All right, I will do it." Richard slapped his thigh.

Taken by surprise, Darcy stared at him. "Do what?"

"Come back to London with you and prowl the ballrooms in search of a wife. Surely there are other ladies out there like the duchess."

"You are joking. Why now?"

Richard leaned forward as if imparting a great secret.

"Aunt Catherine is driving me mad in her quest to find a mistress for Rosings Park. She has lately resorted to inviting all the widows who are scatted about the county. If I remove to London, she might think I am serious in finding a *suitable* woman. After a year of living like a cloistered monk, *any* woman will do for a night. Nay, make that a month," he almost growled out in frustration.

"Regardless of your impetus to finally come to London, Georgiana would appreciate another friendly face in the crowded ballrooms. She still struggles with her shyness."

"Consider it done. Mother will be pleased. She likes the fact I am a gentleman farmer and not a soldier dodging canon fire and bayonets."

"We all are grateful for that, cousin."

The two men joined the ladies and enjoyed an hour of Georgiana playing the pianoforte.

"If Anne had lived, I am sure she would have become a great proficient. It was a dear wish of hers to play, but her health prohibited it."

Darcy shook his head at the two opposing sides of his

aunt's conversation. He didn't contradict her, as it would serve no purpose, but they all knew Anne would not have attempted anything.

"Aunt, I will be leaving with Darcy when he and Georgiana return to London."

"Let me know the time, and I will make sure my trunks are ready."

Richard flashed a desperate look at Darcy.

"I thought you detested town, Aunt Catherine," Darcy commented in a mild voice.

"Only because it made Anne so very sick. I will come to town and help both of you find brides."

"I am not looking for a wife this year, Aunt. My focus is solely on Georgiana and I will not be swayed."

"Balderdash, you are nearly thirty years of age. It is high time you found a mistress for Pemberley. Georgiana can wait."

"No, Madam, she cannot. I will not detract from Georgiana and if it takes more than one season for her to find someone to love, then so be it."

"Do you mean that?" came a soft voice from the direction of the pianoforte.

"What was that? Speak up girl!" Aunt Catherine demanded, banging her cane on the marble floor.

"If I do not find a suitable partner this year, you do not mind?"

Georgiana now stood by the pianoforte; her hands clasped tightly in front of her. Tension rolled off of her in waves. How had he not seen how distressed she was by all this? He stood and walked to her, taking her shaking hands in his.

"I will never make you rush love, Squirt," he whispered. "It is too precious a commodity to waste."

Her stormy gray eyes, awash with unshed tears, met his. A relieved smile lifted the corner of her mouth and her shoulders relaxed.

"Thank you," she said simply, and kissed him on the cheek. "You are the best of brothers."

This one small conversation marked a change in how the brother and sister acted with one another. Although he did feel he had to keep a mental list in his head of who they should be seen with and also who they should *not* be seen with, he was more relaxed when his sister accepted a request for dance set. He was more relaxed, but not stupid. If required, a stern look turned away most reprobates before they even crossed the dance floor. He and Georgiana, along with Richard returned to London and for the first time in years, enjoyed the social life of town.

AN UNWITTING COMPROMISE

Chapter Twelve

FOLLOWING THE WEDDING of Jane and Kit, Henry and Elizabeth remained at Longbourn until the first week of January when they returned to London. Henry wanted to treat his lovely wife to the Argyll Room, where the first concert of the London Philharmonic was scheduled. It was quite a coup to achieve tickets as those who wished to see and be seen had scooped them up as soon as they'd become available.

The night of the concert was the first time Elizabeth had left Andrew alone with his nurse. She trusted Alice very much, but felt a pinch of panic that if anything happened, she would not be in the house to take care of her baby.

"Here you are. I was about to send the footmen on a search of the garden."

Henry entered the nursery where Elizabeth stood, gazing down at their sleeping son.

"I do not know if we should attend the concert. What if he gets a cough? Or falls out of his bassinette?"

"Beth, Andrew is five months old and has only just learned to roll over. He will not fall out of his bassinette. Alice is here, as she always has been, and he will not develop a cough in the few hours we are away."

"But, he might."

"And dragons might come down from the Peaks and cart away a cow or two."

"Do not be ridiculous."

He came behind and wrapped strong arms around her before resting his chin on top of her head. "I promise Andrew will be fine. We will attend the concert and return immediately home."

"I am being foolish."

He placed his hands on her shoulders and turned her to face him. He bent slightly and looked her directly in the eye.

"Yes, you are."

His eyes darkened momentarily and she thought he might kiss her. She raised her chin in anticipation.

"If I kiss you, sweet Beth, we will not make it to the concert on time, if at all."

She placed her hands on his beautifully stitched waistcoat made to match her skirt overlay and rose onto her tiptoes.

"I will not mind if you do not mind," she whispered against his chin.

He swooped her up against his chest and carried her to their room while she feathered kisses along his jaw. They later sent their regrets to Jane and Kit, who had enjoyed the concert immensely and wondered why their brother and sister had missed such an auspicious occasion.

A short ten days later, they hosted a dinner party to celebrate one year of marriage. Their guests included Mary and Kitty, who were visiting the Gardiners much like Jane and Elizabeth used to do when they were their age.

For the first half hour, Elizabeth maintained a close eye on her two sisters as she knew they were a bit overwhelmed by the number of titled guests which included not only their cousin

Percy and his wife, but also Lord and Lady Matlock. However, everyone settled into a comfortable rhythm and she turned her focus to their other guests.

Only once did she feel a bit of shame at not including her parents. It was when Kitty, looking at the milieu before them, whispered, "Mamma could live on this gossip for months."

"I thought she had curbed her habit to gossip."

"She has." Kitty flicked a quick glance at Elizabeth. "Mrs. Gravestone has been so gentle with her corrections. Half the time Mamma does not even realize she has been taken to task. When I said she could live on this gossip, I did not mean in the way she used to... well before she chased off Mr. Bingley and you married Henry. I mean she is... satisfied. Yes, that is a good way to describe things. She is satisfied and is so very proud of her daughters and their *happy* marriages."

"Then I am glad." Elizabeth looped her arm through Kitty's and squeezed. "It helps that the entail was broken and she does not have to fear the hedgerows."

"Papa still will not tell her how that came about. Mamma fainted when he told her."

"I have a strong inclination Henry looked into the entail. He is so very fastidious when it comes to details." She glanced at her husband and found him watching her with a smile on his face. She smiled back. "My husband takes care of those he loves."

Kitty followed her gaze and sighed. "He loves you so very much. Would that I could find someone like him."

"You will. Be patient. *Good men like Henry do not grow on trees, you know,*" Elizabeth said in a perfect imitation of their Mamma.

"There are not many choices in Meryton, as you well remember."

"Then you will be happy to know the duke wishes to hold a ball."

"A ball! When?"

"We were thinking the first of May, before everyone heads back to their country estates to escape the heat."

"Will we *all* be invited?"

By tacit agreement, the sisters rarely talked about Lydia and her ongoing struggles with behaving in a ladylike manner.

"That remains undecided."

"Then I will not discuss the possibility when I write her next."

Their time of sisterly confession was over when Gibson announced dinner was ready to be served.

~~~

"I ASSURE YOU, 'tis nothing, Beth. The doctor is fussing and clucking about like a chicken because he is an old fuddy duddy."

"Fuddy duddy?" Sir Townsend lifted a craggy brow at Henry.

"A curmudgeon?" Henry teased while his personal physician packed up his medical instruments into a small leather satchel. "Crotchety old man?"

"It is a good thing I have known you almost all my life, Henry, otherwise I would be insulted by the fact you have yet to expand your vocabulary. You called me crotchety over three years ago."

"See? Nothing to worry about. If Kenneth was worried, he would have called me, Sir." Henry held out his hand and Elizabeth took hold of it, surprised to find it trembling.

By this time Sir Townsend was prepared to leave the room. Although he'd lightly teased her husband, Elizabeth saw the worry behind his eyes.

"I value our friendship, and that is what makes this hard to say... Sir."

Henry paled and Elizabeth squeezed his hand.

"Your disease has progressed faster than expected. I believe you should retreat to Edgecam Hall and enjoy these final days with your family."

"What are you saying, Kenneth?"

"I am saying you have but a few months." Sir Townsend gave Elizabeth a look of deep pity. "My apologies for being the bearer of bad tidings, but I know you both appreciate the truth. It is what makes you exceptional people and my friends."

Elizabeth escorted Sir Townsend to the front door while Henry finished dressing.

"What can I do to make this easier for him?" she asked.

"He will become excessively fatigued and his appetite will diminish." He shrugged into his great coat. "It is vital that he keeps up his fluids. Encourage him to drink tea, wine, even ale if he so desires. Near the end, you can place a drop or two of laudanum in his drink."

"Is that not addictive?"

"My dear duchess," he said as Gibson opened the front door, "that is the least of his worries."

"Thank you, Sir Townsend. You will come to Edgecam Hall to check on him?"

"Yes, and when he reaches… well, when it is time, I will come and stay to the end."

She turned and ascended the stairs, her heart heavy, stopping partway up when she saw Henry at the top of the staircase watching her. She picked up her skirts and ran the rest of the way. He caught her to his chest and they stood silent for a few minutes, holding one another.

"I am afraid I must break a promise, Beth."

"Whatever do you mean?"

"We will not be hosting a ball where your Mamma can use her new polished manners."

~~~

"I WAS THINKING about having a dinner party."

"We are leaving in less than a week for Edgecam Hall. I have much to do before we go."

"I would like to say goodbye to my friends before we leave."

She paused in her embroidering and assessed her husband. She placed her work in a pretty basket Henry had purchased for her and clasped her hands on her lap.

"Who are you thinking of inviting?"

"Lord Addlesworth, Lord Matlock, and their wives. Also, your cousin Percy and his wife, as well as Kit and Jane. I then thought, if we were going to have extended family around, I would invite Mr. Darcy and his sister."

"Mr. Darcy. You wish to invite Mr. Darcy to our dinner party."

She couldn't help the tension that filled her body. In some small way, she felt betrayed by Henry's plan.

"Beth, you were able to forgive your mother, can you not find it in your heart to forgive Mr. Darcy. This would be the perfect venue as it will be among friends and family."

"Based on that argument, Mr. Darcy must be excluded as I am sure he neither loves, nor respects me as a friend."

"That is where you are wrong. My sources tell me that when you are a topic of discussion, which as a duchess it is to be expected, he has nothing but praise for you. In fact, he points out that when he first met you in Meryton, he knew you were a genteel lady and is not surprised that you caught the attention of a duke."

"That is laying it on a bit thick, Mr. Talbot."

"I tell the truth."

"Mr. Darcy looked upon me with disdain. If you remember, I told you of the first time I laid eyes on him at the Meryton assembly. He said I was handsome, but not handsome enough to tempt him to dance. He did not want to give consequence to a lady who had been slighted by other men."

"Put his foot in it, did he?"

"Most assuredly." She assessed her husband, noting the lines of fatigue around his eyes and how ill his clothes fit. Despite her best efforts, he continued to lose weight. "I see what you are about, Mr. Talbot."

"And what is that, Beth?"

"You wish me to see Mr. Darcy again and become friends."

"He is an honorable man who made a mistake. Everyone has good things to say about him and he should know his son."

"Let him make his own," she pouted.

"Elizabeth," Henry chided. "He did, he just was not aware of it at the time. I like the man, and I like his sister. So did you, not too long ago."

~~~

THE DINNER PARTY was successful. Even though Elizabeth was not as sparkling as her wont, she still maintained a graceful poise and carried her end of the conversations. It wasn't until the dessert course that Henry began laying the foundation of what he wanted built after he left this mortal coil.

"Mr. Darcy. My wife greatly enjoys walking and I am unable to attend her due to my fatigue. Would you be so kind as to provide an escort the last few days we remain in town?"

"If her grace does not mind my company, it would be my honor."

"Thank you." Henry took a deep breath and smiled at Elizabeth. "It does my heart good to know my Beth is in safe hands."

"Your grace," Elizabeth said with a smile that did not reach her eyes, "I am perfectly capable of walking Hyde Park with a trusted footman."

"Of course, you are, my dear, but would it not be pleasant to catch up with an old friend. I am sure you and Mr. Darcy have much to discuss at a venue where you can reminisce to your heart's content."

Elizabeth conceded with a slight nod and resumed eating her dessert.

"What time shall I attend tomorrow, Sir?"

Both Elizabeth and Henry looked to him.

"Come at three o'clock. I would like a word before you and Elizabeth take your stroll on the promenade."

"Very well," Darcy answered.

Every guest's head swiveled between Darcy and the duke and then almost all turned with one accord to look at Elizabeth. She gently dabbed her mouth with a linen napkin and stood.

"Ladies, shall we leave the men to their port?"

Although she smiled demurely, the look she gave her husband warned him they would have a heated exchange later that evening. Henry, the rogue, just winked. Ooh... he was so exasperating at times. She could cheerfully have dumped a full vase of fresh flowers over his infuriating head. To have manipulated a meeting between her and Mr. Darcy... In front of family and friends. And, he picked a time for their walk when all of society would be promenading in the park. She felt like screaming.

Chapter Thirteen

"HIS GRACE WILL see you now," Gibson said and then led him down a wide hall to the duke's study. He opened the door and announced him. "Mr. Darcy, sir."

"Thank you, Gibson."

Darcy stepped inside the room and appreciated the rich wood panelling and the Aubusson rug. The duke stood and came around his desk, extending his hand, which Darcy, after a polite head nod, accepted and shook.

"You are wondering why I asked to speak with you prior to your walk with Beth."

Darcy's eyebrow rose at the shortening of Elizabeth's name, but he said nothing. It was not his place; she was not his wife.

"Your request did surprise me, your grace."

"Call me Tavistock." He indicated with a sweep of his arm for them to sit near the fireplace in comfortable looking chairs. "Care for a brandy?"

"Yes, thank you."

Once they each had a drink and were seated across from one another, he wondered when the duke would begin speaking.

Finally, he broke the silence.

"I know you labored under false assumptions for much of last year and given that my wife, for reasons of her own, did not tell her father everything about the night in question, you were not made to take responsibility." Tavistock raised his hand when Darcy would have spoken. "Do not interrupt. We will discuss this later. Right now, I am giving you the unvarnished truth. What you do with it is your business. Do you wish to hear what I have to say?"

"Yes."

"Then, about that night. Elizabeth was asleep on the couch. From what she remembers, she awakened to find you taking your pleasure. You are considerably larger than her and were quite drunk. Upon finishing your business, you passed out. She could not lift you to escape. Not long after this your friendly lap dog, Bingley, came in the room. With his aid, she was able to escape and leave for her room."

"Your grace, if I may interject. Why did she not tell her father Bingley was a credible witness?"

"You are not a stupid man. Why do you think she stayed silent?"

He didn't have to think about it, he knew the answer.

"She did not want to erect any barriers between a hopeful alliance of Bingley and her eldest sister."

"Hopeful? The word is expected. It was an expected alliance and that expectation was based on *your* friend's behavior toward Jane. She did nothing but act as the refined lady she inherently is. He then compounded his stupidity by not telling you what happened under the roof of his own home."

"The opportunity never arose."

"Never? You did not meet him at White's the day after Mr. Bennet came to your home? You did not have dinner at his townhouse at least five times before you left for Kent and he left for Scarborough? How many times must two good friends get together before an opportunity arises?"

How did Tavistock know his movements? He absolutely did not want this man as his enemy.

"We did have occasions where we met, but in his defense, there were always large ears nearby. The *perfect* opportunity never arose."

"Large ears as in his sister. I will grant you the perfect opportunity may never have arisen, but it was his duty to ensure you knew the truth,"

"I did not want him to talk about the Bennet family. I thought them mercenary and told him so. He then dropped the subject."

"Of course, he did. Why would he antagonize the hand that feeds him?"

"What do you mean?"

"His sister holds high hopes of becoming your wife and he now has aspirations of becoming your brother."

"What!"

"You must have noticed him sniffing about Miss Darcy's skirts. You can guarantee in the privacy of their townhouse, Miss Bingley drops hints with the precision of a military sniper of who the ideal wife is. She has had your sister in her sights for almost four years now."

"I do not believe that."

"No? What if I said there was written proof?" Darcy could only stare at the man. His whole world had been laid bare before him and he had not a thing to say. "I am sure Beth will add to this narrative. She is very angry with me and if I were not mortally ill, I am sure she would take a cudgel and knock my head in. Therefore, during your walk, tread lightly. She may instead use the cudgel on you."

"I will take that under advisement."

Tavistock laughed out loud. "I have always liked you, Darcy. You made mistakes, but who among us has not?"

He stood and pulled a lanyard. The door soon revealing the butler.

"Tell my wife Mr. Darcy is ready for their walk and have the carriage brought around."

"Yes, your grace." The butler bowed and closed the door.

Darcy placed his still full tumbler on a side table and stood. He followed the duke from the room and waited with him in the foyer. Nothing in his life prepared him for the awkwardness of the moment. He knew he loved Elizabeth, and yet he waited with a man who quite possibly loved her more. The duke certainly respected her more than he ever had. The fact that Tavistock married her, knowing she carried another man's child spoke to his superior character. Would that he had that same fortitude, it could have been him telling the butler to call *his* wife so they could go for a walk.

He'd been a fool.

~~~

WITHOUT EVEN LOOKING at Mr. Darcy, Elizabeth sailed through the front door and allowed a footman to help her into the carriage. Always silent, Darcy climbed in after her and they made their way to Hyde Park. Upon arrival, she accepted his aid in exiting the carriage and then proceeded toward the promenade. Whether he followed or not, she did not check. It was only as she walked toward the wide path that he did catch up and keep pace.

"I do not know where to begin, your grace."

She remained silent. It was up to him to begin the conversation.

"I would like to know more about my son."

"No, Mr. Darcy. I and my husband have a son."

"We both know he is my son. *Our* son," he said with a little heat.

"Be that as it may, you have not been involved other than being the unwelcome instrument of his less than illustrious creation and as far as I am concern, can remain that way."

"But he is heir to Pemberley."

"He is heir to Edgecam Hall and all the properties that come with being the twelfth Duke of Tavistock. You may still have a son with your wife."

"I am not married."

"Oh!" She was surprised by that news. "I read your betrothal announcement shortly after you left Hertfordshire."

"My betrothed died before we could marry."

"I am sorry," she said automatically. "Speaking of betrothals, I admit to being surprised when I did not see an announcement for Mr. Bingley and your sister."

"Bingley and Georgiana!"

"Why yes. Miss Bingley was quite explicit in the letter she wrote to Jane explaining your hasty departure from Hertfordshire. She was very proud of the fact that all involved were excited over the joining of your two families."

"I cannot believe she would even hint at such a thing."

"I assure you, she did. Jane might let you read the letter, and the subsequent one if you need to have our honesty and integrity scrutinized, yet again."

"I do not need to read personal correspondence between friends."

"Friends?" Elizabeth gave an indelicate snort. "Not likely. In her last letter to Jane, Miss Bingley boasted joyfully over their increased intimacies with your family. Clearly you were aware of the pleasure she felt over her brother being – how did she word it? Oh, yes – a willing inmate of your house. She expounded on your diligence in purchasing new furniture. One can only assume, given her breathless anticipation of her brother's marital felicity with your sister, the furniture in question was a new bedroom suite. No one wishes to consummate their marriage beneath the frothy pink frills much favored by a then sixteen-year-old girl." Elizabeth gave a delicate shudder. "That would have been in very poor taste."

"There has never been an agreement between Bingley and my sister." Mr. Darcy ground out between clenched teeth. "You met my sister; you know this is true."

"Yes, *I* always knew Caro lied." Elizabeth shifted the parasol on her shoulder and twirled it between her fingers. "Why would you put up with Mr. Bingley mooning over my sister if he was courting yours? Unfortunately, Jane, who believes there is good in everyone, took all of Miss Bingley's viscous words to heart."

By this time, they'd halted in their steps and faced each other.

"This is not the reason your husband arranged for us to speak privately. We have much more to discuss than Bingley's habit of falling in and out of love every two or three months."

"Let us be blunt then. You *are* the father of my son. He is healthy, happy and we are in no need of your assistance." She turned to walk back to the carriage and was brought up short by his hand on her forearm.

"Madam, we are not finished." At her pointed look at his hand, he dropped it from her arm. "I insist on being involved in Andrew's upbringing. He has much to learn before he takes over control of Pemberley."

"Do you think I would jeopardize my son's inheritance as the Duke of Tavistock for Pemberley? You may still find a suitable wife, sir and if you have a son with whomever you wed, they will expect *their* son to be your heir – not the one born on the wrong side of the blanket."

"You would deny our son his birthright?"

"Henry is the legal father of my son and wrote his will accordingly. His birthright has been practically set in stone. You have nothing to offer him, or me."

"I can offer marriage."

When his face darkened in a mixture of rage and embarrassment, Elizabeth realized that she had laughed out loud.

"I am sorry. You were serious?"

"Of course, I am serious. Your husband informed me of his ill health. This is the most logical solution to our dilemma."

"I do not have a dilemma, sir. You do." She began walking, forestalled by his hand on her forearm, yet again. She pivoted and spat out, "Desist in manhandling me. I was unable to stop you the last time, but I most assuredly can now."

He visibly paled before her.

"I have no words for what happened that night. I have never attacked a woman before and have never since. I may have been drunk, but even then, I should have behaved as a gentleman and did not. I would ask that you accept my apologies. I cannot change what happened, but I can change how we address each other going forward."

She took in a deep breath, looking out over the park and the growing crowd of people wandering the paths. She had to behave with decorum or the gossip rags would run out of ink spreading the tale of their public argument. Slowly, she expelled that deep breath as a way to calm her racing heart. She finally took his arm, turned back toward the path, and continued their very public promenade.

"Strangely enough, Mr. Darcy, I have never held you wholly accountable. Yes, you were drunk and I was unable to stop you, but you were never violent. Yes, I was in shock but I never feared you. I feared only my future." She tilted her head and gave him a grace filled smile. "However, my future turned out to be the least of my worries. I met a good man and have a good life with him. I cannot repine what happened because that terrible night gave me Andrew."

"His name is Andrew?"

"Andrew Henry William Talbot."

She was startled to see his eyes mist over when she spoke the name, William.

"Thank you," was all he said, a small smile on his face.

"Do you think we could be friends, Mr. Darcy?"

He looked at her, his expression unfathomable.

"I would dearly love to be your friend, your grace."

"Then, when we are in private, you may call me Elizabeth."

"I expect you to call me Darcy."

A delighted laugh escaped her lips. "Darcy? Not Fitzwilliam?"

"Fitzwilliam was the name my parents used when I was in trouble. Darcy is what all my friends call me."

"Very well, Darcy." She couldn't help the smile which kept appearing on her face. "Although I may call you Willy if you displease me."

"Then I shall do my very best to not displease you, further than I have already," he clarified and she laughed again. "Willy indeed."

~~~

DARCY HANDED HIS CARD to the startled housekeeper and then waited. And waited. And waited. He should have known the stubborn man would behave in this manner, yet Darcy was determined to see the unpleasant task to the end. It was only when he heard the ticking of the grandfather clock, did he realize how silent the manor was. No giggling girls. No hysterical cries for salts. Longbourn was as quiet as Darcy House. It was unsettling. Finally, the housekeeper returned.

"The master will see you now."

He followed her to a room filled to the brim with books. Some of them rare, some of them new. All of them well read. The master of Longbourn remained seated with a newspaper in his hand, not rising to greet him politely. He did not blame the man, even though the lowest form of courtesy should have been extended.

"Mr. Bennet," he said with a slight nod of his head.

Bennet lowered his paper and smirked.

"There is a freshness about you, Mr. Darcy, that comes from living. Last time we spoke, I was explicit in my desire to never lay eyes on you unless you were laid out for viewing. You have rudely shattered my dearest held wish much like you did my daughter's life. Without thought and without consideration."

"I have seen and spoken with her grace, *and* her husband," he hastily added when Bennet's eyes flashed with anger. "I am now come to apologize for the misunderstanding we had the last time we met."

"Misunderstanding! You claimed no part in the creation of – what did you call my grandson – a bastard. We had no misunderstanding, sir."

"At the time, I was not in possession of all the facts and still had not heard from Bingley—"

"What about Mr. Bingley?"

"He was the one who lent aid to your daughter that night."

Bennet rose to his feet for the first time. "Why in god's teeth did she not tell me there was a witness. I would have made you marry her if I had known."

"My understanding is that she was protecting the interests of her eldest sister at the time."

"Foolish child." Bennet flopped back into his chair and

indicated for Darcy to sit down as well. He took the seat across from Bennet's desk.

"It was Tavistock that mediated a discussion between your daughter and I. He is terminally ill and my understanding is he wishes us to have at least a friendship once he is gone."

"Henry is dying?"

"I am sorry. I thought you knew."

"I knew he had been ill at one time, but not this serious. My son-in-law keeps many things to himself and takes prodigious care of those who fall under his umbrella of safekeeping. I am sure he did not want us to worry and fret over nothing we cannot change."

"I have long admired him. My parents knew him well and the word among the *ton* is always one of respect. Not for the title, but for the man himself."

Bennet laced his fingers over his stomach and stared at Darcy.

"I still do not like you, Mr. Darcy. You were proud and disdainful when here last believing that you were above those who have little beauty and no fashion and should receive neither your attention or pleasure. I believe those were your words after meeting us at the Assembly, were they not, sir?"

"I cannot recall saying those exact words," Darcy said through stiff lips.

"Of course, you do. It is a reflection of your base nature. After you left, some of the servants from Netherfield regaled our servants with your little quips and observations. I have written them down in my journal." He tapped a ledger on his desk. "My favorite is when speaking of my Lizzy and her proclaimed beauty, I believe you said, '*She a beauty? I would as soon call her mother a wit.*' Ring any bells?"

He absolutely did say something along those lines and felt a fresh wave of shame wash over him. To think at one time this was how he viewed Elizabeth and her family made him ill.

"Your other insult was not so secretive. Everyone in Meryton knew my Lizzy was not handsome enough to tempt you. That to dance with a young lady who had been slighted by other gentlemen would be a punishment. Do you care for me to continue with how you perceived our quaint, rustic village?"

"No, you have said quite enough, Mr. Bennet."

Having his words tossed back in his face was like having a mirror shoved before his face. A mirror which reflected what was in a person's true heart, and his likeness had shown a demon from hell. It shocked him to the core. When had his pride become so great, he thought himself above so many good and honest people?

"So, you see, Mr. Darcy. I do not like you. One heartfelt apology does not negate the image you projected to us poor, ill-educated savages."

"No, sir. It does not."

"However, I will accept your apologies."

"Thank you." Darcy rose to leave, inherently knowing their meeting was over. About to exit the room, Bennet called after him.

"Tell your faithful follower if he ever comes to his senses, he need not apologize. Not that I expect him to. He seems to be a feckless young man, led about the nose by his wilful sister. However, I would ensure *your* sister stays away from him as he might break her heart. I have been told by Elizabeth that she is as gentle as my Jane and they are the ones he seems to prey upon."

All Darcy could do was nod and take his leave.

~~~

"BETH, YOU DO TOO MUCH."

"Am I not allowed to make my husband comfortable?"

Henry held out his hand. She set down the tea service she'd brought up, took his hand, and sat on the side of the bed, facing him.

"You have run yourself ragged, ensuring my comfort. You chase after Andrew and worry he does not see enough of his mama. Then you come back in here, worrying I am not being cared for properly. At this rate, you will collapse from fatigue and then neither of us will see you."

"I cannot sit idle, Henry. I chafe that I can do nothing to stop this thing happening to you."

"I know that, love. I cherish every minute with you and the jealous lover in me wants all of your time."

Elizabeth crawled onto the bed and snuggled next to her husband, laying her head on his chest. Although comforted by the steady beat of his heart, the crackling and wheezing of his chest was more pronounced than last week. Henry curved an arm around her waist and drew her close. She felt him kiss the top of her head.

"I have missed you, Henry." She hated that his illness kept her from his bed.

"No more than I have missed you. Come to me tonight."

She arched back in surprise and looked at him.

"Are you sure? I do not want you to tire yourself unnecessarily."

"I will taste your sweetness one more time before I die, Beth. It will sustain me until I meet my Maker."

She burrowed her head back into his chest, tears coursing down her cheeks. "I will come," she whispered.

"Thank you."

~~~

"LET US GO FOR A WALK."

"Henry, you can barely make it to the necessary. A walk is

beyond—"

"I will go for a walk and you will attend me."

"Very well, I shall get my bonnet and meet you at the back terrace."

She exited the room and asked a footman to have Bridges attend her private parlor. Within minutes, the butler knocked on the door.

"Your grace." He gave her a polite nod.

"The duke wishes to go for a walk. I would like footmen stationed every ten feet in the garden. Ask them to be as unobtrusive as possible. I also want the portable chair ready because I have a feeling my husband will require it to return to the house." She smiled at Bridges. "As you know, he is a stubborn man."

"Yes, ma'am and has a wife to match his temperament, for which I thank God daily." A dull flush rose on his cheeks, the first time she'd ever seen an emotion cross the staid butler's face. "Forgive me, your grace."

"Do not apologize for telling the truth. Bridges. I sometimes think God gave me Henry specifically so I could be here at this time in his life. I like to believe my courage always rises when faced with adversity."

"I have noticed, your grace."

"Thank you. That will be all, for now."

A half hour later, she and Henry walked arm and arm at a snail's pace.

"It feels so good to get out of that room," he said in a quiet voice.

"Tomorrow, would you like me to set up a chaise on the terrace? Andrew could play on the lawn as long as it does not rain."

"Yes, that would be just what I need to lift me out of these doldrums."

"Consider it done."

He then faltered in his steps and Elizabeth signaled a footman to lend aid.

"I see you came to our walk prepared," Henry teased before a coughing fit had him gasping for air.

"Help his grace back to his room, Walter." She turned and called the other footman lurking near the hedges. "Please have Stevens attend his master in his bedchamber and tell Bridges to call Sir Townsend."

"Yes, ma'am."

"You should be over in France, Beth. The War Office could use another competent general."

"If I solved all the world's problems, you men would have nothing to talk about."

He started to laugh and then stopped to cough again. Two footmen arrived with the portable chair and helped Henry onto it. He held out his hand, and she placed hers in his. He curled their fingers together and she walked beside the chair until they reached the terrace doors where she had to let go. It was the last time her husband ventured outside of Edgecam Hall.

~~~

MRS. HASTINGS PLACED the last black shroud over the clock while Mr. Bridges supervised the footman putting up the hatchments. Although she'd hated their purpose, Elizabeth had some black gowns prepared for this very reason. And that reason was laid out in the ballroom.

"I am taking my leave, your grace."

"Thank you for everything, Sir Townsend."

He gave a polite bow and Bridges closed the door behind him. Elizabeth made her way back to the ballroom and took a seat by Henry's body.

Sir Townsend had spent the last two weeks at Edgecam,

administering increasing doses of pain medication to Henry, who had hated being in and out of delirium. In his lucid moments, he begged forgiveness of her and she'd soothed him best she could.

"You must hate me, Beth. How can you stand to look at this wasted body?"

"I do not hate you, Mr. Talbot. Before me is a man who has loved me body and soul, and I, him."

"I see I am in trouble. You called me Mr. Talbot," he teased in a voice made raspy by his incessant coughing.

"Only when you tell me that what I find beautiful, you think ugly."

"Promise me."

He'd raised a frail hand and she edged forward in her chair and gently twisted their fingers together.

"Promise you what?"

"I want you to promise me." He began to cough and tightened his grip.

"I promise, Henry. Tell me what it is that you want."

"Promise you will love again. Find a man who will love you like I did and never let him go."

"Please, do not ask this of me."

"You promised."

"There is no one for me to love. I have had perfection; how can I seek another?"

"Beth, you are generous, kind, and witty. Much too beautiful to remain alone."

"What if I want to remain alone? You ask too much."

"Andrew needs a father. If you cannot do it for yourself, think of him."

"No, Henry… I cannot. Please do not make me."

"You promised." He took another shallow breath. *"I love you, Elizabeth Rose Talbot."* He exhaled and the grip on her hand loosened.

AN UNWITTING COMPROMISE

She leaned forward and placed her head on his chest. No soothing heartbeat greeted her. No steady rise and fall of his chest. His last breath had been an affirmation of love.

She wept.

Chapter Fourteen

"YOUR GRACE, THE POST HAS ARRIVED."

"Thank you, Mr. Bridges. Just leave it on my desk. I will be in shortly."

"Very well, ma'am."

Elizabeth turned to the sturdy toddler who followed, distracted by all the flowers lining the pathway.

"So, Andrew. What do you think of these pretty flowers? Shall we pick a few and put them in a vase for Mamma's table?"

The toddler clapped his hands and started to run, only to lose his balance and plop down on his bum. He laughed out loud and clapped his hands again.

"Soon, my little man. Soon your balance will improve and then you can run in the garden."

She leaned down and held out her hand. He grasped it with his pudgy one and slowly they walked back into the house. Not once did she regret marrying Henry and finding safe harbor in Buckinghamshire.

"Mamma!"

Andrew never asked a question. It seemed all his sentences were declarations.

"Yes, darling boy."

"Up."

"Up? You want your Mamma to carry you?"

"Up, please."

She smiled at his knowledge that politeness achieved things faster.

"How will you grow big and strong if I carry you?"

"No. I not big."

She laughed and bent down to pick up her son. His command of the language was growing steadily, and she was not surprised to hear the word 'no.' A determined little boy, he used that one syllable word many times during the day while learning new skills. She'd realized very soon after he started speaking, that he was talking to himself, as though chastising his own person for not grasping something fast enough. It lent her much insight into the personality of her son's father.

"Alice? Take Andrew upstairs for his tea and n-a-p."

When Andrew learned to spell, she'd have to find a different way to work around his stubbornness when it came to a required nap.

"Yes, ma'am. Come with me, your grace. I have some tea and biscuits upstairs just for you."

Andrew transferred easily into his nanny's arms.

"Tea?"

"Yes," Alice said as they ascended the stairs. "Tea and biscuits. Can you say biscuit?"

"Bickset," Elizabeth heard as she entered her small study.

Two separate piles were placed neatly on top of the desk. Typically, Mr. Bridges sorted letters of business on the left and personal letters on the right. She settled in the chair that had once been Henry's and started with the pile on the left as her personal letters were a reward for when her work was complete. Estimates on a necessary roof repair was set aside for her head steward, Mr. Mason. She added a note to one of them, advising Mr. Mason she thought the man was trying to up the charges because he saw her as a woman alone and not because of the cost of slate. Invoices for clothing, food, and various other household expenses were sorted and placed with the estimates.

With her business complete, she settled in to read her letters with leisure. The first one she read was from Jane, now Viscountess Telford. She and Kit loved the estate in Derbyshire, Henry's wedding gift to them. He rarely attended the property and Kit, until he inherited his title of Marquis, had no place of his own.

At first Kit had balked, but then Henry deeded the estate in Jane's name and he had no choice but to accept. Elizabeth experienced a small frisson of hope, knowing that if she chose to visit them, another gentleman from Derbyshire might be enticed to come see his son. And her. So far Jane and Kit had not come across him at any local functions. He remained in London escorting his sister in her quest to find a suitable husband.

The next week flew by and soon Elizabeth found herself waiting at the window for Jane's carriage to arrive. Her joy knew no bounds when it trundled around the fountain and not only Jane and Kit descended, but also her father.

"I am so glad you are come!"

She and Jane rocked in each other's arms for several minutes before Papa cleared his throat. Elizabeth released only one arm around Jane and beckoned her father to join them. He shuffled forward and she pulled him in tight, savoring their familiar forms and scents.

"You smell of home."

"We smell of the road and the last posting inn," came Papa's dry reply.

"No, Papa." She fixed a watery look upon his face. "I can

smell your books and your pipe. I smell Longbourn seeping out your pores."

"I have missed you so, Lizzy and wish I could have been here more after you lost dear, dear Henry." Jane said softly.

If anything could break the spell which had woven its way around Elizabeth, it was the stark reminder of her Henry. She caught Papa's eye and he only smiled.

"You have a husband and your own home to look after. We are perfectly fine." She looked to her brother-in-law. "Hello, Kit. Welcome back to Edgecam Hall."

"I am glad to be here." He stepped forward and kissed her on the cheek.

"When can I see my grandson?" Papa asked.

"He is upstairs in the nursery. I had quite the time getting him to take a n.a.p."

"Did you just spell the word nap to us?"

"I guess I did," she laughed out. "Andrew knows that word and fights laying down in the afternoon, so I have taken to spelling out words that upset him. Fortunately, there are not many. The other one is walk. He always wants to come with me, but he still too small and cannot keep up."

"Not many can, dear Lizzy. Well then, to the nursery we shall go and wake him from the dreaded n.a.p."

She linked arms with Jane and led them into the house, straight up to the nursery. Andrew was awake and playing with his wooden soldiers. At the sight of his mother, a wide smile graced his face and his grey eyes brightened. It was only when three near strangers followed that he toddled behind her skirts and peeked out at them. With an adeptness born from familiarity, Elizabeth reached down and swung Andrew up onto her hip.

"Do you remember your aunt Jane, uncle Kit and Grandpapa Bennet?" She asked him. "They have come for your birthday. Can you not say hello?"

He shook his head and burrowed it into her shoulder. Although Andrew was capable of talking her ear off, when among strangers, he became child of few words. Another trait he shared with *him*.

"Very well, then. You can chat with them while we have tea then." She gestured with her hand, indicating her guests to head downstairs. "Mrs. Hastings will have tea and refreshments set out."

"Are you not joining us?" Papa asked.

"I will come down shortly. Right now, I am going to assure Andrew he is safe and has nothing to be afraid of. We will not be long."

"Very well."

Jane, Kit, and Papa left the room and went to the parlor.

She nuzzled her baby's neck, absorbing the smell that was so uniquely her son.

"Andrew, Mamma loves Jane, Kit, and Grandpapa, almost as much as she loves you. Can you be friends with them today." His lower lip protruded and he began to shake his head. "That is too bad, because Mrs. Hastings made sure there were biscuits with our tea, and you know how much you like jam biscuits."

His eyes lit up. "Jam biksets?"

"Hmmm… somehow I knew that would get your attention." She shifted his weight on her hip. "Then, Master Andrew, let us go down and have some *biksets* with our guests."

Andrew agreed with a vigorous nod.

~~~

"LIZZY, I CANNOT tell you enough how glad I am to see you and Andrew again. He has grown much in the past year and looks so much like his father."

Jane's attention was focused on the toddler and missed the

quick look which passed between Elizabeth and Papa. As far as she knew, Kit remained in the dark over Andrew's true parentage. His father, the marquis knew she'd been *enceinte* when she married Henry, but never asked who the father was.

"I would say he seems familiar to you," Papa teased to break the tension. "He is your sister's son. There should be some Bennet coming through his features."

"I definitely see Lizzy's features in his smile. Such a handsome boy, with those exceptional eyes. He is sure to have all the ladies fall at his feet when he gets older."

"His eyes are a unique color," Kit mused out loud. "Henrys were so piercingly blue and Elizabeth's are the Bennet green. I feel like I have seen them before, but their features dance just outside the walls of my memory."

Elizabeth decided it was time her brother knew the truth.

"Kit, there is something you should know. I asked Jane to keep this secret, but one thing I learned from Henry is that a husband and wife should never have things hidden between them."

"What should I know?"

"Are you sure, Lizzy?" Papa cut in before she could tell Kit who Andrew's father was.

"I am sure, Papa. I trust Kit as much as you and Jane." She turned her attention on her cousin as well as brother. "What you do not know is that your father was instrumental in Henry and I meeting, and the reason for that was because I had been compromised and was expecting a baby. Papa reached out to see if he knew of any gentleman who would not mind a ready-made family."

Kit's mouth fell open for a brief second before he snapped it shut.

"Henry has always known the child was not his and made sure Andrew and I will be taken care of the rest of our lives."

"What of his title?"

"He claimed Andrew as his own, the only way the title could be rescinded was if their Majesty's decided to revoke it. The houses, lands and money still remain Andrew's."

"Are they aware Andrew is not Henry's natural son?"

"Yes. As a cousin royal, Henry required their permission to marry. Given that it was short notice and Queen Charlotte knew he had not left Edgecam in almost a year, she pressed for more information. He hid nothing from them. He also took me to meet them shortly after we married."

"You believe they will let the title stand?" Kit asked.

"I do. My son remains the twelfth Duke of Tavistock."

"And a handsome duke you are, Andrew," Jane cooed at the toddler.

At his name, Andrew looked up from where he was playing on the floor and smiled at Jane. How could he not? Everyone loved Jane, Elizabeth thought before her mind trod down a familiar dark path. Everyone except…No. She was not going there. Jane was happy with Kit, and Mr. Bingley made his intentions quite clear by *not* returning to Netherfield as promised.

"Elizabeth, you need not tell me, but I would like to know who Andrew's true father is, in case anything happens in the future. To be forewarned is to be forearmed."

Kit reminded her so much of her uncle Percy. He was a fine earl and would make a magnificent marquis when that event occurred.

"The gentleman is Mr. Darcy."

"Darcy! Fitzwilliam Darcy of Pemberley?" Kit stood in shock, his mouth agape once again. "Never would I have thought he would be involved with a compromise, but to deny his own flesh and blood… I cannot wrap my mind around it."

"In Mr. Darcy's defense, he was quite drunk and has no

recollection of the event. He denied it because he thought I was trying to set him up and have him claim another man's child as his own. His anger was justifiable."

"But, if he knew you even a little, he would surely know you do not lie."

"Sadly, he had only known me a short six weeks and his impressions of our little hamlet were not favorable. His good friend tried to entice him to ask me to dance. He looked in my direction, held my gaze and declared I was not handsome enough to tempt him to dance."

"The arrogant prat!" Kit declared. "He has changed since I knew him at University."

"He then proceeded to scowl and skulk around for the rest of his time there." She laughed at a memory.

"And there were no witnesses to corroborate your story?"

"There was, but I never revealed his identity."

"That is my greatest regret," Papa said, "If I had known there was a witness, I would have made him marry you."

"And I would not have met Henry. At the time, I thought it best to keep the gentleman's name to myself. I wanted nothing to hinder the happiness of a most beloved sister."

"Mr. Bingley," Jane whispered.

"Did you say Bingley?" Kit asked.

"You did not reveal his name in the hope he would return to Netherfield and court me." Jane looked at Elizabeth with tears forming in her eyes. "You should not have sabotaged your own security for me."

"If I had known then Mr. Bingley would abandon you regardless, I might have told Papa, but I was so sure he would return and state his intentions. I wanted at least one of us to be happy." Elizabeth shrugged her shoulders. "As it was, I did not have any desire to marry Mr. Darcy. We all know he did not like me then, and at the time I had no feelings for him either way."

"He came to Longbourn." Papa said out of the blue.

"Who?"

"Mr. Darcy."

"When was this?"

"Last year. Right after Easter."

"That was over a year ago! For what reason?"

"He apologized."

"Apologized! And you are only telling me now!"

"I did not think you would care. His opinions matter not to us."

"His opinion mattered to me, Papa! And to Henry. He wished for us to establish a friendship. I thought Mr. Darcy unbending and rigid. If I had known he would humble himself to ride all the way to Longbourn in order to apologize for his behavior, my perception of him would have altered."

"Well," Papa huffed out, "there is nothing we can do about that now."

"No thanks to you, Mr. Bennet. I am extremely displeased with you."

"You truly are a grand duchess, my Lizzy."

"Bah!" Although peeved at her father, she knew she could not remain angry with him. Like Henry had said, it was a wasted emotion. By this time, it was nearing Andrew's bath time and his nurse arrived to take him to the nursery. "Good night, sweet boy. Mamma will come and give you a kiss before dinner."

"G'night, Mamma," he chirped happily and waved to all of them over nurse Alice's shoulder.

Because it was just the four of them, the men eschewed separating the sexes after dinner and they all progressed to the family parlor and she and Jane both played and sang. Papa soon asked Kit if he'd like to play a game of chess and while their father soundly beat his son-in-law, Elizabeth and Jane sat and caught up on all news.

"Mamma is beside herself with you being a countess?"

"She is as proud as a peacock, as you well know and with her grandson the heir to a dukedom, she is the undisputed queen of Meryton."

"And speaking of heirs, is their any news on that front?"

Elizabeth only dared ask because she'd noticed a familiar roundness to her sister's figure. If Jane had remained tall and svelte, she never would have dared broach the subject.

"There is…" Jane's blush deepened. "I felt the quickening last week. Kit is over the moon."

"Oh, Janey…," she grasped her sister's hands and squeezed. "I am so happy for you. I know you had begun to despair of ever falling with child."

"After nearly a year and a half of marriage, I had begun to wonder if I would ever hold my own baby."

"As I will only ever have Andrew, I am counting on you to have at least ten, so I can spoil them to my heart's content."

"You do not think you will ever remarry, Lizzy?" Jane looked troubled. "You are still so young."

"Until next month, then I am the ripe old age of twenty-four."

"I cannot believe how fast time flies. Only three years ago all of us were still living beneath the eaves of Longbourn."

"You have just come from there. How has Lydia been since she returned home from the seminary?"

"She has been…" Jane huffed out a sigh. "…Lydia, although she applies her stubbornness with more finesse. Thank goodness, the militia decamped from Meryton the year she was sent to the seminary. I firmly believed if Henry had not stepped in when he did, Lydia would have run off with the first soldier who proposed. She was determined to be the first to marry."

"Alas, her plans were foiled before she even started making them. I married weeks before she even tried to sneak out her window." Elizabeth smiled, thinking of Henry. "It is hard to believe he has been gone a year."

"That is why Kit and I insist you come with us to London. Lady Addlesworth's annual Michaelmas ball is next month, and this is a perfect opportunity for you to come back into society."

"I do not know if I am ready, Jane."

"Maybe not, but you need to establish contacts in order to make Andrew's transition into his title easier."

"Andrew only two years old!"

"That may be, but he is still the Duke of Tavistock and if you cultivate friendships now, think how much easier it will be for him when you send him to school."

"I hate when you are right."

"Good, and leaving before the mad rush, we can have our gowns ready in plenty of time."

"Dear Jane, you still do not realize the power of a duchess. A modiste could be lined up past her door and down the road, but if I so much as twitch an eyebrow, she will miraculously have an opening."

"You would not dare do that!"

"No," Elizabeth laughed. "I am still a country squire's daughter at heart and am painstakingly polite, even when my teeth are on edge."

"That is good to know. Aunt Madeline wrote and told me Uncle has the most exquisite fabrics just come in. Our gowns will be talked about for weeks, if not months."

"I am not looking to set London Society on fire with my presence. I look forward to re-establishing some friendships I made through Henry and possibly meet some new people and see where it all leads."

"Will you see any of Henry's cousins?"

"Are you asking me if the Queen has requested my presence?"

"Yes."

"She has. It is another reason why I have agreed to come to London. Her Majesty has invited me to tea."

"Are you worried?"

"That they still might revoke his title?"

"Yes."

"I remain hopeful they will not. However, that decision is within their Majesty's purview if deemed necessary, but everything else is entailed *in fee simple* and Andrew is named as Henry's heir with me as the executor until he comes of age."

"So, if Andrew did lose his title, he would become a rich landowner, much like…" Jane trailed off and Elizabeth knew exactly who she was thinking of.

"Ironic, is it not?"

"And here you thought *I* was the queen of understatement."

~~~

DARCY STOOD AGAINST the wall, watching Georgiana dance with Baron Sidway. A pleasant young man, solid family, good finances. Too bad he had only a minor title, yet his sister enjoyed his company. She actually laughed and became animated, which was more than any other hopeful suitor received.

He would have to speak with her about the baron's intentions and gently turn her attention elsewhere. The Earl of Chilton was always a good catch, although he'd become wilier with age. Darcy glanced across the ballroom and saw him in earnest conversation with Miss Stirling. That was interesting. Miss Stirling had a substantial dowry. She might be of interest to Richard.

The set came to an end and Darcy moved toward Lady Price and her daughters Lady Amelia and Lady Eunice. His next set was with Lady Eunice and he noted that she watched him approach with almost giddy anticipation. He had thought he was being subtle in his courting, not willing to make anything official as he liked the young woman, but was not enamored in any way.

Last month he had casually come across her strolling the promenade, which piqued his interest. He then ensured that he *bumped* into the family at the theater. Tonight, he secured the supper set with her, knowing Georgiana was safe with Richard as her partner for the same set. If things continued as planned, he would consider entering into an informal courtship by early October. He would make no plans for a betrothal until Georgiana was securely married. Would that it happened this year. He'd already suffered through two full seasons; he did not think his patience could take a third.

Also, if he entered into a courtship, Miss Bingley might finally cease hanging on his arm. The Bingley entourage had arrived back in town the week prior, with Charles issuing a dinner invitation as soon as they'd arrived. Now that Darcy knew the contents Miss Bingley's letter to Lady Telford, then Miss Bennet, he had gone alone. He would not subject Georgiana to her machinations. It was bad enough he had to suffer through her pretentions and elevated airs, he would spare his sister the ignominy of her companionship. As it was, the minute he arrived at Bingley's townhouse, the woman had latched onto him never ceasing in her praise of his home, his sister, his company. Truly, if he'd been so ungentlemanly as to pass air in her company, she would have declared it the sweetest essence in all of England.

By now, he had reached Lady Price and her daughters.

"Lady Eunice, I believe this is our set."

"Yes, thank you, Mr. Darcy," she said in a breathy voice.

If he hadn't seen her mouth move, he might not have known she'd even spoken. Come to think of it, she always sounded breathless. Was it because she had a lung ailment, or did her mother advise her that was what gentlemen liked and wanted to hear? Elizabeth had never been breathy. In fact, she always spoke in a forthright manner. She never hedged, nor evaded and had not been afraid to upbraid him over perceived wrongs, or take the opposing side of an argument simply for the delight of a healthy debate.

That may have been one of the main reasons he held her in such high esteem. She gave no false airs. Too late, he'd realized she was his equal, the other side to his coin. No matter, she was out of his reach, safely tucked away in Buckinghamshire. The tentative bond of friendship they had established before the duke passed did not survive the time and distance between them. He now had to look for his future elsewhere.

He escorted Lady Eunice to the line of fellow dancers and spent the next quarter hour in complete silence, completely flummoxed by the fact she was counting under her breath in time with the music. Mistakes she still made, but fortunately he was able to cover up her mishaps and the dance continued unhindered by her seemingly all left feet.

The fact she was not a good dancer was not enough to waylay his plans. He himself did not like dancing all that much. She might be happier living at Pemberley, away from the friendship circles where dancing was a required skill in order to advance yourself in society.

When they were standing opposite one another, while waiting their turn to go down the line, he ventured to have some conversation with her.

"Are you attending Lady Addlesworth's ball next month, Lady Eunice?"

"I am so looking forward to it," she breathed out.

He saw the hopeful glimmer in her eyes, knowing she wanted him to secure her first or supper set. Although tempted, given that he was seriously contemplating her as the future Mistress of Pemberley, he hesitated. Was he truly ready to commit to someone when his heart belonged to another? At times, he felt like a mated swan, with Elizabeth as his chosen partner for life. He'd lain with her once, albeit unknowingly, but his body and soul remembered and could not let go of its primal need to be with her, and her alone.

"Mayhap I shall see you there."

Conversation ceased as they went down the line and he dared not break her concentration or interrupt her counting. The supper which followed, was not much better. She picked at her food, spending more time pushing items around her plate than actually eating. Down the table, Lady Price held court and for a brief moment he was transported back to Netherfield Park when Mrs. Bennet loudly proclaimed to anyone who would listen that her daughter Jane was to be engaged to Bingley.

Lady Price was doing the exact same thing about him with her cronies. At least, she was behaving with more decorum than he'd seen in the past. She had a reputation of shocking her guests with wild behavior and lewd activities. It was fortunate her husband was a powerful man. Anything less, and she'd have been dumped from society like last week's newspaper.

He ignored the tittering, knowing looks and sly nudges to concentrate on his conversation with Richard. His cousin had also been keeping an eye on Lady Price.

He leaned into Darcy and said in a low voice, "I hate to sound like Aunt Catherine, but are the shades of Pemberley to be thus polluted by a member of *that* family?"

"I am considering it," was his reply.

"Fair warning, cousin. If you do, you will not only have Aunt Catherine haranguing you, but my mother will join the chorus. Even Ash's wife, Celia will have words to say."

"Whom I marry does not concern them."

"Yes, it does. We are family and as family we gather together. *That* woman is her mother. She will become family. She will gather with us, as family. Her misdeeds and licentious behavior become our shame. The family's shame. Her husband may turn a blind eye, but my parents will not. I will not. If you move forward in this, you will not only drag your family name through the mud but you could severely hamper Georgiana's chances of a brilliant match." Richard cast a quick glance up the table toward Lady Price who now looked at him, her eyes narrowing. He turned back to Darcy. "Think long and hard before doing something stupid – again."

Chapter Fifteen

ELIZABETH STROLLED THE edges of the drawing room. Now that she'd successfully navigated the receiving line, she wished to get a feel for the room. Gauge the reactions of everyone before entering conversations and having them find out who she was.

The number of people in attendance who knew her as the Duchess of Tavistock were limited. One of them, the Marquis of Dorchester, was still greeting guests and would be there for a while, the others were her cousins, Percy, and Eugenia, as well as Jane and Kit.

She spotted Jane across the room and was about to cross over when she heard a familiar voice. Her nerves scraped at the tone just like it had three years ago. Caroline Bingley. She had no desire to pass in front of the woman and attract her attention. Unfortunately, Miss Bingley turned to speak with her companion, who happened to be Mrs. Hurst, and spied Elizabeth behind them.

"Miss Eliza Bennet! What are *you* doing here?"

The contempt in Miss Bingley's voice was not hidden in any way, shape, or form.

"I am here as a guest of the marquis."

"You know the marquis?" That Miss Bingley did not believe her was quite evident. "Have the borders of Meryton extended beyond Hertfordshire since we wasted two months of our lives there?"

"I met him at my cousin's estate."

"Your cousin has an estate? I thought all your family resided in *Cheapside*, or had little *shops* in quaint towns. How in the world would *you* become acquainted with a titled lord?"

During her snide speech, Percy had come alongside.

"Elizabeth, I have come to collect you."

Obviously, Jane had sent a rescue party. Miss Bingley openly sneered as Percy extended his arm. Elizabeth wondered how Caroline, who'd been in countless ballrooms over the years, could not see that Percy was not only wealthy, given the cut and quality of his evening wear, but was also a person of some consequence as other guests had parted to let him cross the room unhindered.

"Pray excuse me, Miss Bingley. My cousin has come for me."

"Are you not going to introduce us to another one of your *illustrious* cousins, Miss Eliza?" she tittered.

"Miss Eliza?" Percy quirked a brow at his cousin. Elizabeth shrugged an elegant shoulder in response. The unspoken communication apparently irked Miss Bingley because she cleared her throat to catch their attention.

"Pardon me, Caro, where are *my* manners." Elizabeth looped her arm around Percy's, ignoring the venomous look Caroline gave her over the shortening of her name. "Miss Bingley, Mrs. Hurst, may I introduce Percival Manning, the Marquis of Haversham."

Caroline gasped.

"Bingley, you say?" Percy asked, a frown creasing his brow.

"Yes, their brother is Charles Bingley."

"Never thought I would hear that name again."

"You know our brother?" Caroline asked in a bright, hopeful tone.

Percy afforded Miss Bingley a dark look. "I have heard of him." He elaborated no further. "We must... speak with other people."

Without taking his leave, Percy cut them direct and tugged Elizabeth along with him. Not that she minded, but she wanted so badly to turn around and see the reaction of the lady and her sister.

"How do those upstarts continue to gain entrance to these types of events?" Percy ground out between clenched teeth. "When I think of the behavior of their brother to our sweet Jane..."

"Jane bears them no ill will and you must agree that she is beyond happy at this time."

"Yes, I am so pleased she and Kit married." Percy patted her hand on his arm. "He was no man's fool. The minute he had her heart secured, the boy gained her promise and sealed it with a ring."

"And now they are expecting your first grandchild."

"Speaking of children. How is Andrew adjusting to a new home? This is the first time he has been at the duke's townhouse. I guess, that would be *his* townhouse." Percy chuckled.

"Andrew is happy as long as his mamma, his nurse and his toys are nearby. It also helps that he adores nurse Alice."

"Kit said he gave him a pony for his birthday."

"I was aghast. He is only two."

"Kit was that age when I began his riding lessons. I know you have a healthy fear of horses, dear cousin, but do not let that influence him. As a landowner, he needs to know how to ride and take care of his estate."

"I know. I find I cannot abide the thought of him astride a huge beast."

"The pony Kit gave him is small and the boy is tall for his age. He will do just fine."

Yes, her son was tall and athletic, like his father. There was no mistaking him as a Darcy, with his aquiline nose, mop of dark curly hair and eyes the color of a summer storm cloud. Thankfully, Henry had been tall with dark hair. Other than eyes the color of cerulean blue, while hers were the Bennet green, everything else pointed to Andrew being his natural son.

By this time, they'd reached Jane and Kit and soon their host, the Marquis of Dorchester, joined them. Unfortunately, so did Miss Bingley and her sister.

"Miss Bennet!" Miss Bingley enthused and took Jane's hand in hers. "How marvelous you are here. It has been *ages* since we saw you last."

Jane withdrew her hand from Caroline's and looped her arm through Kit's.

"Miss Bingley, Mrs. Hurst. May I introduce you to my husband, the Earl of Telford?" He gave them a curt bow.

At first, they both stood mouths agape, then they dipped into a deep curtsy. Upon rising, Miss Bingley said, in a breathy voice, "The pleasure is all ours, Lord Telford. Louisa and I cannot tell you how delighted we are to see our *dear* friend Jane."

"As delighted as you were three years ago, Miss Bingley? When it took you nearly a month to return her call?"

Elizabeth could not help but challenge her.

"Oh… well… we were quite busy at the time. But I have always remembered Jane with fondness."

"I am sure you have," came Elizabeth's dry reply. "And her name is Lady Telford or you may refer to her as my lady, *Caro*."

"Lizzy," Jane warned in a low voice only she could hear. "Behave."

"Fine." Elizabeth turned to the two sisters; a brilliant smile pasted on her face. "And you? Still trailing around after your friend from Derbyshire?"

"Elizabeth!" Jane's voice was firmer now. "Excuse my sister. She feels she must come to my defense over some small misunderstanding."

"We do not see Mr. Darcy that often, if that is to whom you alluded. He is busy with his estate and with dear Miss Darcy entering her second season, he has his hands full monitoring all the hopeful beaux which cross their threshold."

"I thought your brother was her affianced?" Elizabeth queried.

"Why... Why would you say that?" Miss Bingley raised her fan and began to flick it in hopes of cooling her flushed cheeks.

"When you quit Netherfield, your letter to Lady Telford was quite explicit with regard to how happy both families were over their upcoming union."

Miss Bingley's answer was diverted as the butler came to their host, who watched the conversation with a mischievous glint in his eye, and informed him dinner was ready to be served.

Without saying a word, the marquis extended an arm to Elizabeth. As the lady of highest social standing, she took precedence. A fact which clearly befuddled Miss Bingley. As she made her way to the dining room, she heard Miss Bingley ask, "Why in the world is Eliza Bennet leading the way?"

Oh, how she wished she was an invisible imp on Jane's shoulders. The reaction of the orange shrew would feed her humor for days, if not years.

~~~

FROM WHERE SHE SAT, Elizabeth had almost a front row seat for who paraded into the room. She had a brief moment of disquiet when midway through a tall man entered and took his place halfway down the table. Her nerves fluttered and she briefly entertained the thought of running from the room screaming.

Mr. Fitzwilliam Darcy, true to his nature, barely glanced around the table. She recognized the young lady on his arm as Miss Georgiana Darcy. Further down the table sat Miss Bingley, her sister and husband and Mr. Charles Bingley.

True to *his* nature, Mr. Bingley canvassed the whole table, stopping when he reached Jane seated next to Percy. His face blanched and Elizabeth wondered if he were going to faint. His eyes skittered toward Miss Bingley and she watched them whisper among themselves. Mr. Bingley's head swiveled and he pinned his attention toward the head of the table and herself. His eyes widened and he cast a desperate glance toward Mr. Darcy.

She almost laughed out loud. The guests around them were showing a marked displeasure in the way Miss Bingley behaved, her feathers bouncing atop her head with each word. Mr. Bingley finally said something, accentuated with a cutting hand motion and she sat back in her seat.

"What makes you smile, ma'am?"

She turned her attention to her host, Sebastian, the Marquis of Dorchester.

"Former acquaintances of Jane and I are here and I do not believe they were aware of my elevated status. If the fierce whispering near the end of the table is anything to judge by, the situation has been rectified."

"Ah, you mean the Bingley's. How would they know you?"

"For a brief moment in history, Mr. Bingley rented an estate near my father's. He and his party thought themselves above our company and quit Hertfordshire after a mere ten weeks after taking up the lease."

"I was not aware the Bingley's were invited, but I have heard from many a disgruntled hostess that they tend to ride the coat tails of Mr. Darcy. He must have brought them."

"That does not surprise me. He and Mr. Bingley are great friends."

"You have met Mr. Darcy before?"

"He was one of Bingley's guests in Hertfordshire."

"Let us talk of more pleasant things. How are you settling into Talbot house after such a long absence?"

Elizabeth and the marquis enjoyed a conversation about family and mutual friends before she turned to the other guest on her right.

"Lord Addlesworth. Your wife must be busy, preparing for her annual Michaelmas ball."

"She is, Madam, but after so many years, she has it down to a fine art. Are you planning on attending?"

"I am."

"My wife will be pleased. This will be your first big event since coming out of full mourning."

"Your wife's ball is my grand re-entry into society. Henry said he always enjoyed her sumptuous *fetes*, as he liked to call them. If you like, he told me a few stories I could trot out later to embarrass you."

"Ahh… young lady, your reputation precedes you. Not only have we experienced your charm and wit when last we dined, but Henry warned me in his letters that you were not one to back down from a good tease."

"I do so love to laugh."

"He also warned me not to play chess with you. He wrote your doe eyes hid an intelligent mind and before he knew it, you were knocking over his king while smiling ever so sweetly."

"Did my husband bare all my secrets? Can I not have some intrigue while in town before haring back to Buckinghamshire?"

"He told us nothing other than how proud he was to have you as his duchess and that he never expected to find love again at his age." Lord Addlesworth laid his hand over hers. "You made him so very happy, Madam, and as one of his oldest friends, I thank you."

"Next to our son, he was my greatest love. I miss him."

"I am sure you do."

~~~

THE BUZZ OF CONVERSATION at the end of the table was disconcerting to say the least. Darcy was not surprised to find Miss Bingley as the instigator. With a familiar sense of *ennui*, he watched her feathers bob up and down, then side to side dependent on whether she agreed or disagreed with a topic. Bingley looked almost frantic at one moment and shot him a look which reminded him of a trapped animal.

"I think Miss Bingley has discovered the true identity of the Duchess of Tavistock," Georgiana said in a low voice.

"She is here?" It took all his self control *not* to look toward the head of the table, where she most assuredly would be seated, due to her rank.

"Yes, and her eldest sister."

He canvassed the people seated near him and below but could not find Miss Bennet among them.

"I do not see her."

"Who?"

"Miss Bennet. You said Elizabeth's... I mean, her grace's eldest sister is here."

"Lady Telford is seated next to her father-in-law, the Marquis of Haversham."

He then remembered Elizabeth mentioning her sister had married when they walked Hyde Park at Tavistock's request. She never mentioned to whom she married. By mistake or by design.

Who knew with Elizabeth? As it stood now, Jane was not only a cousin to the marquis and his wife, but also, as their daughter, was a niece to his aunt Lady Matlock.

His head was beginning to ache, the first course had not yet been served and he already longed to return to Darcy House. How many times would his mistakes from the past few years concerning origins and family connections come up and bite him in the arse?

One of his greatest mistakes, other than not believing Elizabeth, had been influencing Charles to abandon Miss Bennet. When he dined with the Bingley siblings the week previous, his friend had hinted, more than once, of his fondness of Hertfordshire. Miss Bingley immediately scoffed and degraded the whole area and all who lived there before zeroing in on every fault she had perceived in Elizabeth and by extension, the complete Bennet family.

At the time, he could have told her of *Miss Eliza's* brilliant marriage but some quirk in his disposition wanted to see her fall on her face in society. He wanted her to have her comeuppance, and if it were at the hands of Elizabeth, all the better.

As she'd spewed her venom in a one-woman monologue, Darcy questioned his sanity in maintaining a friendship with Bingley siblings. What had he seen in them that was so special? Charles was amiable enough and on his own, Darcy enjoyed spending time with someone who didn't drain him emotionally. His sister – that was a completely different story. In the letter he received from Bingley, announcing their return to town, he'd written that Caroline was frantic to marry before her twenty-sixth birthday. Darcy knew all too well her sights remained fixed on him, but he had no intention of ever offering for her. Even if he came across her buck naked, tied to his bed.

A vision of Elizabeth in a state of *dishabille*, bound by silk cravats to his bed flashed through his mind. His body tightened in a familiar way and he fought to gain control.

"William, are you well?" Georgiana asked.

"Yes." He shifted in his chair. "Why do you ask?"

"Your breathing became shallow. I am worried you are becoming ill."

He fought to gain control of his emotions. Having a familiar erotic fantasy next to his naïve sister was beyond idiotic. After nearly three years, he thought for sure he'd purged those exquisite dreams and had finally gone for months without once waking with her name on his lips and his manhood gripped in his fist. And yet, by virtue of knowing she was in the same room as him, he'd reverted to that heartsick fool who had no control over his raging libido. Without even trying, Elizabeth Bennet Talbot still had a hold over his heart.

"Thank you for your concern, Georgiana." He turned to her with a bland smile. "I am well. Ah, here is the first course."

Thank God.

After the ladies had withdrawn to the drawing room, Darcy finally had a chance to speak with Bingley alone.

"I have something very personal to ask, and it cannot wait until we are in a more suitable place." Darcy looked around to make sure they were still isolated near the far end of the room. "Did I accost Miss Elizabeth the night I drank too much while playing billiards?"

Bingley paled and audibly swallowed.

"Yes."

"I need you to tell me everything that occurred."

"Everything?" Bingley repeated, his voice thin with anxiety and he also looked around to make sure no one was near enough to overhear them.

"Everything," Darcy stressed.

"You were well into your cups and declared you needed a book to read. Hurst and I laughed because you were in no shape to find a book, let alone read one, you were that disposed." He trailed off and shifted his weight, clearly uncomfortable with retelling the events of that night. "I was not there for the actual act, but I found you and Miss Elizabeth after... well, after the deed was done."

"Speak plainly, Bingley. We are running out of time here!"

"You were on top of her," he said in a rush. "You were... uhm..." Bingley looked to the ceiling and blushed as he sought words to explain. "You were still... joined," he made a movement pressing his hands together to illustrate the coupling, "and you were passed out on top of her. I had to lift you so she could..." he growled in frustration and glared at Darcy. "So, she could slide out from beneath you."

Bingley's face, by now, had turned a beet red.

"Why did you not tell me?"

He couldn't bear the idea Bingley had seen Elizabeth almost naked.

"I should have, but how do you start *that* conversation? Oh, by the by, Darcy... did you know you took Miss Elizabeth's maidenhead last night?"

"I did what! How do you know that?"

Darcy could not contain his shock.

"There was blood on her nightgown and I had to replace the couch. The stain would not come out."

"Dear God in heaven!" Darcy felt ill. "I all but raped her."

"I do not think that is what happened..." Bingley began in a soothing voice.

"You think not? Let us review facts. I forced myself upon an unmarried maiden in such a state of drunkenness that I cannot remember a single thing, and I most likely was not gentle going about it because I did not... could not know... Argh!"

He couldn't stand the idea that he had forced himself on any woman, let alone Elizabeth.

Their conversation ceased as the Marquis of Haversham and his son, the Earl of Telford approached. Darcy greeted them with a polite nod of the head, as well as Bingley.

"My son and I decided to not dance around distant civilities now that her grace is making her re-introduction into society." He encompassed both Darcy and Bingley in his direct gaze. "We are aware you both know to what we allude."

Darcy was shocked, Bingley even more so.

"I have already apologized, not only to her grace and her father, but also to her husband when he was still alive. I have spoken of this to no one, other than my cousin and Bingley, as he was there the night of the incident."

He refused to rehash what happened with disinterested third-party members, regardless of their relationship.

"In case you are thinking my cousin Elizabeth bandied your name about, I will disabuse you of that notion right now. My son and I only discovered your involvement this past week. She has been very discreet. As far as we know, the duke, her father and sister Jane are the only ones who know the truth."

"Not even her mother?"

"I will not repeat myself again, Mr. Darcy. She has not told anyone other than those she trusts. We understand she did not even tell her father there was a witness." The marquis directed a glare toward Mr. Bingley. "Your pride was your greatest failing, next to your friend not telling you of the deed in a timely manner."

Bingley swallowed hard.

"I urged Miss Elizabeth to contact me if there were consequences. When I did not hear from her, I assumed nothing untoward occurred," he said.

"Mr. Bingley, are you daft? How is a single unmarried woman supposed to write an unmarried man, to tell him she had suspicions? You fled to London and did not return as promised."

"I always assumed one of the Miss Bennets would pay a courtesy call to my sister when in town, especially if there was something they needed to tell me in particular."

"My wife *did* visit your sister in January of the new year following your departure from Netherfield Park, and your youngest sister returned the call after nearly a month," Earl Telford told them.

"A month? She wouldn't!"

"Bingley, I assure you, she did." Darcy said on a heavy sigh.

Bingley turned wide eyes toward Darcy. "You knew? You knew Miss Bennet was in town and said nothing?"

"Although I knew the Bennets were in town, I was not aware she visited your sister. If you recall, I was adamant they were only looking for rich husbands and thought I was protecting you. Your sister told me later she had yet to return the call. Her motives I dare not assume to know."

The marquis gave Darcy a thoughtful look and said, "You knew her motives and silently concurred with them."

Darcy acquiesced with a slight nod of his head. Yes, he had known her motives and had wholeheartedly concurred with them, to his eternal shame.

The marquis turned his attention to Darcy's friend.

"When next you speak with your sister, *Mr.* Bingley kindly advise her that her social calendar will be greatly reduced. Her behavior and spiteful characteristics have not endeared herself to anyone within our circles. Or even lower, for that matter. I would strongly suggest she go back to Scarborough, or further north – the Hebrides, perhaps?"

AN UNWITTING COMPROMISE

Chapter Sixteen

ELIZABETH SAT IN a small grouping of four chairs with Eugenia and Jane. Lady Addlesworth soon joined them, completing their happy quartet. She was glad for this brief moment in time where she could gather her courage because in less than an hour, she quite possibly could be speaking to Mr. Darcy for the first time since their walks in Hyde Park. She had no intentions of avoiding him. She also had no intention of seeking him out.

The ladies were quietly discussing the upcoming annual Michaelmas Ball, when Miss Bingley appeared and hovered at the edge of their conversation circle.

"Miss Eliza, imagine how surprised I was—"

"As surprised as I am that you have yet to address me by my correct name? You never have. I wonder why?"

Caroline stood; mouth slightly agape at being called out so openly. Elizabeth waited for her answer. Patience had never been one of her virtues, but for the sake of putting this woman in her place, she would remain as steady and as silent as the Sphinx.

"I…," Miss Bingley's mouth opened and closed again, reminding Elizabeth of a fish gasping for air and she fought back the smile which threatened to break her stoic mien.

"Your grace," Miss Bingley finally managed and dipped into a deep curtsy, Mrs. Hurst following suit.

"Miss Bingley, Mrs. Hurst," Elizabeth replied with a regal nod of her head.

Oh, how Henry would have laughed at this little parody. He knew she had no love for Miss Bingley or her tag-along sister. She'd regaled him with enough stories of their first meeting at the Meryton assembly and of their supercilious behavior at various events and dinners held by friends in Meryton. She's also shared an amusing vignette of one night at Netherfield when Miss Bingley offered to mend Mr. Darcy's pen in a desperate attempt to capture his attention. Henry had teased by saying, *I bet she wanted to mend more than his pen.* She had teased by back by asking if she could mend *his* pen.

It was good she had been able to laugh about those dark days. Henry had not let her wallow in self pity.

"May I offer you felicitations of your superior marriage, your grace." Miss Bingley simpered, apparently forgetting how much she despised the former country miss although her next comment proved her dislike could not be tempered. "I see your husband did not attend with you. Does he have a pressing engagement elsewhere? Mayhap near the theater or Drury Lane?"

All the ladies gasped, not only because of the fact that Henry was dead, but Miss Bingley had insinuated her husband was with a mistress. Elizabeth's anger began to simmer.

"Miss Bingley," Jane said with her usual calm. "His Grace passed away last July. Elizabeth has just come out of full mourning."

Although her sister's face gave nothing away, Elizabeth noted her right hand had clenched into the shape of a fist, her nails digging into her palm. Oh yes, her sister desperately wanted to slap that smarmy look off of Miss Bingley's face.

"My apologies, your grace."

Elizabeth's one nerve remaining, not yet frayed by the constant simpering interjected with snide comments, was almost stretched to breaking and to maintain her sanity, she chose to ignore Miss Bingley and her twit of a sister. Thankfully, Jane once again came to the rescue, turning to her mother-in-law, Eugenia and asked, "Have you attended Vauxhall Gardens this season?"

"Sadly, not yet. We should all attend and see the famous rope dancer, Madame Sequi," the marchioness enthused. "I have heard she is quite thrilling to watch."

"Yes, cousin Charlotte said as much when I had tea with her the other day." Elizabeth said and was about to ask what night they should all attend when Miss Bingley, once again, inserted herself into the conversation.

"I forgot your friend married your cousin who will inherit the family seat. What was it called again? Langbird?"

"My father's estate is Longbourn and is no longer entailed. And the cousin I referred to was her Majesty, Queen Charlotte."

Miss Bingley's eyes widened to the point where the whites of her eyes were fully exposed and all color leached from her face. Elizabeth stood and looked at her sister.

"I see the men have returned. Come Jane, I am sure your husband is eager to be in your presence. He is not one to leave you waiting for *his* return."

She knew she'd scored a direct hit by the reaction she garnered. Miss Bingley may not have flinched, but Mrs. Hurst did. Frankly, she did not care. By the time she and Jane had nearly reached their cousins, Mr. Darcy approached and bowed very respectfully.

"Duchess, Lady Telford."

"Mr. Darcy."

"Might I inquire if your grace is residing at Talbot House or are you staying with your cousins?"

"I am residing at Talbot House, Mr. Darcy."

"Then I would humbly ask if I may attend one day this week and speak with you."

Her pause was brief, but they both noticed it.

"You may."

"Thank you, Madam."

He bowed again and left the room.

~~~

THE BUTLER TOOK Darcy's card and said he would see if her grace was accepting visitors. While waiting to be escorted, his thoughts tumbled about like a fast-moving river over rocks. Tumultuous, swirling, dangerous if not navigated with care. All of his self-righteous thoughts and attitude over the past few years washed over him like filthy sewer water. He was no better than George Wickham. No. He was worse, for George had never taken a woman against her will.

He could never atone for his sins. He should go. Leave now and let her live her life in peace. He should not be here and taint her child with his sin. About to pivot and open the front door, he stopped when the butler returned.

"This way please."

Like a man being led to the executioner block, Darcy followed in silence. They entered the drawing room and he immediately became aware there were others guests in the room. On one side stood Bingley, near Lady Telford. On the other side was Mr. Bennet, reading a book. Of Elizabeth, there was no sign.

"Lady Telford," he said with a polite half bow.

"Mr. Darcy," she said in return to his greeting.

"Mr. Bennet," he said to Lady Telford's father.

"Mr. Darcy," was all the gentleman from Longbourn said.

"Bring some tea please, Gibson," instructed Lady Telford. "Mr. Bingley has only just arrived himself. Papa, will you not greet Mr. Bingley?"

No response came from the gentleman, who calmly turned a page. Having experienced his own interactions with the gentleman, Darcy couldn't help the small smile that threatened to curve his mouth.

"Papa?"

"For you alone, dear Jane, will I put on the mantle of politeness. Have a seat, Mr. Darcy. You will enjoy this."

Bennet placed the open book across his knee and turned his attention to Bingley.

"Three years ago, you left Netherfield like a thief in the night after paying marked attention to my eldest daughter to the point that everyone, and I repeat, *everyone* in our little town thought you were going to make an offer. Even I, with my jaded intellect and slanted way of looking at life, was certain you would be knocking on my door after your ball."

Completely blindsided, all Bingley could do was open and close his mouth. Not a word passed his lips. Bennet continued over his daughters attempts to catch his attention and make him stop.

"You may wonder what we backward folk thought of as marked attention. Let me lay it all out for you, so you do not repeat your folly in the future. Every gathering we were at, be it a dinner or a card party, you would sequester my daughter in a corner and speak only with her. If there was dancing in the evening, you partnered with her for at least two sets. At your own ball, you opened the event by dancing the first two sets with her. Ah, but you did not stop there, you also claimed the supper set, as well as the final dance. You had the audacity to stand with us, her arm looped through yours, while we waited for our carriage, ignoring all your other guests, *and* you promised my wife you would come to dinner the following week when you returned from London. Was there something we, as a family, as a community missed?

"Papa!" Lady Telford finally cut through his tirade. "We all wish at some time in our life to go back and fix our mistakes. But, we cannot. Let us look to our future. Lizzy is happy. I am happy. I am sure Mr. Bingley and Mr. Darcy are happy."

Darcy and Bingley both looked at one another. They knew. Neither of them was happy and it was their own fault. It was at this moment of yet another epiphany, that Elizabeth entered the room. Darcy immediately came to his feet and gave a formal bow.

"Your grace."

"Mr. Darcy," she said and gave a small nod at Bingley who also properly gave her deference.

He noticed her glance at Bingley's shocked face, then her eyes swept around the room taking in Lady Telford's embarrassed mien and her father's satirical smile. He knew, in a flash, she'd put together what happened before she entered the room.

"I see that everyone has been re-acquainted."

He truly appreciated her wry humor, but poor Bingley looked like he'd been hit by a post coach – twice.

"Your grace, I was going to suggest a walk but I believe my friend and I should take our leave. I shall come back another day if that is acceptable."

Elizabeth nodded in agreement. Mr. Bennet picked up his book and began to read, as though none of them were in the room with him.

"Then I bid you adieu, Madam, Lady Telford, Mr. Bennet."

Darcy gave a curt nod and plucked at Bingley's sleeve. He looked up at Darcy, dazed and confused. Fortunately, he gathered his wits enough to bid everyone a polite good-bye, including Mr. Bennet. As the door closed behind them, Darcy heard Elizabeth say, "Oh, Papa. What did you do?"

Once outside on the front step Bingley stood completely still, quite befuddled.

"Bingley, come to my house for drinks this evening. I think we have much to talk about. Things we should have addressed a long time ago."

"Yes." He shook his head as if do dispel cobwebs from his mind. "I shall meet you there."

~~~

"DARCY, WHEN YOU said you had irrefutable proof the Bennet's were mercenary, what *exactly* was that proof?"

He poured himself and Bingley a drink and they took a seat by the fireplace.

"When Bennet demanded I marry his daughter, saying we had been alone in the library, I was positive they were trying to trap me in a trumped-up compromise."

"Based on that, you assured me Miss Bennet was mercenary and would only accept my offer of marriage to appease her mother."

"I stand by that observation even to this day, Charles. Mrs. Bennet was not quiet about how she expected you to marry her eldest and then throw other rich men in the way of her younger daughters. She trumpeted your betrothal as a done thing. And Miss Bennet, being the gentle creature she is, would never have gainsaid her mother's wishes. She would have accepted your offer because she had been told she must. As far as I could tell, love never entered the equation."

Bingley stared at the reflection of the fireplace on his cut glass. Finally, he roused from his thoughts.

"If a person has a hint of blue in their blood, we all look aside as they trot their daughters from ballroom to ballroom like a prize mare. I am surprised we do not line up the new debutants at Almack's on the first night and check their teeth for any disease. Then, ask them to promenade about the room so we can ascertain if the width of their hips will ensure the delivery of a healthy child."

"Charles, that is disgusting!"

"Is it? Tell me, Darcy, what makes these titled ladies any different from Mrs. Bennet who had five unmarried daughters and an estate entailed away from the female line. What did she do that was so different from those ladies of the *ton*?"

"She is vulgar and uncouth."

"May I remind you of the dinner party we attended after leaving Hertfordshire, whereupon Lady Crenshaw pulled the top of her dress down, exposing her bosoms to everyone in the room. Or shall I turn your attention to something a little closer to home. Lady Price. It is a known fact she has more than one lover, and yet she shoves her two daughters beneath your nose at every event. The gossip mongers are in a feeding frenzy because you have showed marked interest in the youngest, Lady Eunice. Are you not disgusted with *her* mother's behavior?"

"I have some concerns, but I am looking for a wife to help bring Georgiana—"

"Stop. Right. There." Bingley carefully placed his now empty glass on the side table. "You are so damned two-faced. Why did I not see this before? Because Mrs. Bennet's family is from trade and she lives in a small market town, you see everything about her as vulgar and crude. *She* has not exposed her bosoms. *She* is not rumored to have lovers. Yet, in spite of all this, the Miss Bennets were forbidden and Lady Eunice is acceptable."

"Lady Eunice has impeccable pedigree and social standing."

"Pedigree and social standing. Is that all you care about?"

"Your sister and I wished to see you succeed in life."

"How could marrying Miss Bennet have made my life not successful?"

"She did not have connections and brought nothing to the marriage."

"Well, we have seen how wrong we were on that account. At the time, Miss Elizabeth was not the Duchess of Tavistock, but the Bennets *are* related to the Marquis of Haversham and Miss Bennet is now the Countess of Telford." Bingley huffed out a sigh and rested his head on the back of the chair. "That never should have mattered. What type of connections do I need? I am independently wealthy with no debt and no habits that will see me parted from my money like a fool. All I wanted was a woman who loved me for who I am and makes me happy. I had no doubt of her affection until you and Caroline began whispering in my ear, solidified by the fact you said you had irrefutable proof of her mercenary tactics. Based on that, I reluctantly gave Miss Bennet up. How I wished you hadn't interfered."

"At the time, I had to look toward Georgiana's future."

"When did my choice of wife have anything to do with your sister?" Darcy didn't like how exasperated Bingley sounded. "I am not the grandson or nephew of an earl. I am a tradesman's son who is not even one generation away from having earned his wealth. To this day, I still do not own an estate. Marrying Miss Bennet, a gentleman's daughter, would have elevated *me*."

"Bingley, I am sorry. I could not bear the thought of you marrying Miss Bennet. As your friend I might have seen her sister when I visited."

The heavy silence in the room was broken only by the ticking of the grandfather clock. Finally, Charles spoke.

"If I understand this correctly, *you* did not want me to marry the kindest, most beautiful woman – inside and out – because *you* did not want to meet her sister by chance." Bingley stared off into the distance. "It was never about me. You and Caroline never once cared about how I felt," he finally said before he stood and exited the room.

"I am a two-faced fool," Darcy muttered and threw back the rest of his drink.

Had he been wrong to ride roughshod over his friend's choice of wife? Given the examples Bingley provided, and they were but two of many, his answer had to be a resounding yes. How could he overlook Lady Price's abhorrent behavior yet not Mrs. Bennet's? Yes, Mrs. Bennet had loudly proclaimed she expected an offer of marriage for her daughter, but she had not been wrong in that assertion. If he and Caroline had not practically browbeaten Charles upon their hasty arrival in London, he most assuredly would have paid a visit to Longbourn the following week, hat in hand, to speak with Miss Bennet's father.

Miss Bennet had married well and by all accounts in a love match. Charles on the other hand still floundered. Would he have been happy with Miss Bennet? Darcy would never know, and the stain of his pride just kept getting bigger and harder to wash clean.

Chapter Seventeen

ELIZABETH ACCEPTED A warm kiss on the cheek from Lady Addlesworth and a kiss on the back of her gloved hand from Lord Addlesworth when going through the receiving line prior to the opening of their annual Michaelmas ball. Behind her came Kit and Jane, as well as her sister Catherine. At nineteen she was ready to enter society in full, and with Henry settling on her a dowry of twenty thousand pounds, same as all her sisters, she was guaranteed to make a good marriage. Elizabeth had already decided her sister would marry for love. Kitty, as she still liked to be called by family and close friends, deserved nothing less.

As a group, they entered the ball room, already full of society's best. And worse. It was up to Elizabeth to weed out the bad characters and protect her younger, still naïve sister. They hadn't gone far when they spotted Cousins Percy and Eugenia. Next to them were Lord and Lady Matlock and Miss Darcy.

Elizabeth's heart sped up and she fought the inclination to scout around and see if an older brother was holding up a pillar nearby. Either that, or staring out a window. It seemed to be Mr.

Darcy's favorite activity when in large crowds.

Her mind went back to that first evening in Meryton, when he'd prowled the edges of the local assembly so scornful, so full of pride. His pride was still intact, to be sure, albeit softer around the edges. He was not so prone to judge first and ask questions later.

Their walks in Hyde Park, which had paused over the course of Henry's decline in health and their eventual removal to Edgecam Hall, had been re-instated a few short days after the confrontation with Mr. Bingley and during them, she could not help but notice his change in attitude. He lifted his hat when they met ladies walking and nodded in recognition to the dandies parading by in their elaborate phaetons. If she had met this gentleman first, instead of Dour Darcy – as she'd taken to calling him in secret – she could very well have fallen in love with him then.

She stopped short. Then?

Oh, dear.

She loved Mr. Darcy.

"Lizzy, are you well?"

Jane's concerned voice cut into her thoughts. This would not do. Not do at all.

"I am, thank you, Jane."

Get a hold of yourself, Lizzy. Now is not the time to go into histrionics because you love the father of your child.

By this time, they'd reached the Matlocks and Miss Darcy. They all gave her a polite curtsy along with addressing her rank, of which she waved off.

"Please, I am your friend and almost relative through cousins Eugenia and Kit. A simple greeting will suffice." She turned to Miss Darcy. "It is lovely to see you again, Georgiana."

Georgiana had accompanied her brother on two of their walks and Elizabeth had insisted they call each other by their given names as she thought of the young girl as a dear friend.

"Your dress is lovely, Elizabeth," she said in a quiet voice.

"As is yours. We share the same modiste, so I know yours is excellently made."

"Our nephew is running late. He sends his apologies as you were expecting him to partner you for the first dance." Lady Matlock offered.

"I was. He petitioned for it last week."

"Then, his loss is my gain, Madam" Richard Fitzwilliam said, having joined their company. "For King and Country, I will resume my rank of colonel and step into the breach."

"Am I a battleground, Mr. Fitzwilliam?" Elizabeth teased.

"No, but once it is known the elusive Duchess of Tavistock is in want of a dance partner, I may have to sharpen my saber and take a defensive posture."

"Stand down, Richard." A familiar baritone flowed over her shoulder and the hairs on the back of her neck raised. "No need to protect the prize of her grace."

"Dash it all, Darcy. You move so quiet for a large man. You would have made an excellent spy."

Elizabeth swatted Richard Fitzwilliam on the arm.

"Do not dare recruit the only man who has asked me to dance tonight. Napoleon has no fury like a woman scorned, or stood up for a set."

Mr. Fitzwilliam playfully backed away; his hands partially raised as though in surrender. He then saw Catherine and halted. Seeing where his gaze had landed, Elizabeth took hold of Kitty's hand and drew her forward.

"Mr. Fitzwilliam, may I present my sister, Miss Catherine Bennet of Longbourn, Hertfordshire. Catherine, Mr. Richard Fitzwilliam of Rosings Park, Kent."

"I had the pleasure of meeting Miss Bennet when she visited her friend at Hunsford. The pleasure then and now is all mine." He bowed low, never taking his gaze off her now rosy hued face. "As I have experienced a rout in garnering the first dance with your sister, may I petition your hand for the first set?"

Elizabeth almost laughed out loud at the narrowing of her sister's eyes and was not surprised by her answer.

"I am unwilling to play second fiddle to any of my sisters, sir, but if I decline your less than adequate request, I will be required to sit out the rest of the ball. Therefore, as needs must, I will dance the first set with you."

Georgiana's mouth had opened slightly in surprise before closing, and Lady Matlock hid a smile behind her fan. Lord Matlock guffawed out loud.

"You have been put in your place, my son. And about time, I might add." Lord Matlock then turned to Kitty. "Miss Bennet, I know I am an old dog, but would you do me the honor of the second set? That is if my bumbling son has not trodden your toes into the floor."

"Yes, my lord. I would be delighted to dance with you."

Mr. Darcy then secured her third set and Kit asked for the fourth. All this time, Mr. Fitzwilliam watched, seemingly in shock over such a young girl taking him to task.

"Miss Bennet," he finally managed to gain her attention. "I apologize for treating you so cavalier on our introduction. I will excuse myself from your first set and not bother you again for the evening."

"Mr. Fitzwilliam, I thank you for the apology, but please do not make it worse by now casting me aside over a bit of good-natured teasing."

"You were teasing?"

"I might have been. You will have to learn my nature before you know for certain."

Mr. Fitzwilliam turned to Elizabeth and said, "Please tell

me there are no more Bennet ladies to chastise me over my behavior. My ego cannot be deflated so quickly or so concisely any longer."

"I have two more sisters, Mr. Fitzwilliam." She smiled widely when he clutched his chest as though wounded. "Fear not, Mary and Lydia are not here. You may prepare yourself for their introductions later this year when they come to spend Christmas with Andrew and me."

"How is Andrew, your grace?" Darcy asked.

"I have been told when a child reaches the age of two, they make a parent ever wonder where their loving baby has gone. As of last month, Andrew reached that stage and exudes everything you may have heard about toddlers pushing their boundaries."

"I remember when my sons were about his age. Oh, the things they got into," Lady Matlock said with a smile. "At one time we could not find our eldest, Edmund. We searched and searched. Robert was ready to call in the constable, convinced someone had kidnapped him."

"I remember this," Lord Matlock said and chuckled.

Lady Matlock continued. "My husband and I were in my chambers. I was heartbroken and weeping uncontrollably, convinced my baby had been taken when we heard a little voice saying, *here I am*. It took a few times calling his name, with him saying over and over, *here I am*, that we discovered him in my dressing room armoire."

"Lucinda snatched him up and said, *we have been looking everywhere for you*. Edmund, pointing at his own chest, replied with a child's logic. *I was here, Mama*, he said, *I was always here*. You see, in his eyes he was not lost, he was waiting for us to find him."

"I aged ten years from that." Lady Matlock shook her head, lost in memories.

"Andrew has discovered his toys can be hidden inside of

things. The maids are forever finding them in vases, potted plants. One morning as I poured tea, the lid popped off and a wooden pony ended up in my cup."

"I have yet to meet… your son," Darcy said.

Their group fell silent, the exception being Georgiana and Catherine who continued chatting. Soon, even they realized no one else was speaking and looked about in confusion. All eyes turned to Elizabeth. She took a deep breath. It was now or never.

"Will you not join us tomorrow for our walk, Mr. Darcy? You would be welcome to stay for dinner."

Everyone knew what Elizabeth had offered Darcy. A chance to know his son in a personal, private manner. A chance to see if they could be family.

~~~

SHE INVITED HIM to meet their son. His heart constricted. With joy or fear, he knew not. Tomorrow he would finally see Andrew and bit the inside of his cheek to keep his eyes from tearing up. It would not do for Fitzwilliam Darcy to begin weeping in a ballroom.

The orchestra signalled the first set was about to start. He stepped forward and extended his arm.

"I believe this set is ours."

"It is."

They stood for some time at the head of the line without speaking a word and he began to imagine their silence could stretch through the two dances, much like it had at Netherfield. This made him realize it had been almost three years complete since they'd first met and two months later, their first dance. This was his chance to rewrite their shared history.

"Lady Addlesworth's annual ball is a popular event."

Elizabeth remained silent as she promenaded around the

lady next to her. He almost grinned as the memories of their first dance began to replay in his mind. When she returned to her spot, he jumped in again before she could speak.

"It is your turn to say something, your grace. I talked about the dance, you should make a remark about the size of the room, or the numbers of couples…"

Her eyes flashed and then she smiled as she stepped forward to sashay around him.

"Whatever you wish for me to say, it shall be said."

"That will do for the present. Perhaps you still observe private balls are much pleasanter than public ones. But, pay me no mind, we can remain silent if that is your pleasure."

"Much has changed since we last met on the floor of a ballroom. However, I see that you still wish to talk while dancing with me."

"One must speak a little. As all eyes are on us, it would look odd if we remained entirely silent for half an hour together."

She made no answer, and they were again silent till they had gone down the dance.

"Do you and Andrew walk every day?"

"We try. Of course, weather is a mitigating factor and I have two days where I receive visitors and two days when I must return calls. That leaves precious time to spend with him."

"But you are there to see him every morning and knowing your character, I think I am correct in presuming you are there to tuck him into bed every night."

"That is my favorite time of day with him." She gasped when she caught his expression. "Forgive me, Mr. Darcy, that was unknowingly cruel. You have not had the chance to meet my son and knowing *your* character, having seen how you raised Georgiana, you would covet even a minute of his time."

"That is true, and tomorrow one of my deepest held wishes will come true."

"You have more than one deeply held wish?"

He held her gaze without saying a word. Her eyes widened and a light blush touched her cheeks and she whispered a soft, 'Oh.'

They went down the dance again and he could see her poise was regained when they reached the head of the line.

"I remember hearing you once say, Mr. Darcy, that you hardly ever forgave, that your resentment once created was unappeasable."

"I did say that," he replied with caution, wondering where she was going with this conversation.

"And you have never allowed yourself to be blinded by prejudice?"

"I did in the past. I hope I have learned valuable lessons these past three years." They stepped forward in the dance, then retreated back to the line. "May I ask where your questions are headed?"

"I was once blinded by prejudices and a wilful pride," she replied. "Because of that, I kept a vital secret which did not allow you to discover exactly what happened."

"Are you asking if I have forgiven your past prejudice?"

"Yes, I also wanted you to know that I, too, have changed much these past three years and have learned to speak my mind more clearly."

"Madam," he barely managed to control a smile, "you have *never* had to learn that skill. You most definitely have always spoken your opinions quite clearly."

She flashed a quick smile and then smoothed her face before saying, "I do believe I should be affronted."

"Did you, or did you not, on the night we all were at Sir William Lucas's home, call me out for listening in on your conversation with your friend, Miss Lucas?"

"How do you remember these things?"

Because every conversation, every minute I spent with you in Meryton is burned into my memory banks.

"To me, they were memorable," was all he allowed himself to say out loud.

"I vaguely recall Charlotte made me play the pianoforte." They moved down the line again. "At those moments, I questioned her friendship."

"There was nothing lacking in your performance."

"Were you deaf? Compared to your sister, I am but a child plunking the keys in a random fashion."

"I found your singing and playing exquisite. You are being too hard on yourself."

By this time the dance had ended and they turned to applaud the orchestra and he took her hand and began leading her back to their group of friends and family.

"I look forward to a time when I can hear you sing and play again," he said as approached their friends and family and then continued in a low voice. "I will say one thing before we part. There is nothing you have done which requires me to forgive you. All the blame lays with me." They had now reached their group. "Thank you for the dance, Madam."

With a polite bow over her hand, he took his place by his Aunt Lucinda and watched as Elizabeth was led to the floor by her brother-in-law, Earl Telford.

"You and her grace are becoming more comfortable around each other," Aunt Lucinda began conversationally. "She is a powerful woman in her own right and there will be many fortune hunters and power-hungry men who will work to earn her good will."

"The duchess *is* formidable, Aunt. She will not make a hasty decision, nor will she be swayed by a pretty face and polite manners. If they try to coddle her, or sing false platitudes in her presence, she will cut them to pieces. Of that, I have no doubt."

"She holds you in high esteem."

"At one time, she did not."

"That may be true, but she does now."

"Aye, she does now and I will not forfeit the ground I have gained."

"Good. She deserves a strong man in her life. One that compliments her character without smothering it." Aunt Lucinda turned to face him and held his gaze. "The duke was such a man. Whether you like it or not, those are very big shoes to try and fill. I wish you to succeed in this quest – do not give me that look Fitzwilliam Darcy – I have seen the way your eyes follow her. You love her deeply and I believe she is beginning to understand that."

"From your lips to God's ears, Aunt."

Chapter Eighteen

ELIZABETH STOOD IN front of the large mirror, twisting this way and that and then scowled.

"Let me see the blue silk, Hattie." In the reflecting glass, she saw her selfless maid slightly roll her eyes before blowing a wisp of hair from her forehead. "I am being ridiculous."

Hattie's eyes widened.

"No, ma'am."

"Yes, I am. Fussing over a simple day dress." She continued to look at herself in the light green gown. "This will do. Thank you for indulging me."

Hattie curtsied and began to hang up the other four dresses Elizabeth had tried on while getting ready for Mr. Darcy's arrival. She would be the first to admit her nerves were taut with excitement. She dreaded, yet tingled with excitement over him finally meeting Andrew.

Why had she never felt this nervous with Henry? From the minute she'd met the duke, she had always experienced a strange confidence. Not once did she ever regret marrying him, or loving him as she did. Yet, knowing that in a few short hours Mr. Darcy would darken the doors of her home had her stomach tied up in knots and her breath catching in her throat. She almost began wringing her hands, similar to Mamma when she had a fit of vapors and nervous fluttering.

At the thought of acting like her mother, she finally laughed.

If Papa could see her now. His eyes would roll heavenward and his sly grin would let her know he had some cryptic quip on the tip of his tongue. She sighed. There were times she missed her family so much. It was lovely having Catherine, Jane, and Kit with her at Talbot House for part of the season, but next week they would all return to Longbourn. From there, Mary would join Jane and Kit and leave for their estate in Derbyshire. Jane, at almost six months pregnant, did not want to travel during the dead of winter, nor at a time when her discomfort would be increased.

Jane had asked her to join their merry party. Mayhap this year she would accept their gracious invitation. Also, their estate was close enough to Pemberley that Mr. Darcy could spend Christmas day with Andrew. *And me.*

She took one last look in the mirror, squared her shoulders, and left the room to wait in the parlor she used for her receiving day. Jane met her at the bottom of the stairs.

"Are you excited or nervous," she asked as they turned together and walked toward the parlor.

"Both." She forced herself to smile as normal.

"You will do splendid. I have great faith in you."

By this time, they'd reached the parlor. Kit stood as they entered and pulled the lanyard to signal a maid bring them tea. She had barely sat when Gibson appeared in the open doorway.

"Mr. Darcy, your grace."

She smoothed down the front of her gown and inhaled a deep, cleansing breath. Before she could blink, he entered the room and approached, giving her a low, courtly bow.

"Your grace," he said.

Gooseflesh rose on her arms at his mellow baritone. How could just his voice elicit such a response?

"Mr. Darcy," she replied, thanking everything she held holy that her voice hadn't quivered like an untried maiden with her first beau.

He quickly greeted Jane and Kit and the four of them had tea and conversed on mundane things such as the weather, Parliament and of course the latest escapades of the prince Regent. Elizabeth's mind briefly settled on her Majesty. Surely, she heard about the rumors. What did a royal mother do about a badly behaving son? What would she do if Andrew behaved in same manner? Thank goodness he was just a little over two and still a loving, happy child.

Her thoughts were interrupted by the chiming of the clock, letting her know that over half an hour had lapsed since Mr. Darcy had arrived and Andrew would be rising from his nap.

"My son will have been awakened from his nap and his nurse will be getting him ready for our walk, Mr. Darcy. Would you care to join me in the nursery before we leave?"

He rose to his feet, as did Jane and Kit. They were on their way out to have dinner with his parents. She was very aware of the large, silent man following her up the stairs to the nursery. The attraction between them pulled at her, much like it had with Henry. At the top of the staircase, left would take them to her bedchamber. Right would lead to their son. For a split second she hesitated, then tamped down her natural desires and turned right. She was a gentlewoman, born and bred as well as a duchess. She would not behave in a manner worthy of a courtesan even though Henry had instructed her in the finer arts of pleasing a man. He had explained that what happened between man and wife was natural and just and she should never be ashamed of giving and receiving pleasure.

It may have been her heightened awareness, but it seemed like Mr. Darcy was suddenly closer. The heat emanating from his body warmed her back and a delicious shiver coursed through her. Her hand was on the doorknob when he covered it with his own large one, staying her movement.

Warm breath feathered her neck and a kiss brushed the lobe of her ear. She tilted her head back, giving him fuller access to her neck. His arm inched its way around her waist and drew her against his body.

"I have dreamed of you, Elizabeth. Every night you come to me and I taste your sweetness. Am I wrong to want you so badly?"

"No," she whispered and twisted the doorknob, breaking the spell. It was too soon. They barely knew one another and today was about their son. She forced herself to smile in the merry way Andrew expected and opened the door.

~~~

WHAT WERE YOU thinking, man! Seducing the mother of your child in the hall where any servant could stumble upon them. If there were a desk nearby, he would have gladly banged his head on the surface, so irate was he at himself.

He waited as Elizabeth composed herself then opened the door. Time slowed down when he entered the room. He looked across the room and by the large window was a young boy, playing with his nurse. At the sight of his mother, the boy jumped to his feet and ran to her. Darcy could hardly breathe. Feet rooted to the floor, he could only stare at a child that was his exact duplicate, right down to the color of his eyes.

Elizabeth stooped down to accept sweet little kisses and hugs before straightening and taking hold of his hand. Together they faced him, her face wreathed in smiles, Andrew's one of hesitation.

"Andrew, I would like you to meet a special friend of Mamma's." She looked down at Andrew, then up at him. "This is Mr. Fitzwilliam Darcy of Pemberley, Derbyshire. Mr. Darcy, may I present to you his grace, Andrew Henry William Talbot, twelfth Duke of Tavistock."

"Your grace." Darcy took a step forward and gave his son a polite half bow.

Andrew attempted to copy his bow, then looked up at Elizabeth for approval.

"Well done, Andrew. You are such a gentleman, but as a duke, you are not required to return the bow unless that person is royalty. Can you show Mr. Darcy your toy soldiers? I am sure he will think they are the finest he has ever seen."

At the mention of his toy soldiers, which seemed to be his beloved treasure, his face lit up and all formality was tossed out the window. He raced to the back wall where a shelf was situated. In neat rows, all his soldiers were lined up.

"Did you arrange your soldiers, your grace?"

"Yes," Andrew said with an accompanying nod. "I do not like them all mixed up."

Darcy afforded Elizabeth a quick glance and saw her smile. He was not surprised by his son's little quirk. He also had to have structure with his toys and belongings growing up. Even now, he kept a neat desk where everything had its place and he experienced disquiet when things were not arranged to his specifications.

The two of them sat on the floor and discussed the merits of foot soldiers to calvary soldiers. One thing which did come out of their conversation was the fact his son was mad about his pony. Next to his books and his toys, riding his little horse daily as his favorite activity.

"If your mother is amendable, I would very much like to attend your next riding lesson."

Andrew looked to his mother.

"Mamma?"

"Of course. Is tomorrow agreeable?"

Andrew looked back at him and he nodded.

"Theodore is a bestest pony ever, Mitter Darcy."

"Theodore?"

"A character from one of his books," Elizabeth explained.

"I am sure Theodore is a fine pony, your grace."

Andrew turned to his mother once more.

"Mamma, Mitter Darcy called me Grace."

Elizabeth raised a hand to cover her smile. As soon as she was composed, she said, "When someone calls you, 'your grace', they are calling you by your title. You are his grace, the Duke of Tavistock."

"No, I am Andrew."

"You are still Andrew. You are also your grace."

"We talk about this later, Mamma." Darcy could almost hear Elizabeth in those few words. Now, he also had to hide a smile. "Can Mitter Darcy call me Andrew?"

"Yes, he may."

Andrew faced Darcy.

"You call me Andrew, Mitter Darcy."

Determined. He son was a determined young man, not to be swayed. His heart melted even further, if possible.

"Thank you… Andrew."

"Mr. Darcy wished to join us on our walk before dinner. May he come with us to the park?"

Andrew jumped to his feet, clapping his hands.

"Yes! Please!"

Within the half hour, they were all in a non-descript carriage. Darcy quickly realized they were not headed to Hyde Park but traveling further east.

"We are not going to Regent's or Hyde Park?"

"No." Elizabeth straightened Andrew's cap on his mop of curls. "When I take Andrew for a walk, I like the little park near where my aunt and uncle Gardiner live. It is more peaceful and no one cares who Andrew is. He is allowed to be a little boy who feed the ducks, sometimes floats a toy boat, and can get as muddy as he likes."

The carriage pulled to stop in front of an elegant looking house. Andrew scrambled to his feet, clearly impatient to escape and visit the park. A footman opened the door of the carriage and Darcy exited, turning around to hand out Elizabeth and then picked up Andrew, holding him close to his chest. This was the first time he'd touched his son and he nearly wept.

"You squeeze too hard, Mitter Darcy," Andrew complained and he loosened his hold.

He set his son down on sturdy legs and straightened, catching Elizabeth's gaze. She too, had a distinct sheen about her eyes. The door of the townhouse opened and a woman Darcy had come to know as Mrs. Gardiner stepped out, two younger children with her.

"You are late, Lizzy," she said, pulling on gloves while coming down the stairs. "The children thought you might have forgotten your promise to come today."

"I had not forgotten. Aunt, have you met Mr. Darcy?"

"A long time ago and he would not remember."

At his confused expression, she said with a smile, "I grew up in Lambton. I knew your mother and father – well, as much as anyone who lived in Lambton knew the Darcy's of Pemberley. My father, Mr. Haywood, was the vicar. We often saw the family at services."

"You look very much like your father."

"I shall take that as a compliment, Mr. Darcy as my father was a handsome man."

"No offense meant. You have his smile and eyes."

The next hour flew by. Elizabeth and her aunt settled on a bench and she did not interfere or direct how he interacted with Andrew. Every now and then, his son would check back to the bench to ensure his mother was still there. If she happened to look his way when he did, she always smiled and waved. Otherwise, they were free to feed the ducks, fly the kite the Gardiner lad had brought with him, or try to catch a colorful butterfly with only his hat as the net.

All in all, it was the most satisfying afternoon he'd ever spend his entire life. When they were done, both he and his son had muddy knees, leaves in their hair from disentangling the kite from one of the trees, and sun-kissed cheeks. He wouldn't exchange it for anything.

He then caught sight of Elizabeth and readjusted his thoughts. There was one thing he would exchange it for. A lifetime of nights with the mother of his child. If the good Lord and Elizabeth thought he'd done enough penance for his arrogance and pride, his deepest wish might come true.

He waited until they were back in the carriage and Andrew fell into a fitful sleep before he broached the subject.

"Thank you for letting me have this day."

"I will not deny you access to Andrew, Mr. Darcy."

"Even if I want to see him every day?"

"Every day?"

"Yes."

"Difficult when I live most of the year at Edgecam Hall and you reside at Pemberley."

"Not so difficult if we lived in one of them together."

"What are you saying, exactly."

"I find I am wanting more than a friendship with you."

"What if friendship is all I am willing to offer? I have only come out of full mourning less than two months ago."

"If we were to hearken back to Meryton in the year of 1811 when a group of terrible snobs descended upon the local assembly—"

"You might not wish to go back that far, Mr. Darcy. You did not leave a good impression the first time around."

So, we are back to Mr. Darcy. It seemed like a portion of his son's stubbornness did not come solely from the Darcy side of the family. He would not give up. She was worth more than having a little bit of figurative egg splattered on his face.

"I will continue, if the lady allows."

She gave a regal nod and he wanted to kiss her so much he ached.

"Ahem… as I was saying. Let us presume we had been introduced and I *had* danced with you that night, would it have been reasonable that within a few short weeks of acquaintance I might have asked for an opportunity to know you better?"

"Yes," she answered slowly.

"It is true I made a hash of things right from the beginning. If given a second chance, I would do things different."

"And what would you change?"

"For one, I would court you. We have done everything backward and I would like to do at least this one thing right."

"If we are going to enter into a courtship, then you must call me Duchess." His eyes widened in surprise and she laughed with glee. How he loved her laugh. "You are so easy to tease, Mr. Darcy. Please, call me Elizabeth."

"We already established, before you left for Edgecam Hall, that you would call me Darcy, but I think I prefer William."

"Alas, I assume I am still not allowed to call you Willy."

"No." His answer was short and to the point. She was going to be the death of him.

"Then, William it is."

"May I court you, Elizabeth?"

She paused for such an extended period of time, he thought for sure she was formulating words to let him down gently. Finally, she answered.

"You may."

"This courtship is not for me as I know my own heart and desires. This time is set aside for you and one month from today, I shall pose my next question."

"I would ask that you wait until the new year."

"That is three months from now!"

He'd never last that long. As it was, he barely made it from one day to the next.

"Yes, but I have never been courted. Courting is a time of surprise and delight in discovering new things about your intended. As you said, we have done everything backward. I would like one thing to proceed in a normal fashion."

She was right. Of course. He had already wasted three years. What was another ninety days, plus long lonely nights in an empty bed?

"Then, you shall have your three months."

And so, the courtship of Elizabeth Rose Talbot, Duchess of Tavistock began. With precision he mapped out his plan and plotted well into the night. Richard would have been proud.

Chapter Nineteen

"WILL YOU NOT TRY ANOTHER FLAVOR?"

"I like lemon. Surely you know by now how much."

"I do know you like lemon. Lemon tarts, lemon cake, lemonade – the more tart the better – I only wondered if you would like to broaden your horizon."

"Broaden my horizon?" She acted as though shocked and placed a hand on her chest. "There are some things that are perfection. Lemon ices at Gunter's is one of them and you do not mess with perfection."

"And yet, you will not wear yellow."

"Have you ever seen me in yellow? I have what is called a buttercup chin."

"Buttercup chin?"

"Yes, when yellow is close to my neck, it reflects upon my face and my complexion turns sallow. You would think I was on death's door. Quite gruesome. Mamma forbade me from ever purchasing dresses, ribbons, or other accoutrements in that color."

"I concede. I will buy you a lemon ice."

"Thank you, William. Will we have this argument the next time we come here?"

"Most likely."

"Good. I like that we know what to expect."

~~~

"GOOD MORNING, WILLIAM, GEORGIANA."

"Good morning, Elizabeth."

Elizabeth stepped lightly away from her carriage, accepting the arm of Mr. Darcy to enter St. George's Cathedral for morning service. They were very aware of the craning necks and surprised expressions of fellow parishioners as he escorted her, Georgiana, and Catherine to the Duke of Tavistock's reserved pew. Elizabeth indicated for Catherine and Georgiana to enter first, then she followed with William close behind.

"How many pages do you think we shall garner in the society column of this week's *Gazette*?" she queried in a low voice, not minding that he had to lean into her in order to hear the saucy question.

"The *Gazette* will have but a few lines. It is the *Tattler* that will cover half a page."

The four of them settled into their seats and when they sang the hymnal, she was pleasantly surprised by his full-bodied baritone and Georgiana's clear soprano. The siblings could sing, and sing well. While the bishop preached from the book of John, William slid his hand over hers and left it there for the whole service. They were one of the first ones to exit the church, greeting the bishop and complimenting him on his sermon. She then turned to William.

"Kitty and I are joining our aunt and uncle for lunch and a visit this afternoon. You and Georgiana are welcome to attend with us. I sent her a note yesterday advising Aunt Madeline I was going to extend an invitation to the both of you."

"Georgiana, do you have plans for this afternoon?" William turned to his sister.

"No, I had thought to practice the new music I purchased the other day, but it can wait until the morrow."

William turned back to Elizabeth.

My sister and I are delighted to join you and your family for the day."

"Excellent." She dared to smile up at him and was rewarded with a warm smile of his own. "We shall meet you there. I must first gather up Andrew. He adores his cousins and if I went without him, he would surely pout for days on end."

"He certainly had fun the day we went on our walk."

"His excitement also included you. I heard nothing but 'Mitter Darcy did this,' or 'Mitter Darcy said that' for days. You left him with a good impression and a strong desire to know you better."

"And does this desire also extend to his mother?"

At his low words, a flush of heat shot through her, as though she'd stepped too close to a roaring fireplace. Good heavens. They were on the steps of a church. God should smite her dead at the hedonistic thoughts traipsing about her mind right now. She raised wary eyes to his and was once again struck mute by the banked heat from his.

"Brother, Elizabeth's carriage has arrived."

She startled back into an awareness of her surroundings, saved by the sweet voice of Georgiana. Thank goodness. Not only had she almost succumbed to an unfamiliar longing and begged William to kiss her, but she seemed unable to hold a coherent thought and form words. Who knew how long she would have stood there, held captive by his gaze? And, did William just growl?

~~~

"BROTHER, ELIZABETH'S CARRIAGE has arrived."

Elizabeth's eyes widened in surprise and he realized what he'd more than hinted at.

He was going to Hell, for surely God would not be pleased that he openly lusted after the mother of his child and dared touch on the subject of desire on the steps of a church. A church! What was he thinking? The answer was obvious. He was thinking of spending the afternoon with Elizabeth. In a room that held only a bed, and Elizabeth. With locked doors. And no servants. And no distractions. Just him, and Elizabeth, and a bed that would be well used until they were completely sated.

How long could they go without food or water? That might be the only thing that would drag him from this imaginary room. Sustenance so he could continue to pleasure her. He growled in frustration.

"Thank you, Georgiana," he finally managed to say and tore his gaze from Elizabeth's.

With quiet dignity, or whatever dignity he had remaining, he offered his arm and escorted her to her conveyance and saw her safely situated. Miss Bennet had elected to come with them.

"Until later, Madam." He gave a polite nod of the head toward Elizabeth.

The carriage moved on and the next carriage, which was his, came to a stop. He turned to give a hand to Georgiana and Miss Bennet, then gave the driver directions to take him and his sister to an elegant address in Cheapside.

"Drive on," he called out once settled in the dark velvet squabs cross from his sister and her friend. Hopefully, in a little over three months, he could also call Miss Bennet his sister. As the two young ladies talked about things important to them, he stared out the window.

Only days into their courtship, and he was already chafing at the bit. Much like Arion, he wanted to gallop, to run free with his emotions. It may prove difficult, but he had to bring his heart and mind to a gentle canter. She wanted him to woo her, not toss her up into a high racing phaeton and careen pell-mell toward the altar. He was not a randy youth, unable to control himself. He dared smile to himself and admitted, he was randy. But he was not a youth, he was a gentleman and would behave as one. And if granted the privilege, he would raise his son as one.

~~~

"YOU HAVE NEVER READ THIS BOOK?"

"No, Papa expressly forbade me from ever picking up that volume and reading it."

William assessed her with knowing eyes.

"Hmmm... did you, by chance, prop it up against a pillow and use some device to turn the pages?"

She laughed gaily.

"You have found me out! Yes, I did. Lydia carried it to my room and turned the pages for me. I had to promise her three month's allowances in order for her to do so, but she did."

"She did not read it!"

"No. Between turning the pages, she tore apart a bonnet and re-trimmed it. She had quite the talent for doing things like that. It was very fetching on her. When Papa asked how she could afford all the little trims and shoe roses she suddenly had money for, she said she helping her sister with a project and he left it at that."

She and William browsed the aisles for a while longer and it wasn't until they were in the carriage, he presented her with a wrapped package.

"What is this?" she asked, turning the package over in her hand.

"I am not sure, it might be a book, but the clerk seemed

underhanded. He may have slipped in a wooden block."

"Did you just tease me?"

"I believe I did."

"Well done, William. There is still hope for you."

"That is all I cling to lately, Elizabeth. It has become my faithful companion."

She didn't think her heart could soften any further with this man, yet he confounded her at every turn.

"May I open it now?"

"Please, do."

Like a child with a gift at Christmas, she tore the wrapper off, her eyes lighting up when she read the title.

"*Sense and Sensibility*, by a lady. I have long wanted to read her books. I am told her other novel is also very popular."

"Georgiana raves about her, but I fail to see why educated people would wish to read a story about a prideful man and a prejudice lady… or was it a prejudiced man and a prideful lady? Regardless, this can be some light reading which I hope you enjoy."

"I am sure I shall." A small piece of paper fluttered onto her lap. "What is this?"

William settled back into the seat of the carriage and watched her with hooded eyes.

"Oh…," she managed to finally whisper out after reading the note. "I shall give this much thought."

He'd totally discombobulated her and she felt the heat rise to her cheeks. Teasing, teasing man. Once safe in her bedchamber, she brought the note out and read what William had borrowed from the bard, her fingertips tracing the words.

She is beautiful, and therefore to be wooed;
She is woman, and therefore to be won

~~~

"THANK YOU FOR inviting me for tea, Georgiana. Kitty tells me the you have discovered a new blend and I simply must give it a try."

Catherine and Georgiana had struck up a strong friendship. Fortunately, their houses were not that far apart and were able to meet up on a regular basis for shopping, playing the pianoforte or taking a carriage to promenade in Hyde Park. The two of them were highly desirable matches. Georgian had a dowry of thirty thousand pounds while Kitty had twenty. It did not take a genius to know they would be sought by not only good men, but nefarious ones as well. Their specially trained companions and the four burly footmen Elizabeth hired to escort them were always on guard.

"It is an imported blend with a hint of lemon. William said you would like the tea before you even tasted it."

"William found this tea?"

"He enlisted the aid of your Uncle Gardiner."

"That sneaky man. I swear, he is scouring the whole of London, nay all of England, for anything lemon."

"You do have an affinity for that flavor, Elizabeth. Anybody who knows you is aware."

She huffed out a soft sigh. "Yes, 'tis true. It is one of my weaknesses."

"And you cannot be surprised at his quest to make you happy."

"Are you not the brave girl today?"

"Girl?"

Elizabeth almost chuckled at the look on Georgiana's face. At that moment, she was fully a Darcy. "Woman, then. A brave woman."

"I am brave, but I am also happy. He loves you so, Elizabeth. You do see that, do you not?"

"I do, but he has promised to not rush this time in our life. I am enjoying our courtship."

"I cannot wait to have my own courtship."

"Does any young man stand out above the others, and not by height alone. I saw that quirk of your brow."

Georgiana grinned. "There is one, Baron Sidway. I know he does not have the title my family expected for me, but he makes me smile and when I am with him, I feel safe. And happy."

"And he returns these feelings?"

"I believe he does."

Elizabeth gazed at her friend, and hopefully future sister, with great affection. When she'd first met the young lady, she had been so painfully shy. Today, although still quiet, she exuded a quiet confidence that came with knowing her family supported her in every way possible.

At one time, Georgiana had confessed to a youthful folly with a man who was her father's godson. She didn't say much other than she had learned the hard way the notorious womanizer had only been interested in the dowry which came along with her marriage. That alone was shocking enough, but when Georgiana told her she had been all but fifteen at the time, Elizabeth was horrified. The same age as Lydia when she attempted to climb out the window after Mr. Wickham.

She also realized, given the time frame, the incident with her father's godson must have occurred prior to William attending Netherfield with the Bingleys. Which explained his less than admirable look on life. It did not excuse his abhorrent manners, but did give reason for his distrust in people's motives as the godson must have been a close member of the family.

Their tea over, she gathered her things together and after a kiss on the cheek from Georgiana exited Darcy House and entered her carriage. She could have easily walked home, but she had been invited to dinner at her aunt and Uncle Gardiner's. She settled against the squabs and heard a familiar rustling. In the discrete pocket of her redingote, was a folded slip of paper.

William. He'd left her another note.

Doubt thou the stars are fire; Doubt that the sun doth move; Doubt truth to be a liar; But never doubt I love.

Of his love, she had no doubt. She had asked for a courtship and he continued to exceed every hope and secret desire. Why, oh why had she stipulated three months?

~~~

"WHO ARE THOSE FLOWERS FROM, GIBSON?"

"Mr. Darcy, your grace."

"Why are you putting them all the way across the room?"

"He left explicit instructions to place them near the window and provided an explanation."

Her butler handed her a small folded note. Elizabeth laughed out loud after reading it, then watched as Gibson arranged the three dozen yellow roses on a table in front of the window. They were achingly beautiful. She glanced down at the note again.

Elizabeth,

I cannot fix on the hour, or the spot, or the look or the words, which laid the foundation of my love. It is too long ago. I was in the middle before I knew that I had begun.

You may look all you like at these beautiful flowers, but are not allowed to sit near them.

Yours,
F.D.

P.S.: I did try to find buttercups, but was woefully unsuccessful.

~~~

"MR. DARCY AWAITS you in the blue parlor, ma'am," Gibson told her when she bid him enter her study.

"Thank you, Gibson, but I believe I shall meet him in the south drawing room, it is such a beautiful day I wish to enjoy the sunshine. Can you have Mrs. Prentiss bring tea in about a half hour?

"Yes, ma'am." He bowed and exited the room.

She smoothed down her skirts and forced herself to not look in a mirror. Nothing would have changed since Hattie dressed her earlier. With that in mind, she made her way to the drawing room, arriving before William by a few minutes. She knew who entered the room before the door had even shut.

She hadn't the chance to turn in greeting when he moved in behind her. The warmth of his body seeped through the back of her dress, completely at odds with the goose bumps which had risen on her flesh. His arms slid around her, drawing her even closer and he nuzzled her neck.

"How I long to kiss you."

"You ask my permission?" She was glad he had his arms around her middle. If not for them, she'd have melted into a puddle of desire. "Consider it granted."

"The question is, do I kiss you standing up, or seated, or laying down?" he murmured against the tender lobe of her ear.

She turned, still within the cocoon of his embrace and looked up at him.

"You debate how you will kiss me?"

"Elizabeth, you have no idea how often, or how long I have thought about kissing you."

"You... you thought about this?"

"*This* fills my every waking hour. Every night, before I fall asleep my body burns with thoughts of *this*."

"Oh..."

"My thoughts are consumed by you. Only you," he said and captured her mouth with his own.

~~~

ELIZABETH ROSE FROM her deep curtsy and approached the Queen, who waved her to come and sit in the chair opposite her.

"Thank you for inviting me, your Majesty."

"We are always pleased to see you. Next time, we shall arrange something so the new Duke of Tavistock may attend."

"Thank you, that would be lovely," Elizabeth said with a gracious nod of her head.

"We have much to discuss. You are now a very wealthy woman with a very young duke to raise."

"Your Majesty, may I be so bold as to speak plainly?"

Queen Charlotte's eyebrows raised a fraction before her face smoothed out.

"It would depend on how forthright you wish to be."

"Very forthright."

"Interesting. My cousin said you were a rare treasure, and if you knew how jaded the man was you would know what a compliment that was."

"My love and respect for his grace knew no bounds and it is because of that respect, I feel I must canvas an issue which is difficult to speak of, at best."

"I like you, Elizabeth Talbot. State your business then."

"Madam, as you know my son is not Henry's natural child.

I had been compromised and was *enceinte* when he offered marriage. With Henry's blessing, my son's father and I have resumed our friendship."

"This friendship is leading to an offer of marriage?"

"Yes, I believe strongly it is. For that reason, I must ask for Andrew to have his title revoked. He is well cared for with Henry's various estates and wealth, but he is not entitled to such a prestigious title and heritage."

Her Majesty was silent for so long Elizabeth worried she might have offended the woman.

"Have you any idea how many great bloodlines of England are populated with the offspring of strapping young footmen?"

"Pardon me?"

"We have shocked you. No mind. The fact of the matter is Henry Talbot acknowledged your son as his. He made us aware of this fact when he sought permission to marry you. We were surprised, but he shared with us how he met you at your cousin's estate and remembered you as a lovely young woman. Truth be told, he was a little in love with you long before he came to London, but thought he was too old for you."

"Age was never an issue with my husband. All I ever saw was a man who loved me and made me feel as though I was special."

"Go back to Talbot House with a clear conscience, Duchess. We see no need to strip your son of his title. With luck, he will grow up and represent the best of you and Mr. Darcy."

Elizabeth's eyes widened at her Majesty knowing who Andrew's father truly was.

"Yes. We know and approve. Please send our secretary an invitation to your wedding. If we are able, one of us will attend. You will make a pretty bride."

Elizabeth knew she'd been dismissed and stood, curtsying deeply before exiting the room, her knees shaking.

~~~

"YOU ARE STUPID, MY BLOCKS ARE STUPID!"

Elizabeth entered the room just as a wooden block hit the wall by the very door frame she stood within. Andrew, standing in the middle of the room, still had another block in his hand. His nurse stood wringing her hands, near where other toys had been thrown, obviously upset by his anger.

"What do you think you are doing?"

"I hate my blocks. I hate this room and I hate Alice."

"Nurse Alice, has he done this before?"

"Only once."

"Once is one time too many."

She marched over to Andrew and wrested the block from his fingers. He began to scream and fell to the floor, kicking his legs. Shocked, she could only stare and wonder where her cherubic little boy had gone. She shot a hard look at his nurse.

"Next time, you will tell me when he misbehaves in this manner."

"But, your grace, the duke is only vocalizing his displeasure."

Elizabeth's eyebrows rose in disbelief. Frustrated beyond reason, she leaned down and snatched her wailing son's arm, lifted him to his feet and forced him to walk with her out of the play room to the nursery, calling over her shoulder as she stormed down the hall.

"His grace is having a temper tantrum and needs to have his bottom warmed by my hand. You are dismissed and may return in an hour once he has settled and understands this type of behavior is unacceptable."

"Yes, ma'am," was all she heard before she entered the nursery and dragged Andrew in behind her.

Her son faced her, a dark scowl marring his handsome face. He planted his feet shoulder width apart, crossed his arms over his chest and jutted his chin out. Her breath caught. He reminded her so much of William, it was uncanny.

"Oh, my son, you had better take this petulant attitude and hide it somewhere deep and dark. You and I are going to have a long talk after I have spanked you."

"You not gonna spank me."

"Yes, I am and once I am done, I will tell you why."

"No."

She sat upon one of the chairs near his bed and held out her hand. He stared her down.

"Andrew Henry William Talbot, you will obey your mamma or another punishment shall be added. You choose. Come here now, or be punished further."

She tried hard not to smile as she watched her stubborn son war within himself. He desperately wanted to obey, but had reached a stage in his life where he was beginning to test the boundaries. She remembered many a time her bottom had been warmed by her Mamma's hand.

She knew she'd won the battle when he shuffled forward and stopped near her knees.

"Andrew, I am going to give you one good tap on your bottom, and it will hurt. After that, you must choose. Either be a good boy and do not throw your toys when you do not get your way or we shall come back here and I will give you two taps on the bottom *and* you will not ride Theodore for two days."

"Two days?"

It was so hard not to laugh. He cared not that his bottom was going to get a spanking, his only worry was that he couldn't ride his pony. She tucked that vital piece of information away, knowing it would be used in the future.

"Yes. Two whole days." She held out her hand. "Come, lay across my lap on your tummy."

He complied and she quickly brought down her hand. He

jerked when she made contact, but didn't cry out. She helped him to his feet and he immediately wrapped his arms around her middle and buried his head in her shoulder.

"I am sorry, Mamma," he sobbed out.

"I know, Andrew. I know you are." She hugged and rocked him until he quieted. "Mamma is sorry, too. I do not want to spank you, but you cannot behave in that manner. If you are angry, you must take yourself into a quiet corner and think about why you are angry. What if you had hit Nurse Alice in the face with one of your blocks? You could have hurt her very badly."

"I not wanna throw blocks."

"You must have, because you did. Can you tell Mamma why you became so angry?"

"They would *not* stay up. They felled down."

"I am going to tell you a great secret. Do you think you can keep a secret with Mamma?"

He nodded and wiped his nose with the sleeve of his shirt. *Oh, dear Andrew, you are so like your Mamma.*

"You are a little boy who one day will become a gentleman."

"Like Papa and Mitter Darcy?"

"Yes, like Papa and Mister Darcy." Her heart pinched at the thought of Henry and how Andrew would never really know that wonderful man. "And while you grow into this gentleman, your body will learn new skills. Sometimes, as you learn, you will make mistakes. Your blocks will refuse stay on top of one another."

"Stupid blocks."

"Andrew," she said in a firm voice. "The blocks do not stay on top of one another because your body has not learned how to place them correctly. Next time, you will stack them higher."

She took Andrew back to the play room and left him with Nurse Alice. As she walked downstairs to her study, she felt an unbearable regret. When something new happened with her son, or a new achievement was unlocked, she longed for Henry's presence. This time her regret held a difference, for although she missed Henry with a palpable ache in her heart, her thoughts had flown to William. She wanted him to see his son grow and mature into a handsome, confident young man. She wanted him to share in Andrew's triumphs as well as failures. In short, she wanted him here, with them, every day.

William had patiently courted her for over thirty days. He never wavered and never lost a chance to tell her how much he loved her. The little piles of notes now reached a total of seventeen. Where he found all the quotes and snippets of romantic poems, she had no idea. His estate work had to be suffering from neglect.

She reached into her drawer and brought out the notes, looking at the last one he'd had a footman tuck inside her linen napkin for her to discover at breakfast this morning.

No sooner met but they looked, no sooner looked but they loved, no sooner loved but they sighed, no sooner sighed but they asked one another the reason, no sooner knew the reason but they sought the remedy; and in these degrees have they made a pair of stairs to marriage.

Sixty-one days, my love, and then we shall build our own stairs to marriage.

Yours always,
FD

P.S.: I beg you to make it a short staircase. Two or three steps at most...

She placed the notes back into her drawer and brought out her personalized stationery and inkwell. It was time.

Chapter Twenty

DARCY SAT AT HIS DESK; a book written by Cowper open before him. October had been mostly Shakespeare, this month he would delve into more bucolic prose. Perhaps Wordsworth. His gaze flitted to his own journal where he wrote his thoughts down. Would she appreciate his own words? He flipped the journal open and began to scan his own poems. A polite knock on the door from Burke had him pause.

"A letter from her grace, sir."

Burke advanced and placed the sealed note on his desk, then left with a polite nod. This was the first time his love had written him, other than formal invitations. He broke the seal and unfolded the paper.

William,

Thirty-two days have passed since we began this journey. It is time for a serious conversation about our courtship and where it is headed. To that end, please attend Talbot House at precisely three o-clock.

Elizabeth

He couldn't breathe. Her words seemed so formal. Was she calling off the courtship with only sixty days remaining? Where had he failed? He stood and paced to the window, back to the desk, back to the window, back to the desk, falling into his chair. Despair ripped at his chest. The clock chimed twelve bells. Three hours until his possible eviction from her life.

Would she allow him to continue seeing his Andrew? He loved the boy with all his heart and would do anything to ensure his safety and happiness. Surely, he'd be allowed to have some form of contact with him.

At precisely three o'clock, he presented himself to the butler.

"Good afternoon, Gibson."

"Good afternoon, Mr. Darcy. Her grace is in the south drawing room and asked for you to proceed there directly." Darcy crossed the marbled floor to the hall which led to one of Elizabeth's favorite rooms, overlooking her garden. The last time he was here, he and Elizabeth had ended up in a passionate embrace, broken apart by the arrival of the housekeeper with tea. Today, she could be sending him home with no hope of return.

He came to a complete stop upon entry. Not only was Elizabeth in attendance, but so was her father, sister Jane and her husband Kit, as well as his uncle Matlock and his aunt. He turned at a slight noise and saw not only Georgiana, but Elizabeth's sister Catherine, and her cousin Percy and his wife Eugenia. A nurse held Andrew's hand who tugged until he broke free and ran to him. He stooped down and swung Andrew up into his arms. Holding his son tight, he cast his surprised gaze about the room.

"Good afternoon," he managed to finally say.

Everyone was smiling and returning his greeting, so his

rapid heartrate began to ease. Elizabeth could not mean to cast him aside if she'd called all the family in as witness.

"Andrew, Mamma needs to talk to William. Can you please stay with Nurse Alice for a little longer and maybe tell Grandpapa Bennet about your pony?"

"I will."

Andrew squirmed and Darcy reluctantly set him on his feet. Although he'd joined Elizabeth for countless walks and bedtime readings, his son had never asked to be held by him.

"Will you join me in the garden, William?" Elizabeth held out her hand and he gladly took it in his, ignoring the knowing smiles and nods of their family members.

Together they traversed the terrace steps and moved onto the grass. Could she feel his trembling?

~~~

"ELIZABETH, I WAS convinced you brought me here to say we were finished. That I had lost you."

"You did not lose me. I am here, William." She faced him, took his large hand, and pressed it over her heart. Did he feel her trembling? "I have always been here, waiting for you to find me."

His eyes darkened and he said in a low voice, "I am not looking for a two-year-old child in his mother's armoire, Elizabeth. I am looking for a woman who will accept me with all my faults."

"Then, it appears today your search is over."

"I wish did not have ten sets of eyes on us."

"This is the perfect place for us to talk things through."

"How so?"

"No one is lurking in the corners, trying to listen into our conversation. In the most public of places, we are afforded the greatest amount of privacy."

"Your logic astounds me at times."

"In a good way?"

"Yes! You have always talked circles around me and my friends. It is one of the things I first loved about you." He stopped walking and kissed her forehead. At this rate, they'd never reach the reach the sheltered gazebo – her ultimate goal for that afternoon. "There are times I wished I had not sent your father packing and offered for your hand in marriage."

"I always thought you knew."

"Knew what?"

"What you had done that night in the library."

"Elizabeth, I confess to my eternal shame that I was drunk. So drunk I had no recollection of the event."

They walked a little further and finally entered the gazebo. She guided him further inside and soon tall cedars hid them from anyone who might look out the terrace doors, or the windows, or venture out into the garden...

"What made you think I was aware? Bingley... poor fellow, was so embarrassed when I asked him to explain. He told me I had passed out and was dead to the world."

"You whispered my name." She blushed a delicate red. "At the time of your... completion, you whispered my name. That is why I always felt you had some knowledge."

"No," he shook his head, his countenance one full of sorrow. "I had strange dreams over the years and once the truth began to surface, they intensified. However, at the time your father confronted me, I was completely ignorant of my participation. Indeed, at one time I was led to believe Mr. Collins was the reason for your ruin."

"What! Why would you have thought that?"

"As distasteful as this subject is, you should know he alluded to having immoral relations with you while at Longbourn. Because I knew you were with child when he more or less bragged about his conquest, I assumed he was the father. The timing was too convenient. This further fed my anger as I thought you had tried to shift the blame to me in order to catch a bigger fish."

"Odious man. Did you know he had the gall to propose and then would not accept no for an answer? I had to quit the room because he persisted, saying I was trying to *entice him with my elegant female airs* and my refusals were a *ploy to heighten his anticipation.* Fortunately, Papa supported my decision."

"You must have hesitated over your refusal. You would not have known for certain if you were with child. It must have given you pause."

"It did give me pause, but at the end of the day, child, or no child, I would have been bound to Mr. Collins and he would have had full rights to me, body, and soul. I could not do it. I despised him and the thought of being with him 'til death do us part' was worse than being thought immoral." William put his large hand over hers that rested on his forearm and squeezed. "As it was, once I knew for certain, I asked Papa to see if Uncle Gardiner knew of any gentleman, be they tradesperson or not, who might need a wife. Papa also sent a letter to our cousin, Percy and from there, I met Henry."

"Did the duke tell you I had a conversation with him shortly after you wed?"

"No." Elizabeth looked up at him in surprise. "He did not."

"I was at the modiste with Georgiana and he was there with his new bride. When I asked if you were known to me, Tavistock made vague references about your cousin, the Marquis of Haversham and said there would come a time when I would recall meeting you. He was very cryptic and not until much later did I figure out his meaning."

"He said not a word."

"He was protective of you. Even though I wish I had not spurned your father's demand, I am forever grateful the duke took you into his protection. I could not have wished you to have a more thoughtful, elegant husband."

"Not even yourself?"

They stopped and faced each other.

"Were I able to go back through time and change each mistake I would, but then, I would not have grown into a better man. If we had married, I very likely would have remained disdainful and always looked down on you as the woman who caught me in a compromise. The possibility of me not being a faithful lover should also be considered, so great was my anger. The only thing that eats at my soul is that you loved him. I have to learn to deal with that fact."

"William, it is true I loved Henry. He was everything good in my life, but I was never *in love* with him as I am with you. You hold my heart and I ask that you treat it with care, for it is very fragile.

"Elizabeth." She adored the way he said her name in that low voice. "You have bewitched me body and soul. I felt the danger of falling in love with you when we were at Netherfield. No – I cannot continue with this untruth. The night I first laid eyes on you at that little country assembly, I found myself without breath. When I told Bingley, you were not handsome enough to tempt me, it was a pitiful attempt to stop myself from falling at your feet. Oh! – how I fought the attraction. I made fun of your family, I criticized your good looks and never once stopped Miss Bingley from abusing both you and your sister. All to no avail. On the night in which I compromised you, I now realized that I had finally given into my deepest held desires. What I imagined only in dreams, I acted on in person. I still do not understand how I could not fully recollect the event."

"You *were* very drunk, Mr. Darcy."

"To my everlasting shame. We wasted so much time!"

"I will not say they were wasted. There is a reason for everything and I firmly believe I was there for Henry. He had peace and joy the last few years of his life and I would not trade that for anything."

"Once again, you are the better person. I have always been a selfish being and hate any hour of the day where I was not in your life."

"Ah, but Mr. Darcy, you have been with me every hour and every day since that fateful night in the guise of our son. Every time I look at that beautiful boy, I see you." She stepped closer and raised her face to his. "One might say I have been falling in love with you for a very long time."

"Words borrowed from others or of my own cannot begin to plumb the depths of my love for you. I cannot hold out much longer."

"What of our courtship?"

"Fifty-nine days remain." He brought her hands to his mouth and kissed them. "This will be the first time in my life I fervently wish to break a promise."

"It appears thirty-two days was all you required to earn my love and respect."

"*Lady, as you are mine, I am yours. I give away myself for you and dote upon the exchange.* Marry me."

Emboldened by his declaration of love, she dared to slide her arms around his waist and burrowed her face into his chest. He drew back far enough to look down at her.

"Is this all the answer I can expect to receive?"

"I am savoring the moment, Darcy. Do not disturb me."

He gathered her close and cupped the back of her head with his palm, securing her against his beating heart. "Your wish is my command, although I would like an answer to my question."

"Mmm hmmm…" was all she said as she snuggled even closer.

"Was that yes?"

"Mmm hmmm…" she hummed again accompanied by a nod of her head.

"Woman, I need to hear the words before my heart gives out."

Now she was the one who drew back far enough so she could look up at him.

"Yes." She raised herself onto her toes and kissed the cleft of his chin. "Yes, I will marry you, Fitzwilliam Darcy."

With an inarticulate growl, he pulled her up and kissed her firmly on the mouth. She wound her arms around his neck, tangling her fingers in his dark curls, and met him kiss for kiss. His mouth and tongue sought out the pulse at the base of her neck and he reverently grazed his lips along her jaw line, across her collarbone and farther. With one hand he cupped her breast and brought the creamy swell to his mouth, his tongue seeking its own delight beneath the edges of her gown.

When she gasped in pleasure, he brought his mouth back to hers, his kisses hard and unyielding. Exhibiting no restraint, she surrendered to his passionate plunder and was panting for air when he ceased his ardent lovemaking with an audible groan and stepped away from their heated embrace.

"Marry me." He rested his forehead on hers, his breathing labored.

"I believe I already said yes," she replied, her breath as choppy as his, her chest heaving.

"Today. Marry me today. I will get a special license. I will hound the archbishop and we can be wed by this evening. As it is, almost everybody we wish to invite is already assembled in your drawing room."

She longed to give into him.

"I want a proper wedding, Fitzwilliam. I was denied the first time, which was expected as time was of the essence and I did not love Henry *then*, but I do love you and want all the pomp and circumstance that comes with declaring said love. I want the flowers and the doves and the wedding breakfast—"

Her declaration was cut off because he kissed her again. A passionate kiss that devasted her equilibrium and made her lose her train of thought.

"One month," he said in a tight voice. "I will give you three weeks for the banns to be read and another week to decorate every building in London if that is what you desire. Then you will be mine."

She cupped his cheeks and held his gaze.

"I am already yours. The wedding will only make it official. Two months."

"What! No, I will not survive that long. Five weeks."

"Six weeks. It takes time to find all the doves I require to release."

"Elizabeth," he groaned out. "I cannot wait that long. As it is, I have been waiting for years already. I burn for you."

"Fine. I shall forego the doves and marry you in four weeks."

"I would rather only wait a month — Wait! What? — You said four weeks."

"Yes, my darling. Four weeks."

"How I love you woman and on our wedding night," he growled seductively, "I will show you how much."

She shivered in anticipation. Mayhap he should purchase that special license. No, she had to stand firm. He was an obstinate man and boundaries needed to be set from the beginning. She laced her fingers with his as they strolled out of the gazebo and back to the house and waiting family, her head resting against his shoulder. She adored this tall, silent man. Her unwitting compromise had turned out to be the best thing that ever happened in her life.

Chapter Twenty-One

"ELIZABETH? HIS GRACE wishes to leave Pemberley and become a pirate. Have we any eye patches to pack in his bag?"

Elizabeth choked back a giggle and continued to rock Henrietta while she suckled. Ever since delivering her daughter five months prior, Andrew had grown increasingly moody, unwilling to share the attention with his baby sister, even though he hadn't balked at Bennet's birth almost nine months to the day following her and William's marriage, which Queen Charlotte herself attended.

By this time both William and Andrew had arrived in the nursery. At five, Andrew was even more like his father, whom he now called Papa. Her son planted his feet with arms crossed, a deep frown marring his brow. His lips were turned down and nothing but disgust emanated from his tight little body when he spotted the baby being held so close to her mother.

"Andrew." She addressed her son directly and shifted Henrietta onto her lap. With one hand beneath her chin to support her neck and head, she gently patted the baby's back to help expel air. "Please have a seat. I wish to speak with you."

"No."

"No?"

"Yes. I mean, no."

"You have a choice, my son. Either you sit now and talk, or you will receive a punishment and be forced to sit down on a sore bottom, because we *will* have a talk. Do I make myself clear?"

He did not speak, but grudgingly sat in the chair opposite her.

"Are you looking forward to the new pony for your birthday tomorrow?"

"Yes."

"He cannot go with you, if you become a pirate."

"Why not?"

"Because pirates do not like horses. It is why they live on ships."

Andrew digested her words.

"I am still going to be a pirate."

"Very well." Elizabeth stood and placed the freshly burped Henrietta into Andrew's arms. "Hold your sister while I find something to make an eyepatch with."

"I cannot hold a baby!" he cried out, his eyes and mouth wide open in sheer terror.

"Yes, you can. Now be careful, she trusts you as her big brother to make sure she is safe."

All this time William had said nothing, but now he moved to take the baby. She lightly touched his forearm and shook her head. In tandem, they moved into the hall and listened carefully by the open door. For the longest time Andrew's short, choppy breaths were the only sound. Then, Henrietta gurgled.

"Did you smile at me?"

The wonder in Andrew's voice almost made Elizabeth want to cry. She was such a watering pot when it came to her children.

"Careful, Henrietta. If you move too much, you might fall." They heard him shifting in his chair. "There. Now you are safe. I will not let anything happen to you, even though I am going to be a pirate." There was a long pause. "But then, I do not know how I will protect you."

Elizabeth signaled they should re-enter the room.

"I am sorry, Andrew. I could not find anything to make an eyepatch. However, your Papa said the cobbler in town could make something out of leather. That would look dashing on you as you stand on the edge of the deck, waiting for the next big wave to crash over the side of your ship."

Andrew sat very still, but she could see that he was chewing the inside of his mouth, something he did when deep in thought. Something his father did when deep in thought. She waited him out, much like she did the father.

"I do not think I will be a pirate."

"Why not?" She sat in the rocking chair, not even making a move to take back her daughter. "I was certain you were determined to be a pirate. You were even willing to leave your new pony behind."

"Henrietta needs a protector."

"Yes, every fair maiden needs a protector." She looked to the ceiling as though deep in thought. "Mayhap you could be a knight. One who fights dragons and slays all the beasts that would hurt a fair maiden."

"Can a knight still be a duke?"

"Of course. They make the very best kind of knight." She rose and lifted Henrietta from his arms. With the baby snuggled in her arms, she looked down at her son. "To be a good knight, you must learn to ride exceptionally well, which is good because you will have a new pony to ride. Then you must learn how to fence and shoot. Papa can teach you those things. He is secretly a knight. Did he tell you?"

Andrew looked to William, awe and wonder lighting his grey eyes.

"Papa, you are a knight?"

"Only for your mamma."

"Papa, will you read me a book about knights when I go to bed?"

"I believe I have something in the library."

"I should hope so," Elizabeth teased. "I have heard it is the work of many generations."

Andrew and William left the room and she laid Henriette into her bassinette. She walked down to the nursery to check in on Bennet, who was holding onto furniture, testing out his newest skill of walking. Well, walking and falling on his well-padded behind. Nurse Alice looked up and smiled.

"He is walking at almost the same age his grace did."

"I am not surprised."

She bent over and held out her arms, hoping Bennet would attempt to walk into her arms. He surprised her by plopping down onto his bottom, then crawled at a rapid pace before tugging at her skirts to pull himself up. She rewarded him by lifting him high over her head, then brought him down to kiss his chubby cheek.

My son, she thought and hugged him close. Another replica of William, the exception being his green eyes. They wouldn't know the color of Henrietta's for another few months, but it looked as though she would also have the Darcy grey.

The sound of a carriage drew her to the window and she and Bennet watched as Jane and Kit, along with their two children disembarked. Right behind them was Papa, Mamma, and Mary. Kitty and Richard and their twin boys would arrive later in the day along with Lord and Lady Matlock and the Viscount Ashton. Percy and Eugenia were arriving tomorrow making for a full house in honor of Bennet and Andrew's birthdays, celebrated together even though they were eight days apart. The only one missing was Lydia and that was because she had married a naval captain and traveled with him on his ship. Which may have been where Andrew got his idea to be a pirate. Lydia's letters were always full of adventure.

She looked at the young child in her arms.

"Are you ready to see Grandpapa and Grandmamma?"

Bennet answered by sticking his thumb in his mouth.

"You are? Let us go then and greet our guests."

Later that night, when she and William were finally alone in his room, he pulled her onto his lap.

"How did you know to do that?" he asked after a few minutes of kissing and cuddling.

"Do what?"

"Know how to turn around Andrew's determination to be a pirate."

"Papa did the same to me. I was about Andrew's age, having already suffered the birth of Mary when along came Catherine. Not that I was jealous of Mamma's attentions, but I was heartily tired of wailing babies."

"So, you were going to be a pirate?"

"No, I was going to join a traveling band of gypsies." She laughed at the memory. "Papa said I would have a difficult time as a gypsy because I did not play the fiddle and then asked if there was something else I could do instead. I had no ready answer and before I could think of anything, he plopped Kitty into my arms."

"Your father knew you well."

"Yes, he did."

"Ah, but I know you better…" his hand slid beneath the hem of her nightgown and began to caress the inside of her thigh. "…and I am intimately more familiar with your body.

"I should hope so, Mr. Darcy. After all, you are my

husband and the father of my three children." She began to squirm from his touch, strengthening his arousal.

"Speaking of children." His fingers dipped into her warmth and she gasped. "Have you anything you care to share."

"Oh, good heavens, William. I cannot think when you do that."

"Then we shall canvass the subject later... much later."

He rose with her in his arms and laid her gently on the bed. Obediently, she raised her arms and let him strip off her nightgown and then watched, with rising desire, as he divested himself of his clothing.

He began by kissing her ankles, moving up her legs at a snail's pace before settling in between her thighs. He suckled and kissed, dove in with his fingers and tongue, teasing her pearl until she reached her apex and lay spent on the counterpane.

"You are driving me to distraction, my love."

"I am only returning the favor from last night."

She felt a delicious quiver at the memory of taking him in her mouth, bringing him to raptures with her tongue alone. The bed dipped as he crawled over her and with one thrust entered her fully.

It was only when she was curled against his side, her head on his chest that he asked, "When were you going to tell me about the babe?"

She lifted her head and stared up at him. "How did you know?"

"You have not had your courses since Henrietta was birthed. You should have had at least one by now."

"I still cannot fathom how you know. I myself only began to suspect today."

"Elizabeth, we make love every night and sometimes several times a day other than when you are indisposed. I have mapped the contours of your body with my hands, lips, and tongue. There is no part of you that I am not intimately familiar with. I cannot get enough of you."

"I have noticed, Mr. Darcy. You make a habit of accosting me in various rooms of the house. You delight in having your wicked way with me."

"Yes, I have had my wicked way with you and shall again." He reached into his nightstand and brought out a familiar silk cravat. He wound the slim cloth around her wrists then raised her arms above her head, securing the ends to the headboard.

Deliciously helpless, she could only receive his undivided attention, reaching her completion several times until, with one final thrust, he called out her name and collapsed on her body. This time she was a willing captive and knew he was very aware that she lay beneath him. She wouldn't have it any other way.

THE END

ASLO BY SUE BARR

Pride & Prejudice continued…. Series

Caroline
Catherine
Georgiana

Pride & Prejudice Variations

Pride & Perception
An Unwitting Compromise
Compromise & Consequence
In Essentials
Longbourn's Angels

A Pride & Prejudice Alternate Universe

Fitzwilliam Darcy ~ Undone

CONTEMPORARY ROMANCE

According to Plan
Man of Her Dreams
Fiancé for Hire